Seeing Voices

Seeing Voices

OLIVIA SMIT

WhiteSpark

This is a work of fiction. All characters and events portrayed in this novel are either fictitious or used fictitiously.

SEEING VOICES
Copyright © 2020, Olivia Smit

Cover design and interior layout by Roseanna White Designs
Cover images from Shutterstock

WhiteSpark Publishing,
a division of WhiteFire Publishing
13607 Bedford Rd NE
Cumberland, MD 21502
www.WhiteSpark-Publishing.com

ISBN: 978-1-946531-62-9 (paperback)
      978-1-946531-64-3 (hardcover)
      978-1-946531-63-6 (digital)

Praise for *Seeing Voices*

"*Seeing Voices* by Olivia Smit has what a lot of YA romances have: new girl in a new town, cute boy, past pain, but Smit's sophisticated and engaging writing elevates the story while reaching into some deeper places. The story features Skylar Brady, a 16-year-old girl who has lost her hearing due to what might have been a deadly accident. So, along with the usual difficulties of adjusting to life in a new place, she is also learning to adjust to life with a new disability. Smit takes us into the world of a deaf protagonist with astonishing honesty. Skylar is at different times frustrated, angry, and even forgetful of the fact that she has lost her hearing. And while, yes, we have the budding romance of the town's cute boy, Cam, my favorite part of the story was watching the very complicated, very nuanced relationship between Skylar and her older brother, Mike, who seems to be falling apart. In some ways, he is more damaged by the accident than Skylar is, and Smit brings this relationship to the page expertly, with the kind of love that can only be built from confrontation. It's a beautiful story that proves the point that our senses become stronger when one is lost. In this case, it's not just the loss of Skylar's hearing, but the loss of comfort and familiarity and trust. With faith, friendship, and family, even these can be restored."

Allison Pittman, author of *The Seamstress*

"How Olivia Smit is able to take us so deeply and realistically into a world of silence without living in that world herself is as much a magical mystery as anything that takes place in *Seeing Voices*—which is saying something! Those of us who love true to life YA fiction welcome HER new voice with a big 'Yes!'"

Nancy Rue, Christy award-winning author

"A touching story of love, family, and friendship, and how they help us heal after tragedy. Skylar is a main character who's easy to root for and who will stay with readers long after they finish the book. A wonderful debut!"

STEPHANIE MORRILL,
author of *Within These Lines* and *The Lost Girl of Astor Street*

"In a book that balances the hopeful with the bittersweet, Olivia Smit has crafted a lovely portrait of beauty and tenacity reminiscent of Nicola Yoon and Jennifer Niven. Tight familial bonds are strained and new relationships forged when we journey through an unexpected change that forces us to--alongside our indomitable heroine-- to reimagine our concepts of beauty and fulfillment. Smit's assured voice makes Seeing Voices an immersive and compelling debut certain to stand out in the marketplace."

RACHEL MCMILLAN, *The London Restoration*

For my parents, who helped me find my way here,
and for God. This has always been His book, not mine.

Chapter ONE

THERE AREN'T ANY STREETLIGHTS ON COUNTRY ROADS. I LEAN MY FOREhead against the glass window of our family minivan as the fields blur past and wonder how I've never noticed this before. The dark road stretches calmly out in front and behind us, field upon field of corn swaying past the window, with no stark pools of lamplight to mark the distance.

My thoughts dance lazily from one idea to the next as the van hums along, my parents talking softly in the front seats. It would be nice to run out here. I let my eyes drift shut, and as I slip between waking and sleeping, I imagine the feel of loose gravel under my sneakers, the gentle shushing of corn stalks rubbing together, and the sun warm on my skin.

My heartbeat pounds in my chest, and my breathing is even as I strike out for the hill, one foot in front of the other. And then, before I've even realized that I'm dreaming, the scene changes. I'm at home now, running down the road by our house with my older brother, Mike, and suddenly I know exactly where this is going to end.

Wake up, Skylar. I try to shake off the dream before I'm caught reliving my last hearing moment over and over again. I need to wake up before the headache starts. Before my family notices that something's wrong.

"Are we there yet?"

From the backseat, my younger sister's voice shrills through the amplifier of my left hearing aid, and my eyes fly open, my hand going straight to the left side of my head and the small plastic casing buried beneath my hair.

Mike twitches beside me, but when I glance across at him, he's looking the other way. My twin siblings, six years old but convinced they're almost twenty-five, lean over my shoulder from the backseat, and when Sara keeps talking, her mouth too close to my ear, I jump away from them, fingers scrabbling to turn the sound on my hearing aids down. Even after almost eight months of wearing them, it still takes me a few seconds to find the volume button, and I feel a migraine begin to throb somewheree deep inside my left ear.

"Not yet," Mom says, turning around in the front seat to answer. Her voice is a low hum in the back of my head, but it's still light enough outside that I can see her lips to piece together the rest of her sentence. "Remember, Aunt Kay's house is how many hours away?"

I don't look to see what the twins say in response, rubbing the ache behind my ears that comes after a day with my hearing aids in. As I dig my fingers a little deeper, the hook that tucks around the top of my ear shifts to the side, the plastic caught on a stray hair, and tiny pinpricks of pain sprinkle across my scalp. Forget this. I pull the hearing aid out of my ear and then reach for its mate before dropping both into my lap.

"Right." Mom's lips move soundlessly as she holds up six fingers—it's a six-hour trip. Bits and pieces of the next sentence drift away from me, but when she holds up one finger, then bends it halfway, it's clear that we have only half an hour left to go.

I feel, rather than hear, my older brother sigh from the seat beside mine, but when I glance across at him, his eyes are closed. He has his headphones on, his toe tapping along to the beat of whatever music is playing.

"Mike," I say, almost choking on the silence of the words leaving my mouth. It's funny, losing your hearing—you always expect the biggest surprise to be when you can't hear what's going on in the world around you, but for me it's more shocking to miss the sound of my own voice. I can still feel it, deep inside my chest, but sometimes I feel trapped there, like I'm spinning and spinning within the confines of my ribcage, and no matter how loud I shout, no matter how deeply my voice vibrates in my throat, it can't get out.

My brother doesn't open his eyes, so I nudge him with the edge of my right foot, bumping my cold toes against his shin. "Hey." In hindsight, maybe I shouldn't have taken my hearing aids out, but the relief is palpable, the aching sensation in my ears already fading.

"What, Skylar?" Mike opens his eyes, and when I'm met with a glare, I catch myself leaning back, widening the distance between us. Why is he angry? I motion to him that he should pull his headphones off, which he does, although with one sharp movement that's probably a warning sign not to bug him.

"What do you remember about Aunt Kay?" I'm trying to make conversation, forgetting I won't be able to hear the response. Whoops. Mike won't care, though—he and I have always understood each other, almost as if we were twins.

"She has a big house in a small town and never answers her phone," Mike says, face turned to me so I can see his lips, but his eyes on his hands. He pulls his headphones back up again.

My face stings, almost as though I've been slapped. I play my question to him over in my mind, wondering if I just phrased it wrong. If I had used different words, would he have acted like himself? Is it my fault Mike has practically become a stranger?

Before I can get too lost in this depressing spiral, Mom puts her hand on my knee, tapping her long fingers up and down on my skin to get my attention.

"I took them out," I say, holding up my hearing aids before she can ask. "They were giving me a headache."

"Are you looking forward to seeing Aunt Kay again?" she asks, enunciating clearly so I can read her lips. Mom doesn't miss a thing—even if she's in the middle of another conversation, she's always listening to us in the background, picking up the loose threads of a conversation even minutes later. It's uncanny and, sometimes, exhausting.

"I guess," I say, glancing out the window then back to Mom again. "All I remember is from when we were kids and she played tag with us after dark after Thanksgiving dinner."

"And she sat at the kids' table instead of eating with the adults," Mom says, an amused smile playing across her lips. She's right—I remember that, too, because she ate the brussels sprouts I was hiding under my mashed potatoes and never told my parents I didn't finish them myself. As Mom turns to say something to Dad, I look out the window again. The country roads have changed to small houses, and then storefronts begin to slide by—a Main Street grocery store, a library, and then a small café flick past before we get stuck at a red light, waiting to turn.

My phone buzzes against my hip, vibrating in the pocket of my shorts, and when I pull it into the palm of my hand, I find a message from my best friend waiting for me.

Janie: How big is your aunt's house?? Send pix! Miss u!

I smile in spite of myself, fingers hovering over the keypad as I try to decide how to reply. Finally, the light turns green, Dad makes the turn, and then after a quick right, we're on a street driving directly toward the water—I can see it, right out the front window. My text back to Janie is short, because I just want to keep looking.

Still driving—text u later. Wish u were here!

After a moment, I send another text.

have you seen Gavin?

I want to ask if he's said anything about me, but that seems like it would be going a little too far. My heartbeat picks up simply from the act of typing in his name, and I turn my phone off, glad Janie can't see the blush on my face. We'd always been best friends—and we're not dating now or anything, but before we left, I thought things were heading in that direction. Of course, now we're halfway across the province on the shores of Lake Ontario for the summer, so who knows. Maybe I've lost my chance completely.

I jump when Sara taps my shoulder from behind, her lips moving too fast to track in the dark that has fallen outside the car windows.

"Hang on," I say and wedge the speaker back into my ear, waiting for the four successive beeps that mean I've rejoined the hearing world.

"We're here!" Sara shrieks from behind me, and I cup my hands over my ears, turning the sound down another few clicks. "We're here, we're here, we're here!"

"I'm hungry," Aiden says from the seat behind Mike, his voice muted and faraway compared to Sara's. "And I have to go pee."

"Just a few more minutes." Mom's voice is miles away, too. "But look at the neighborhood. Isn't it beautiful?"

Bungalow cottages slide by the windows, beach houses with balconies next to little colored cabins; each one has tall, open windows, like they're trying to see past the other houses to the lake. Our minivan crests the top of the hill. And then it's all spread out below us, the moonlight tracing a path across the water straight to the beach. Aunt Kay's house is at the end of the street, with white siding and blue shutters, and one window right below the point of the roof. It's big and sprawling, but adorable, and I fall in love with it in a heartbeat. I can tell that Mom loves it, too, by the way she lifts one hand to her mouth, the other one reaching for Dad's arm. I can't see her lips, so I don't know if she's spoken, but if she has, I'd be willing to bet it was just a sigh, or maybe Dad's first name.

Almost before the van has stopped, Aiden and Sara are out the side doors, followed closely by Mom. Dad parks and turns to Mike, who pulls off his headphones again.

"Can you and Skylar help me with the luggage?" He squints at the two of us. "And have either of you seen my glasses? I had them just a moment ago."

"They're on your head," I say, as Mike gets out of the van. I wait for him to glance at me so I can roll my eyes in Dad's direction, but he doesn't look up, doesn't say a word to anyone.

"So they are." Dad pulls them down to the bridge of his nose. "Imagine that."

Mike, a suitcase in each hand, marches past with his eyes on the ground. As Dad reaches for the last two, I waver in between car and house, and then something moves—just a shadow, really—in the corner of the porch. Arms crossed against the evening chill, I tiptoe forward, peering into the dimly lit space. Without Mike to talk to, I feel awkward in my own family, lost, almost. Dad says something as he passes, his voice snatched by a gust of wind, and then two gleaming eyes appear in the light from the doorway.

"Come here, kitty," I say as my eyes adjust and the crouched figure of a cat is visible, the white patches in his coat standing out. He pads across the porch to me right away, pressing his head against my hand when I reach out to pet him. I'm leaning forward with two hands to lift him into my arms when Sara appears in the doorway. The cat flinches as she yanks the door open, but he doesn't run away, and I scoop him up.

"Come on!" Her voice is just barely audible under the obnoxious crackling of the outdoor air against the speakers that rest behind my ears. "Aunt Kay isn't here, but she left waffles in the freezer."

"Okay." I follow her into the hall, shifting the cat to my left arm so I can exchange my hearing aids, which have begun to ache behind my ears again, for my phone on the way by my backpack. When I press the home button, it lights up, four new messages waiting for me.

I smile in spite of myself—probably the whole gang back home clamoring for pictures of the house and of Golden Sound, the cute little beach town where my "mysterious aunt" lives. If I'm lucky, there will be one from Gavin, too.

I wander down the hall, sliding my phone into my back pocket so I can bury both hands in the cat's soft fur. The wood floor feels stiff beneath my feet, and I tiptoe in case the boards are creaking. Aunt Kay's house is full of wood; the floors, walls, and even the beams of the ceiling are rich chestnut in colour, and smooth to the touch. I follow the glow of light into the kitchen. The twins have already pulled the waffles out of the freezer and spread them across the table, counting to see which ones have the most blueberries. Mike and Dad continue to load the front hall with luggage, and Mom climbs the stairs, probably to search for our absent aunt.

"Aiden, Sara," I say, rubbing the cat's ears, "just take the top ones."

They either can't hear me or pretend not to, still rummaging through, pushing waffles across the thin layer of dust that lines every flat surface in this house.

"Gross, you guys," I mumble, sitting down at the table, but the protest is feeble.

They choose their dust-covered waffles and slide them into the toaster, arguing over who gets to push the buttons. I'm sitting with my back to the doorway, so it's only when they both stiffen and look behind me that I realize someone else is there.

"Hey," I say, turning to see Mike standing in the threshold. Aiden, Sara, and I are all varying shades of ginger, but Mike has hair like our mom. It's dark brown and tousled, sticking up on one side where his headphones were.

"Hey," he mutters without meeting my eyes, his backpack dangling from one hand. His lips are stiff, and after the one-word greeting escapes him, he rubs his thumb across the lower half of his face. It's an unconscious movement, the same way someone will compulsively rub their own cheek if they see a stray crumb on their friend's, like he knows I'm watching him speak, and he's trying to wipe my gaze away.

"Did you pick your bedroom?" I try to sound casual, but everything feels too stiff and polite. I can't even figure out how to talk to the people in my own family.

"I don't care. You can pick." Mike reaches past me and snags the milk jug out of the open fridge before nudging it closed with his foot.

I try to figure out where to take the conversation next, but by the time I look up to ask what his plans are for tomorrow (still lame, I know), my three siblings are chattering away to each other, faster than I can follow.

I catch Sara saying, "How many times do you think … … ?" but miss the rest.

Aiden laughs at her question, whatever it was, and then rattles off a reply, turning away from me so I can't see his lips at all. I think of my hearing aids, buried deep in the pocket of my backpack. It's too late to get them now. I have to settle for interrupted lip-reading.

"… … last night, when … … and Aunt Kay … … !" Mike wipes his mouth with the back of his hand. He seems to have no trouble finding more than one word to use when he's talking to the twins.

"Skylar?" Aiden tugs my hand, and I tear my frustrated gaze from my older brother to my younger one.

"What did you say?" I blink—hard—and focus on his lips. I'm not a great lip-reader, but even though I don't understand every single word that is spoken when I don't have my hearing aids in, usually if I grasp the context, I can put the pieces together.

"Where is Aunt Kay?"

The simplicity of the question makes it easy to smile back at him. "I don't know, but I'm sure she'll be back soon. I'm glad she asked us to come and visit."

"Me too," he says, and then pulls free of me and runs back to the table, where Mike has taken pity on the breakfast-for-dinner endeavors and is putting the freshly toasted waffles onto two paper plates.

Their three heads are bent over the table together, Mike totally focused on filling every single waffle square with syrup, as per Sara's instructions. I try to convince myself that I'm happy as I watch the moment take place, that the pang inside my heart is one of affection and not of pain. All I can think is how perfect they look, huddled around the table without me.

And that's when Sara's flailing arm catches the glass syrup bottle and sends it smashing down, glass shards and brown liquid oozing across the floor. The four of us freeze, and by the way my siblings' heads turn toward the doorway, I know they hear footsteps. I'm expecting my parents to be exasperated or upset with us for making a mess after barely five minutes inside, but instead, they're preoccupied with a piece of paper Dad is holding in his hand.

"Listen to this," he says, not even looking down at the floor—Mom has to put her hand out to stop him before he walks right across the kitchen. Sometimes I think she has a sixth sense when it comes to looking out for my dad, since she always seems to know when to step in and save him from himself. Now, his glasses dangle from one hand, the handwritten letter held close to his face with the other. He's been reading aloud, judging by the attentive look on Mike's face, but whatever he said can't be good.

"What is it?" I ask, and the cat pads through the kitchen doorway, ears pricked.

"My sister—" Dad starts, and then stops, staring at the note in front of him. He finishes his sentence, but the note obscures his mouth, making it impossible for me to understand.

"What?"

"She moved to Africa," Mike says, so startled that he actually makes eye contact with me as he's speaking. "Three weeks ago."

Chapter
TWO

To my wonderful brother and his wonderful family:
Hey, kiddos!

I'm so glad you made it to Golden Sound and my dear little house, which is actually quite large, but likes to pretend that it is a small cottage. I'm sorry that I'm not here to greet you in person, but I've had the most incredible opportunity to spend the summer traveling South Africa with a friend, and I simply must go! I thought perhaps taking the summer to yourselves, especially after the events of the past year, would be good for all of you, and you don't need me around to have a lovely time, that's for sure!

Feel free to explore the town and say hello to the neighbors—I asked them to pop over for the next few weeks and keep the fridge stocked, until they see your car in the driveway. I'm afraid I'll miss my flight if I spend much more time writing, so I'll be brief in my instructions for you all:

David: get your nose out of a book and look up, brother dearest! (Imagine me affectionately tousling your hair while you're reading this.) Promise me you'll watch at least one beach sunrise while you're here?

Marisa: Make sure David takes me seriously!

Mike: I have a couple of old guitars in the upstairs closet, if you've still got an ear for music!

Skylar: I love you, honey. "Golden Sound Public Library, 15 Main Street. Open 9 a.m.–4:30 p.m. on weekdays only." There's a summer job opening with your name on it, if you want it!

Aiden and Sara: There's a secret stash of chocolate behind the farm painting in the entryway. Don't tell your dad or he'll eat it all!

Miss you all and love you lots'n'lots,

Kaylie / Aunt Kay

P.S. The cat is called Tom. He belongs to me but prefers the neighbors, since they're the ones who feed him. Feel free to re-adopt him if you like! I'm sure they won't mind.

AFTER I FINISH READING, THERE IS A MOMENT OF COMPLETE STILLNESS BEfore my entire family explodes into chaotic action. They're all talking at once, lips moving too fast to read, arms flying in a multitude of directions, while I stay frozen at the table, Aunt Kay's letter still clutched in my left fist.

"Okay," Mom finally says, laying a hand on my shoulder. Her words are slow and exaggerated, lips perfectly formed to make sure I don't miss anything. "Everyone needs to take a deep breath. Aiden, Sara—sit down. No," she continues, before they even begin to ask a question, "you may not go and check for chocolate right this very minute. Your dad and I are going to have a private discussion, and the two of you are going to head upstairs and go to bed. The chocolate can wait until tomorrow morning."

Aiden pouts. "But what about Mike and Skylar?"

Mom glances down at the syrup and glass mess spread across the kitchen floor, and I can't see her lips, but I'm pretty sure I know what Mike and I are going to be doing for the next few minutes. I'm more preoccupied with the random list of instructions Aunt Kay has left for us—especially mine.

"Why a library?"

Maybe no one hears my question because I've spoken too quietly. Or maybe no one else knows the answer. Either way, I get no answer, but I don't bother repeating myself. From what I know of Aunt Kay, she's been like this forever; sometimes she just does things without having any particular reason at all.

A hand comes down firmly on my arm, and I jump in my seat, eyes flying open, heartbeat tripling as I spin around. Mike has the grace to look ashamed, but the way he pulls his hand back as though it's burned him makes my stomach do an uncomfortable flip.

"What?" I say, perhaps more sharply than I mean to.

"Never mind." Although his gaze starts at my face, it quickly jumps to just over my shoulder, and then across the kitchen, before settling on the table in front of me. "About the mopping. I'll just do it."

"I can help," I say, pushing my chair back from the table so I can look him in the eyes.

Mike winces, and I stop the movement of the wood against the tile floor with my hand.

"Too loud?"

He doesn't answer.

"I don't mind helping." For a moment I feel like he's the one who can't hear, like my words are being swallowed up by the void between us.

"It's fine," he says, shoving his hands deep into his pockets in a motion he usually reserves for talking to people he doesn't really like.

I know this because I am his sister, and until the accident, I understood him better than anyone. I know things about Mike that no one else does, but I never expected to see one of his tells, little movements that signify discomfort, used in approximation to me.

"Okay," I say at last. Why is this so hard? Why does he feel so inaccessible? We're standing two feet away from each other, but Mike might as well be standing on the moon. He's my best friend, and it feels like we don't even speak the same language anymore.

"Okay," I say again, as if repeating myself will help, somehow.

Mike doesn't even wait long enough to ask what I'm going to do. Instead, he just shoves his head down and makes a beeline for the living room and, presumably, a closet somewhere with cleaning supplies.

I sigh. "I'll just go to bed, then." I wait in the doorway to the kitchen for a few seconds to see if he'll turn around, change his mind, or tell me that he wants the front bedroom. My brother does none of these things, and so I'm left with no choice but to climb the staircase alone, the wood steps cool underneath my bare feet.

The bedroom is big and sparsely furnished, but the bed is made and the sheets are crisp and white. My suitcase lies by the foot of the bed, but I don't bother unzipping it. I just climb straight under the covers and flick off the light.

I'm asleep in a matter of minutes, and although a red car drives in and out of my dreams all night, I wake up the next morning without a headache. Ten points to Skylar, I guess.

I haul myself up, exchanging last night's wrinkled clothes for a pair of yoga pants and a hoodie before sliding my hearing aids into place and jogging down the stairs to the kitchen. Mike is already there, eating a piece of toast and leaning against the stove, but when I step through the doorway, he walks toward the living room. I try to pretend that this is a coincidence as I snag an apple from the bowl on the table and follow him into the adjacent room, where our parents are engrossed in a discussion by the front window. The volume on my hearing aids is up as high as it will go, but someone's turned the radio on, and I can't quite hear the individual words being spoken, just a general hum that is punctuated occasionally by a cymbal crash from the radio or an exclamation from one of my parents.

Dad's playing with his glasses and squinting at Mom, who is monopolizing the conversation and accenting her words with enthusiastic hand gestures. She always looks like my grandma when she talks like this: her hands flying, words too fast to follow. I stand in the doorway for a minute, watching the two of them talk, but the longer I watch their soundless interactions, the more I feel like I'm inside a glass bubble.

"Mom," I say, and then realize as her hands freeze mid-gesture that I've interrupted something more than a discussion about breakfast. The bubble shrinks, and I have the horrible feeling that I can't draw a full breath, but somehow, I do. "Do I have to go today?" I don't specify that I'm talking about Aunt Kay's library mission, but they instantly know what I mean.

My parents exchange glances, and then Dad slides his glasses on and studies me for a moment, pinching the bridge of his nose. "No," he says, after a pause so long it's almost painful. "But are you going to want to go tomorrow? Or the day after that?"

I shove my hands deep into the pocket of my hoodie, wishing I'd waited to catch one of them alone, instead of walking right into a tag-team parent effort. "Do I have to go at all?"

Mom looks at Dad, and then back to me. "David," she says, and I can't actually hear her, but I recognize the way the word looks on her lips, "maybe…"

Dad meets her gaze, and she places a hand over her mouth so I can't read her lips. My stomach tightens; I bet I can guess what she's saying. She's asking if it's too soon, if they're really right to push me. If Mike hates my deafness, my Mom is afraid of it, but where Mike flees, Mom leans in. She over-enunciates everything, and even when she's not in the house, I swear I can feel her just over my shoulder, trying to protect me. Trying to make up for the fact that I got hurt in the first place.

My parents resolve whatever conversation they were having behind their hands, but it's Dad who addresses me next.

"We're not going to force you to go," he says, and while he speaks carefully, his lips don't have the desperate precision I've come to associate with my mother. "You're seventeen years old, and your mom and I have decided that you can make your own decision."

I hate it when they say that, because they're still not giving me much of a choice.

"But," he says, as though proving my thoughts—sometimes I think he can read them. "We think it would be a good idea."

Mom's tight-lipped expression betrays her, but she doesn't contradict my father.

"Why?" I ask, and glance over at Mike, hoping for support. This is normally when he'd jump to my defence, coming to stand beside me to plead my case with our parents. He's only a year older than me, but for some reason, they're more inclined to listen to me if I can get Mike on my side.

Instead, I catch him looking at the three of us with an expression I can't place. When he sees me looking back, his lips press together in a thin line, like Mom's, and he turns his back on us, reaching for the TV remote.

The lost feeling seeps in, stronger, and I swallow hard.

"We don't want you to mope around the house all summer," Dad says when I turn back around, but his eyes wander after Mike, and I know he's seen his strange behavior, too. "A lot has changed in the past few months—"

"I know." I run my hands through my hair, yank out the tie at the end of my braid, and comb my fingers through the snarls at my roots. Anything to distract me from how much I feel like an outsider even here, where I'm supposed to be at home. "I know, Dad."

"And," he continues gently, waiting until I'm watching him again, "we don't want you to feel trapped in the house all summer. This is a new place for all of us, but especially you." He holds up a finger against my heaved sigh. "And we're just trying to help. Aunt Kay didn't leave many details, but I know she loves you."

"Why didn't she leave instructions for anyone else?" I grumble, getting to my feet. "Except for Dad and his watch-the-sunrise order. What if *I* just want to sit outside in the morning and look at the sun?"

Mom breaks her silence to meet me halfway across the room and plants a kiss on my forehead before I can duck away, stepping back so I can read her lips again. "Then you can watch the sunrise, too." Her hands are still on my shoulders, and I try to convince myself that I feel comforted, rather than stifled.

I'm about to reply when her head turns away from me, shoulders stiffening, and I know she's either heard something in another room, or her sixth sense has picked up some sort of distress among my siblings. She says something, either to me or to whoever is calling her, but with her face turned away, the radio and television swallow her words.

Sara comes wailing into the room and buries her face in Mom's shoulder, and after doing a cursory check for blood and finding nothing, I lose interest. She and Aiden are probably fighting over the long-lost chocolate, and I leave them behind me as I climb the stairs to my bedroom and flop onto my bed.

To distract myself, I pull out my phone and scroll through my old text messages, stopping at last night's conversation with Janie. My friends would love it here, I find myself thinking, staring at the wooden rafters that crisscross the ceiling. And if Janie was here, she'd call this whole library thing an adventure and march me straight across town to get started.

But I'm scared, I realize suddenly, and the thought makes me angry. *Since when?* I demand furiously of myself, rolling onto my side so I can look out the window. Since when does Skylar Brady get scared of anything?

Since she stopped feeling comfortable in her own skin, whispers a little voice inside my head. *Since she lost one sense and felt the other four slip away, fuzzy and out-of-place. Since she couldn't tell her own words from the silence inside her head, couldn't tell if people were laughing at her behind her back and for the first time wondered if they were.*

Trying to shake these thoughts free from my mind, I roll over, letting my gaze dance across the wood walls to the floor, where a brightly colored rug lies crookedly next to the bed, the edge puckered where it's been pushed against the side table. I reach to smooth it out and notice a small card lying face-down on the floor beside the rug. I must have knocked it over when I switched the light off last night. When I pick it up and turn it over, I find my name on the front, written in my aunt's handwriting. The note inside is a little scattered, but sweet, in the typical fashion of Aunt Kay.

> *Dear Skylar,*
>
> *I thought you might choose this bedroom. It's always been my favorite. If you didn't, and someone else simply handed you this note, that's fine too. I make a point of liking all the rooms in my house, although I admit to playing favorites with that front bedroom from time to time. Anyway, dear, the point of this note is just to tell you not to be afraid to try new things. I pulled a few strings at the library (I meet there with my knitting club from time to time) to set up this job for you, but if it doesn't tickle your fancy, find something else! Just don't let the accident define you. You're bigger than the events of your past, and*

you can go on to do great things no matter what stands in your way.

I believe in you, and I love you!
Aunt Kay

I hold the note for a few minutes, staring down at the scrawl of her handwriting. She's right. This kind of stuff never used to scare me. It's only the thought of navigating it without my hearing that keeps me from throwing caution to the wind and chasing down the things that I want.

That's when I decide to go.

I grab a more professional change of clothes and go off in search of a bathroom, my hair still greasy from last night's long car ride. My head is held high, as though I can banish my fears simply by pretending that they don't exist. Aunt Kay is right—I know I can do this.

● ● ●

My rickety sense of confidence lasts exactly thirty-eight minutes, the amount of time it takes me to shower (ten minutes), get dressed and pull up my hair (another ten), plus walk from Aunt Kay's house to the Golden Sound Public Library (eighteen minutes). It's when the automatic doors slide silently open in front of me, a wave of air-conditioning slapping my face, that I remember I have almost no idea what I'm doing here. All Aunt Kay left me was an address and a vague note about getting hired—no other instructions or directions or even a name.

"Great," I mutter to myself and, chin up, walk in. It's quiet, I think, before realizing that of course I would have no idea how loud it actually is.

There are only a few people in the building, several sitting in chairs by the back window, and one or two browsing the display by the front counter. There are big windows along every wall, and the morning sun streams in and leaves streaks of light across the worn carpeting.

I like it instantly, feel drawn to the easy atmosphere and slow tempo of the air, a mood I can actually keep up with—a place I can understand. There's only one librarian behind the desk, and I force myself to stride confidently toward her, my hands unclenched, shoulders relaxed, easy smile on my face. *You've done this a million times*, I remind myself, and I have.

Last summer, a whole group of us who decided we wanted summer jobs went around to all the restaurants and grocery stores in town, taking turns marching ourselves in and handing over our resumes. We knew that even if we screwed up, we could laugh it off after it was over. Gavin was the quiet encourager of the group, always clapping the victor on the back, or offering a smile.

This is just the same as then, just as if I could hear. I grit my teeth and try to believe it as I make my way down the aisle. The young woman behind the front desk catches my eye and smiles, still too far away to hear. I smile comfortably back at her. I'm trying to go for a calm mood, like, *Oh hey, just hanging out here. No hurry*, but when she tilts her head inquiringly toward me, my brain goes on standby and all I can think is, there's no way I'm faking my way through this one.

I'm deaf.

"… … help you?" Her face is friendly, and even though she's speaking too quickly, I catch most of her words. I relax a bit and let my hands uncurl at my sides, taking a deep breath to steady myself.

"Hi," I start to say, and when she doesn't flinch, I keep going. "I'm Skylar Brady, and I'm here for a job interview."

Her brow furrows, and she turns to the computer, resting one hand lightly over her lips as she clicks the mouse back and forth. *Please take your hand away from your mouth*, I think with some desperation, staring at her perfectly manicured hands—nails painted bright pink to match her lipstick—as she taps one long nail against her upper lip.

"Well," she says next, still staring at the computer, and then she coughs into her elbow, opens the desk drawer, and drums her fingers on the counter, all while continuing to speak. Any chance I had of understanding what she's telling me is gone, lost in a thousand little noises of movement.

The butterflies in my stomach bunch together and then spiral outward, beating their wings against the underside of my heart. When at last she finishes whatever she was saying, her eyebrows are raised, and I know she's expecting an answer. I tuck my hair behind my ear, feeling the pounding of my heart against my ribcage, and take a stab in the dark.

"Um," I say, grasping for the right words. "My Aunt Kay sent me. I mean, she left me a note and told me to apply here, at the library."

This appears to help matters, and the librarian taps her fingers against her lips again as she begins talking, her lips moving faster and faster, her voice a hum in the back of my head that I can't quite fit words to. I can feel myself beginning to panic, like when I was six and lost sight of Mom in the grocery store. I want to plop myself down on the floor and cry until someone comes to rescue me, but no. That's not going to happen. I'm still the same person, the same Skylar who marched into six grocery stores in one night and came out of it with five job offers. I recall Aunt Kay's words in the note by my bed and think them fiercely, as though by repeating them over and over, I can make them true. *My past does not define me. I can still do great things.*

"I'm deaf," I blurt out, and watch her freeze in front of me, her fingers paused mid-tap at the keyboard, her pointer fingers hung stiffly in midair, hovering over the keys.

"I mean," I say, struggling to backtrack, trying to get it right, "like, not completely. I'm technically hard of hearing. But that's why I didn't hear what you were saying before."

It was quiet before, but the dead silence settling over the library now is poignant, people's heads turning from the bookshelves all the way by the front windows, and as everyone physically stills, a hot blush creeps up the back of my neck.

Oops. Maybe not quite the first impression that I wanted to make.

The librarian, her face still and drawn in an expression of concentration, extends her arm, one finger raised in the universal sign for "wait one minute," and then begins to back away, lips exaggerating her words.

"I'll be right back." This is spoken far too loudly. I can actually hear, but the way she's forming her words, lengthening the vowels and spitting the consonants out like they taste bad, it comes across more like: Iiieeee-yuuulll beee riiiight baaaack.

It's almost as disorienting as her fingernails, but I manage a smile. "I'll wait right here," I say.

Judging by the surprised lift of her brows, I'm guessing it came out at roughly the right volume, and as she scurries away toward the back of the library, I take a few more deep breaths and try to relax my shoulders.

I can do this. I close my eyes for a moment and try to pretend that I'm at home, that this is just another job interview and Janie and Gavin and the rest of our friend group are waiting outside the front door. They're probably peeking through the window, I tell myself, laughing at the way Skylar always manages to command the room, to make a fool out of herself and still get offered the job.

They asked me once how I did it, after I slipped in a puddle in the entrance to a Food Planet and knocked over a full display of apples. Glossy red fruit went rolling down four different aisles, into people, kicked under shelves, and caught in the wheels of shopping carts. It took six employees, plus me, about fifteen minutes scrambling around on hands and knees to catch them all again, and most of them were bruised and ugly, skin splitting and already turning purple. When I asked to speak to the manager, the gangly boy who'd been stacking the display looked relieved, probably thinking that I was going to explain the mess I'd made, but the first thing I did when I walked into his office was to ask for a job. I explained about the apples after he'd already leafed through my resume and told me he'd "be in touch."

So lost in my memories that I forgot I'd closed my eyes, I'm sufficiently startled when someone gently touches my elbow. I'm even more startled when I open my eyes and find a boy about my age standing in front of me, the sleeves of his long sleeve shirt rolled up to his elbows. The words "John 3:16" are wrinkled slightly across his chest, like he yanked the nearest shirt out of his closet without worrying about whether it had been folded or not when it was put away.

He smiles at me and then, before I fully grasp what's happening, begins to sign, hands moving fluidly in front of him, so fast I can barely tell where one sign ends and the next begins. I've seen people use American Sign Language in videos before, even tried out a few signs myself after I took the hospital-run course, but I couldn't wrap my head around it. Even though I brought an ASL/English dictionary buried in the bottom of my suitcase, I haven't exactly been dying to flip through it again.

"Sorry," I say, and then without thinking, I grab his hands, pulling him to a stop like he's a runaway horse and I'm yanking back hard on the reins. "Sorry," I say again, pitching my voice lower. "I don't speak—I don't know how to sign."

After a pause, I realize that I'm still holding onto his hands, the fingers of my right hand around the cords of his wrist. I let go, a blush creeping up my cheeks.

"It's fine," he says, and relief washes over me. Not only can I read his lips, but I can actually hear him—his words slow and clear.

He enunciates precisely, but not carefully, has no facial hair, doesn't squint or twitch when he speaks, and has now put his hands safely into his pockets, where they can in no way obscure his mouth. I want to hug him.

"Hi, ma'am," he says, drawing one hand back out to shake, and I wonder briefly if he speaks with a Southern accent. Maybe he's a rancher or something, from the States. Or maybe he just wants to be a cowboy.

"Um, hello." I shake his hand, and he waits, still holding mine, expectant.

"What's your name?" he asks, finally.

"Skylar," I say, relieved to be asked a question that I can finally answer. "And you are?"

"I'm Cam," he says, and this time I catch the subtle difference, the hard consonant cupped in the back of his throat. Oh. He hadn't said "Hi, ma'am" before, after all. So, not a cowboy. He didn't really look like a southern drawl kind of guy anyway.

"It's nice to meet you," I reply, feeling very formal and stilted. "I'm trying to apply for a job, but it doesn't seem to be going very well so far."

Cam grins, and I feel my shoulders relax a little bit more. He reminds me of Mike—my brother has always been able to ease the tension in a room after just a few seconds. He used to smile that easily, too. "Let's go sit in the staff room for a minute," Cam says, and then after a heartbeat, "you're Kaylie's niece, right?"

It takes me a minute to process that by Kaylie, he means Aunt Kay.

"Oh," I say, following him into the staff room, which has an overstuffed old couch that I instantly fall in love with, a small wooden table, and three mismatched chairs. "I mean, yes. I am. She's my aunt."

"Excellent." He slings his long body into one of the chairs.

"She's in here almost every week, so I'm not surprised she sent you here to get a job."

"Oh?" Why can't I think of anything else to say?

Cam nods. "And she always remembers everyone's birthday." He smiles, as if remembering something, and then gives his head a shake. "Anyway," he says, "as Anastasia was trying to tell you earlier—"

"Anastasia?"

"Sorry," he says, smiling a little sheepishly. "The librarian at the front. Anastasia—Ana for short."

I fit her face to the name inside my head and feel as though I've understood more than a simple introduction, as though something more significant has unlocked within me. It feels so good. With a start, I realize that I haven't been paying much attention to whatever else Cam has been telling me, tuning the low hum that is his voice out as I pictured Anastasia's face.

"Sorry," he says, apparently seeing my confusion. "Am I speaking too quickly?"

"No, it's fine." I clear my throat, nodding as if to confirm to him that he's doing just fine. "You're very good at this."

He tilts his head to one side. "Good at what?"

"The whole talking-to-someone-who-can't-hear thing," I say, because I'm nothing if not eloquent. "I mean, you don't have facial hair or anything."

Cam doesn't really respond to this, which is a good thing because I have no idea why I said it.

"I mean," I hasten to add, "your lips are very easy to read. Because you have no facial hair. And you sign, too." Which I can't do, I want to add.

"Oh," he says, grinning. "My older sister's deaf. We—my whole family, I mean—we all sign."

"It's beautiful," I say, though I'd never really paused to think about it before. It's true though.

"I can show you a few signs sometime," he says offhandedly. "When you start work."

"When I what?"

"Sorry," he says, circling a fist over his heart in what I assume is to be my first sign. "If you want the job, that is."

"I've never worked in a library before," I say, dubiously.

"Oh, it's easy." He shrugs. "If I can do it, anyone can. You shelve a few books, talk to a couple of people, mostly just point them back to the front desk. And you get first pick of the new releases, if you like that sort of thing."

I've never been a big reader—Mike's the bookworm out of the two of us—but Mom's right. I don't want to be stuck in the house all day.

"Okay," I say, chin up because this is something the old Skylar would do—this is something I can do. "I'll take the job."

Cam's grin widens, which I didn't think was possible, and I try to smile back broadly enough to cover my inner doubt. If Aunt Kay thinks I can do this, I can, right?

Chapter THREE

I WAKE UP BEFORE MY ALARM THE NEXT MORNING, AND FOR A COUPLE OF minutes I think I'm still at home. Without opening my eyes, I roll over onto my side, reaching for the glass of water that's always beside my bed. When my fingers fail to find the cup or even the table, I crack open one eye and almost fall out of bed when I see that I'm not in my house at all, but in my little bedroom at Aunt Kay's.

"What time is it?" I mumble to myself, morning-clumsy fingers fumbling for my phone. It's early, I realize, and then reluctantly admit to myself that it's early enough to fit in both a run and a shower before my first day of work.

Mike and I used to run every day before school, waking up at six in order to get a good workout in, but after the accident, I wasn't well enough to run. By the time we got to Aunt Kay's, both of us had fallen out of the habit. For a moment I ponder the idea of waking him up, even though it's normally him who knocked on my door. Sometimes he came in and tore the blankets away from me so I'd get up on time.

But today, still riding the high from yesterday's success at the library, I feel like running by myself. I hoist myself up and out of bed, staggering across the floor to my pile of clean clothes heaped on the floor, where I scold myself for not having them folded and put away yet. I tug on the first pair of spandex shorts my fingers touch and my favorite green athletic tank top, purposefully leaving my hearing aids on the dresser so I don't have to listen to the wind howling against the speakers. Then I tiptoe to the end of the hall and down the stairs, hoping like mad that my footsteps won't wake anyone else up.

It isn't until I reach the bottom of the stairs that I realize someone else is already up. Mike is lying on the couch, his back to the room, and at first I think he's asleep—until I see his shoulders shaking.

"Mike?"

He starts at the sound of my voice but doesn't roll over.

"Are you okay?"

My brother doesn't respond—at least, not that I can hear.

"If you're talking to me, I can't hear you," I say, conscious of the non-volume of my own voice, the silent vibrations rolling in my chest.

He rolls over at last, rubbing a hand over his face, and for a moment I think I was wrong, he was asleep, and I woke him after all.

"Sorry," I say, and then I get a good look at his face.

His cheeks are flaming red, eyes puffy and swollen, neck blotchy. He sniffs, getting to his feet, and pulls up the hem of his shirt to wipe his face as though he'd merely been sleeping after all, but I know better.

Mike's been crying, and I don't know why.

"What happened?"

"Nothing," he replies shortly, pushing past me into the kitchen.

"It's not nothing," I say, following him. "Are you okay?"

"Leave me alone, Skylar," he says, turning away from me so I have to guess at the last few words. His lips are trembling, but I know what my name looks like when he says it. I've just never seen it like this before.

"No!" I grab his arm, but he shakes me off. "Mike!" I can tell that my voice is rising, but I don't care anymore. "Tell me!" I've never had to ask him to talk to me before. I used to be the first one he'd come to.

"Shut up!" He actually pushes me away, takes me by the shoulders and shoves me backward. I stumble, and then, thanks to my eternally weak ankles, I trip and fall, landing flat on my butt.

"What is wrong with you?" I'm gasping for breath, my chest jarred uncomfortably by the fall, and I cough a little bit, trying to convince my lungs to start working again.

Mike stares defiantly past me, lips pressed in a thin white line, but he's trembling. I wait.

"Do you ever dream about it?" he asks finally, and something in the posture of his throat tells me this has come out in a whisper, strangled. It's only because I know Mike so well that I can read his lips at all.

"About what?" I make no move to get to my feet, and as he refuses to meet my eyes, I understand.

"I dream about it every night. You scream, and I hear it. Every night," he says, and this is strangled too. Finally, he's looking at me again, jaw clenched in his effort to hold his emotions in check. "Do you still hear things in your dreams? Or is that gone, too?"

"I don't know," I whisper.

"Oh, God," he bursts out. "Oh God." And I can't tell if it's a prayer or a plea, but the look on his face scares me, his eyes wider than I have ever seen them, desperate for something I can't name.

"Mike," I say, but his face closes off and I can tell he regrets his outburst.

"It's fine, Skylar," he snaps. "I'm fine. Sorry, I just…"

Neither one of us says anything.

"Don't tell Mom and Dad, okay?" He swipes at his eyes again, presses the heels of his hands against his forehead. "I just…it's fine. I'll get over it."

"I've dreamed about it, too," I say, but Mike shakes his head, cutting me off.

"I don't want to talk about this anymore." A muscle jumps in his jaw, then is still, and whatever I just saw is buried again. Mike opens the fridge and pulls out the peanut butter before turning to look at me. "Are you going for a run?"

"I was," I answer, still sitting on the floor. And then, after a minute, I add, "Do you want to come?"

He shakes his head and then turns his back to me completely, methodically spreading peanut butter on two pieces of bread and beginning to eat. I'm being shunned, and it stings. I get to my feet slowly, wanting to say something, to bring back the brother who was also my friend, instead of this stranger. My heart is still thumping, both from my fall and from being confronted by the look on his face, and I curl and uncurl my fingers a few times—they're stiff from being balled into fists.

I check over my shoulder twice on my way to the front door, but he doesn't turn around, and when I finally step onto the front porch, I've given up hope that he's going to. Instead of stretching, I leap straight off the top step and into a sprint, pounding down the driveway as though I could actually run away from the mess of my feelings. My thighs sear with the unexpected strain, but instead of slowing down—which, in this situation, would be the smart thing to do—I speed up, feeling myself tip forward as gravity begins to pull me just a little bit faster than my legs can run.

I ease up enough to stay on my feet and start to turn left. It's automatic after so many mornings of running with Mike. Today, just as I'm about to cross the street I pull back and veer off in the opposite direction. I don't want to think about Mike right now, don't want to think about turning left and where that took us both on one particular morning.

In trying not to think about it, the whole morning of the accident leaps prominently into the front of my mind, and although I try to banish it, the images flood my consciousness, dizzy in their poignancy. I run a few more steps but nearly fall, tripping over nothing, and slow to a walk, my hands on my knees. My chest is heaving, but not from exertion. I want the memories to stop. I want these feelings to go away. I just want to go for a run, the way I used to, and not have to think about anything except what I'm going to eat for breakfast when I get back.

After the worst of the dizziness has passed, I start walking again, making my way down Main Street. The town looks quiet; no one's awake yet at this hour as I limp down the street passing the library in a blur of morning light and crossing through multiple vacant intersections.

Where are the people? I want to scream, just to fill in the overwhelming silence. I need people to be here. I need visual noise if nothing else, I need a distraction from the fact that there is something wrong with my older brother and I don't know how to fix it.

I get a cramp in my abdomen, even though I'm not running anymore, the stitch knotting my insides together. I bend over, scrubbing my hand against the sore spot, gasping for air on my knees by the side of the road.

There is no one awake to see.

• ● •

I have to walk all the way home, hand pressed to my stomach, which means that by the time I've had a shower I'm already late for work. I grab my hearing aids off the dresser and run down the stairs, where I snag a Pop-Tart and slide my feet into flip-flops. My sundress whirls around my knees, and I hope it won't catch an incoming breeze and expose my underwear. Then, stomach still aching, I limp out to the van, where Dad is already behind the wheel, adjusting the mirrors.

"Okay, kiddo?" he asks, checking over his shoulder before reversing down the driveway.

"Fine," I mumble, buckling in and sinking my teeth into my poor substitute for breakfast. "Tired."

Dad writes children's books, and when he's in the middle of a first draft, he's often distracted and easily satisfied with my one-word answers. Right now, he spends the most time with Aiden and Sara, asking them serious questions about why brown dogs are happier than spotted dogs, or which swing on the swing set back home is their favorite, or why it's so hilarious to see an illustration of a kitten holding an umbrella.

"You were up early," he continues, which surprises me, but I don't feel like having this conversation right now, so I pretend that I didn't hear him. I can feel him looking at me, his red hair uncombed, glasses slightly crooked and perched on the bridge of his nose, but I stare at the window, watching the telephone poles flick past on Main Street.

"How's your book going?" Another attempt to distract him, but he doesn't take the bait.

"It's going well," he says, but the look he shoots me is unusually focused. He knows what I'm trying to do.

The drive to the Golden Sound Public Library is mercifully short, and when we finally pull up, I leap out of the front seat, smoothing down the green polka dots on my dress.

"See you later," I toss over my shoulder, purposefully not turning back to see if Dad has anything to say in return.

By the time the automatic doors slide open to admit me into the heart of the library, the clock over the front desk reads 9:20. I'm almost half an hour late.

"Sorry," I blurt out to Anastasia as I pass the counter, stumbling into the little gate when the latch sticks. "I'm really sorry I'm late, I went for a run and then…" *Don't tell her about Mike.* I grasp for something else to say instead. "And then I ate a Pop-Tart, but I was already late at that point. I mean, I ate it in the car on the way here, to save time, because I didn't want to be late, but it was already after nine. Because I…something happened." I try to sound off-handed, but by the way her eyes widened during the course of my little speech, I assume I'm not quite succeeding. "Something un-expected happened, and now I'm late, and I'm really sorry. Please don't fire me."

She says something in response but I'm moving past her, too fast to hear what it is. I turn back to try to read her lips, catch enough context to figure out the first half of her sentence, and I feel my right foot catch a rough spot in the floor. I struggle to recover, but the damage has been done, and I feel the room tip ever-so-slightly to one side.

The doctors say the balance issues are because of some scien-tific teeter-totter inside my ear, but I know better. I can't stand up straight because little slivers of *me* have been hacked away, I totter after every other step because each time my foot hits the ground, it's missing something. I grip the doorframe until my knuckles turn white because I've lost so much more than sound. I've lost essence, judgment, any sense of feeling or grasp on reality. It's as if I'm floating in time, hovering on a diagonal edge, reaching out for help but missing, like an optical illusion that reads "items closer than they appear."

Off-balance, I skitter to one side and career straight into Cam, who's carrying a tall stack of books. Or he was carrying them, until I rammed into him and knocked us both to the floor. Hardcovers slam into the tile floor beneath us, and Cam's arms pinwheel for a second, mouth open in surprise, before he topples to the floor, hard. His descent isn't made any easier by the fact that I actually fall on top of him, my chin on his chest and a book jammed into my side.

His frame compacts under me, and for a moment I think I've

killed him. Plus, I'm almost positive that my underwear is showing after all. I'm not sure which concept upsets me more.

For one very long second, nobody moves. Then Cam sits up, places his hands on my shoulders, and not unkindly—not like Mike—pushes me off of him. I sit on my butt and stare at him in horror, my skirt twisted over my knees and my chin throbbing. One of my hearing aids has fallen out and is lying on the floor beside me. I pick it up but don't put it back in right away. By the look on Cam's face, I can tell he's hurting too—probably in a few places he'd rather not reveal.

"Sorry," I say for the second time in two minutes. I can barely choke the word out past the realization that we met only yesterday and now I've knocked him over and fallen on top of him and practically almost committed murder on my first day at work. "I'm really sorry, Cam, I—"

He shakes his head at me to stop talking, leaning back on his arms, then his gaze shifts up to Ana, and reluctantly I look up too.

Both hands are placed over her mouth, but her eyes are horrified. I give up on trying to understand whatever it is that she's saying and look back at Cam.

"Yeah," he grunts, rubbing the back of his head. "We're okay. Skylar?" He turns to me, reaching for the book that I only now realize is clutched in my hands. I love him for saying "we," like both of us were casual victims of some outside occurrence and I didn't more or less assault him. "Are you good?"

I open my mouth to reply, to apologize again and say that I'm fine, mostly thanks to Cam for breaking my fall, but when I try to speak, the words won't come.

Instead, I sneeze.

And then, after drawing a shuddery breath, I have the terrifying feeling that I'm going to burst into tears. "Um," I say, holding one hand to my nose in what I hope is a casual sort of way, "I need to, um, use the restroom. I'll be back in a minute."

Ducking around Cam, I stride to the bathroom and only take my hands away from my face when the door is locked safely behind me.

Okay, Skylar Brady. I stare at my blotchy face in the mirror. *You need to pull it together.*

With two fingers, I find my pulse and hang on to it, feeling the steady beat of my heart as it slows back to a rate that can be deemed normal. There's no clock in the staff bathroom, I notice as I'm splashing water on my face, willing the puffy red bags underneath my eyes to go away.

It's not like I was on time anyway. I'd rather stay in here for the rest of the day, but the longer I delay my return, the weirder it's going to be. So after only a few minutes, I dry my hands, unlock the door, and step back into the library, where Anastasia almost instantly enfolds me in a tight, warm hug.

"I'm sorry," I say anyway, but I can feel her shaking her head, her earring slapping against my neck. So I just stand and let her hug me, taking deep breaths and trying to portray the image of a normal teenage girl who definitely has not been fighting tears in the bathroom for the past five minutes.

At last, Anastasia releases me, holding up one finger before I can start talking again. Picking her way around the still-spilled books and back over to her desk, she pulls out a small whiteboard.

Are you okay? She scrawls this in pink, bubbly letters. *Did you get hurt when you fell?*

"I'm okay," I answer, licking my lips.

Will she write that I've been fired on the whiteboard, too, or will I get an official letter? Do people write official letters when you get fired from a summer job?

"It wasn't the fall; I mostly landed on top of Cam, anyway."

Cam, standing at the front desk, nods emphatically. I can't decide if this is a good thing or not.

Do you want to talk about it?

"Not really," I say, relieved to discover that I don't feel like crying anymore. "I just…it was a rough morning. I'm not a morning person," I add, like that's a suitable explanation and everyone who hates mornings comes into work late, knocks down their co-worker, and then flees to the bathroom for no apparent reason.

Although who knows? Maybe that's the norm.

"I wanted to call your parents," Anastasia says, her eyes still wide. "And the Workplace Health and Safety Board, and maybe an ambulance, but Cam said that we should wait at least fifteen minutes before doing something that we might all regret later."

The last few words are said so quickly that it takes me a minute to understand, and when I finally glance up at Cam, he offers me a small smile.

"I have three sisters," he admits. "I thought it was worth a try."

"But you're feeling better now?" Anastasia asks, and I realize with a pleasant shock that she actually cares. She so badly would like for everything to be okay, and as I see this in her face, something in my chest relaxes. Maybe it will work out, after all.

"I'm feeling better," I say, and then swipe under my eyes one more time to check for mascara before I remember that due to my late start, I'm not actually wearing any. It's a small mercy on a morning like today.

"Well," Cam says, leaning back against the counter, facing away from the rest of the library so he can look at me. "Wanna get started on your training? It's nice and quiet now that you've scared everyone away."

I glance sharply at him and see a teasing look on his face; he's not angry, but as he waits for a response, I know he's testing me, trying to figure me out. He wants to know how I'll respond, who I really am.

Good luck. When you find out, let me know.

Out loud, I say, "I do tend to have that effect on people." As a joke, it's pretty pathetic, but for some reason Cam grins back at me anyway.

"We'll start with the returned books."

• ● •

After two hours, I've sung the alphabet so many times in my head, I'm pretty sure I'll be reciting it in my sleep, and the book titles have all started to blur together.

"Okay?" Cam pauses in the act of handing me a stack of paperbacks to scan through.

"Uh-huh," I reply numbly, sliding them under the red beam of light before stacking them by author's last name and setting them down on the nearby cart.

He touches my arm so I'll look up at him. "Do you need a break?"

"Nope," I say, determined to keep going. I can do this. I can.

Cam watches me try to scan in the next book three times before smoothing down the barcode label that was curling up on one side.

"Thanks," I say, and when I reach for the next book, it's not there.

"I need a break," Cam says and grins. "After a while, they all start to look the same."

"They sure do," I gasp out, resting my forehead on the counter before remembering that I'm supposed to be pretending that I'm handling this well. "I mean, kind of. It's okay. I'm getting the hang of it."

Cam laughs, and for the first time since the accident I find myself enjoying the sight of it before I realize the loss of the sound. His head tips back, eyes closed, and his shoulders hitch just a little bit when he gasps for breath, winded. The individual tones and nuances of his voice are filtered out by the little machines behind my ears that do so much, and at the same time, so little. But they can't take away the sight of his joy, and for that, I am thankful. I wonder what his voice really sounds like, without being mangled by my hearing aids. I'm so surprised by this thought that I have to re-stack an already ordered tower of books to disguise my interest.

I think instantly of Mike, the teenage male I am most familiar with, but dismiss the comparison almost instantly. Cam is tall and slim like Mike, but not as skinny. My brother is bony and full of sharp edges and corners, especially lately. Cam is more relaxed, more flexible than Mike. He looks like an athlete—not wiry enough to be a runner, but maybe a soccer player. Before the accident, I would have said they were alike, but now, Mike is practically a stranger. Cam seems more like Mike the way he used to be—maybe even more like Mike than Mike himself. Trying not to think about him, I wonder if Cam is anything like Gavin, but I can't think of a time when he's laughed like this, so free and relaxed.

I wonder, picking up another book and adding it to the stack in no particular order, what that says about Cam's voice? Gavin's is tenor and sort of monotone—not the way I imagine Cam's at all. I imagine Cam's voice, like the rest of him, would be even and natural, one of those voices you like to listen to without really knowing what it sounds like or being able to properly describe it when asked.

His hand reaches for the book I've incorrectly arranged, breaking into my daydream. "Skylar?"

"Yeah," I say, relinquishing the pile and tucking my hair behind my ears. "I'm good."

At this very opportune point in time, Anastasia comes around the corner of the counter, waving a paper Tim Hortons bag in the air. "I bought muffins! Are you two hungry?"

As if in answer, my stomach does a pathetic little flip, and when I glance at the clock I'm shocked to find it's after one P.M. "I'm starving." I accept the chocolate chip muffin that slides across the counter toward me.

"I think now is the perfect time to take our lunch hour." Ana hands me a little wooden sign that reads CLOSED FOR LUNCH (PROBABLY READING). "Just pop that … …" She scratches her nose, coughs into her elbow, and then takes a bite off the top of her muffin before finishing her sentence. "… would you please, Skylar?"

"Sorry," I say. "I, uh, didn't quite catch that."

"You can hang it over the door," Cam says, the faintest twitch of a smile hovering on his lips.

"Ah," I reply, straight-faced. "How could I have missed it." The playful jab goes unnoticed by Ana, but Cam laughs again, his head tipped back, eyes closed, and my smile begins in my chest long before it reaches my lips.

I like Cam, I decide. He feels like the kind of person I could be friends with, and as someone who hasn't needed to make a new friend since elementary school, this means a lot.

I kick my shoes off behind the counter and jog down the center aisle, worn carpeting against the soles of my feet as I reach the door and, after a moment of hesitation, flip the locks. I rest the sign against the front window and then walk leisurely back to the front desk, where Cam and Anastasia are deep in conversation. I wait, not wanting to interrupt, until I catch the word *sister*.

"You said you have a sister, right?" I shove my hip against the gate and walk behind the desk.

"Yeah," Cam says, reaching under the counter for his lunch. "There are six of us at home, if you count my parents."

"Seven if you count Elyse," Anastasia says proudly, as though Cam's siblings are her own personal achievement.

"Elyse?"

"My oldest sister." Cam rubs an apple on his shirt. "She's married and lives out of town."

"She's deaf," Anastasia says, and then pauses, and I think I see the words *just like you!* hovering around her lips. The space where those words would have fallen, had they been spoken aloud, stretches awkwardly.

I take pity on her and change the subject. "How about you, Ana? What about your family?"

Ana shrugs, reaching for something underneath the counter. "My parents live here in town, just a couple of blocks away from me."

"So it's just the three of you, then?" I run my finger along the edge of my lip, watching her face. "Do you have any siblings?"

A strange look flits across her face, the faintest twitch of a frown, a twisted lip, two rapid blinks, and then her expression smooths out into a neutral little smile. "One," she says, shrugging as though her words are supposed to be easy. Instead, they just look stiff. "I have an older sister."

I wait for more details and, when none are forthcoming, turn to Cam. He looks up from the counter, mouth full—he wasn't watching her, he didn't see her reaction—and traces the letter S in the air in front of me. "Her name is Sophia."

"Sophia," I say, sounding out the soft "ph," liking the way it feels, and I'm startled when Anastasia flinches in response. "What's she like?" I ask, and then think that maybe this is like poking an open wound. Maybe I should have left her alone.

"She's wonderful," is Ana's instant response, and I relax. "When we were growing up, she was my best friend."

I notice the past tense but bite back a comment and watch as Anastasia's lips slow, her gaze far away. I wonder what happened between the two of them that would put that look on her face, how you could spend your life growing up beside someone and then only be able to refer to them with stiff shrugs and one-word answers. She said they used to be best friends. So what happened?

Mike used to be my best friend, too. This thought comes unbidden, and I jerk back as though someone has physically touched me. He still *is* my best friend, I want to say, defensive without quite knowing why. He and I are nothing like Sophia and Anastasia. Probably. Nothing between us has really changed.

But I know that isn't true. Lots of things are different now, and smack-dab on top of the list is my relationship with my older brother.

Chapter
FOUR

IT TAKES ALMOST TWO WEEKS FOR ME TO SETTLE INTO THE ROUTINE AT THE library, but working with Cam and Ana is so natural that I almost don't mind making a mistake or two. Or twenty. After the first few days I barely have to focus on reading Cam's lips, and Anastasia learns by the end of the first week to face me when she speaks.

In turn, I figure out how to decipher the words of someone who is constantly in motion, creating little background noises of her own wherever she goes. It's like a dance, always back and forth, a battle to choose which noises matter and which don't. By the time week two wraps up, I feel like we've been doing it forever. Sometimes Anastasia and I walk part of the way home together.

On Monday afternoon, after our first shift of my third week, there's an unexpected rain shower coming down, so Cam offers to drive us all home. We all pile into the van. Ana claims the front seat, and I slide into the back, shoving a coloring book and several broken crayons out of the way so I can buckle myself in.

"Did you guys go on a road trip?" I regret my question as soon as I open my mouth, because Cam's driving, and over the road noise and my inability to see his lips, it's unlikely I'll understand his reply.

"Look," Ana says, twisting in her seat to face me. "I've never seen so many CDs in my life."

She pulls a box out from underneath her seat and begins to leaf through them. Cam shoots a quick glance down and then keeps his eyes on the road.

"They're what?" Ana's looking at him, but her face is still toward me. "What's VBS?"

Cam says something else to her, with that sheepish smile on his face again, and she slaps his shoulder. "Enough with you and the crazy Jesus music!"

"Jesus music?" I ask, giggling, and by the time the car stops outside Ana's house we're all laughing as she bounces up to her front door, waving her keys at us in farewell.

"Yeah," Cam says, after I move up to the front seat where I can hear him a little more clearly. "I like it. I mean, it's good music."

I'm not really sure how to respond, but I feel awkward just sitting there, so I ask the first thing that comes into my head. "So, you're a Christian?"

I instantly feel stupid as things click into place—the T-shirts, the music, other small hints. Obviously, he's a Christian, and just as obviously, I'm an idiot. To his credit, Cam doesn't laugh, but I see his lips tighten as he reins in a tiny smile.

"Yeah, I'm a Christian."

"Cool," I say, and want to kick myself for bringing it up. "And, uh…how's that working out for you? Do you like it?" What kind of a question is that?

This time, he does laugh. "Sometimes I like it, but I don't think that matters very much."

"Why not?" For some reason, I appear to be incapable of stopping this conversation. "If you don't like it, what's the point?"

He shrugs. "I believe it's the truth. I mean, I genuinely think Jesus is God." He darts another glance at me as he says it, and it's such an *awkward* moment I could just cringe. I mean, I guess God is fine for some people, but I've never given Him much thought before, and I don't think I want to start now.

To distract myself, I pull out my phone and find an unread text from Janie. Eagerly, I tap my way into the message, expecting paragraph after paragraph of details, all the juicy summer gossip, and hopefully more than a few details about Gavin, who I still haven't heard from since we left.

Instead, I find a hastily typed invitation to a party tonight.

It's addressed to someone named Daria.

Obviously a wrong number, I tell myself, tapping out a snarky response, but I feel shaken. Uneasy. I know we haven't talked much since the accident, but when did Janie have time to meet people without me? Especially people she'd want to invite to one of our parties. We always prided ourselves on having more fun than everyone else, because we only invited people we actually knew. Mike had come to a few, and Gavin, who lived down the street from one of our other friends, had been asked along as well. But who was this Daria? The pit of my stomach clenches uneasily, a hard rock right beneath my belly button.

I don't say anything else for a little while, thinking about Gavin and Janie, and then about Cam. This minivan smells like bubble gum and baby shampoo, and I have no idea how to restart the conversation without making it awkward, since I've been silent for so long.

"So," I say at last, still not sure what's going to come out of my mouth next. "Anastasia."

Cam grins. "She's pretty great, right?"

"Yeah," I say, relieved he's letting the God thing go so easily. "How long have you known her?"

"She was close with Elyse when I was growing up." He slows the van to a halt at Golden Sound's only stoplight, which always seems to be red, no matter what direction you're coming from.

"When she got her own place and started running the library, we started hanging out more."

"How old is she?" I realize too late that this isn't a polite question to ask someone, but I want to know, and Cam doesn't seem to mind.

"About ten years older than me," Cam says, slowly. "So, mid to late twenties? Maybe twenty-nine?"

"She seems younger than that," I say, and then I think of the look on her face when I mentioned Sophia two weeks ago. Just hearing the name aged her instantly. Again, that niggling worry—in ten years, will I talk about Mike that way, too?—appears before me, and I do my best to shrug it away, turning to look at Cam. *We are not the same!* I shout these words at myself over and over again, but I can't quite believe them.

"She does seem younger," Cam agrees, and then turns so I can see his lips, a small wrinkle between his eyebrows as if he's still thinking through what he's going to say next. "She's different than us," is what finally comes out, his voice clear and careful.

"I noticed," I say wryly, thinking of the sky-high heels, the pink letters on the whiteboard, and her incessant need for physical motion.

"I've known her since I was a kid," Cam goes on, as the light finally turns green. "And she's always been like this. She was born here, grew up here, even went to college online from home. I can't imagine her anywhere else. She belongs here, you know?"

"I know," I answer softly, and even though I've only been here for two weeks, only known her for fourteen days and haven't even walked to the end of Main Street yet, I understand that it's true.

"She went away once," he says, driving up Aunt Kay's street and then turning into the driveway. "She was gone for a year to live with her sister, and it felt weird. The whole town missed her." He pulls the keys out of the ignition and drops them into the cupholder between us. "Maybe it seems silly to a city girl—"

"Normally, it would," I say, making no move to get out of the van. "But with Ana, it makes sense. She's…" I hesitate, looking for the right word. "I don't know. You get the feeling that there's only one of her, and no matter where you go you'll never meet someone else like her. Like," I rush on, struggling to clarify, "you could go anywhere and meet someone like me. I'm just a jock, I fit the stereotype pretty much to the letter." Or at least, I used to. "And maybe you could go anywhere and meet someone like you too. But you get the feeling there will never be anybody else who you meet and go, 'Oh, I used to know someone just like you. Her name was Anastasia and you're the spitting image of her,' or whatever. I just don't see that happening."

Cam nods, drumming his fingers softly against the rubber of the steering wheel, and at the front of Aunt Kay's house, the curtains twitch as Aiden and Sara's faces appear at the window.

"What happened between them?" I ask after a pause, ignoring my younger siblings. "Sophia and Anastasia, I mean. She said they used to be best friends, and if they lived together for a year…"

I let the sentence trail off. Every time I say Sophia's name, I think of Mike. And then I try not to think about Mike, but I just can't help it somehow. Since it was my accident that caused this rift between us, I should be the one to repair it. But how do you fix a relationship when the other person won't even talk to you?

Cam shifts in his seat, cracking his knuckles—or at least, it looks like they're cracking—as he considers this. Aiden's half of the window is fogged up, and he's busy drawing smiley faces, but Sara is still watching us, eyes wide.

"I don't really know," he admits at last. "After the year was up, Anastasia came back and bought a house, and Sophia didn't, and no one's ever really asked why. Ana doesn't like to talk about it."

"I noticed," I say, so low I'm not sure he hears me.

"They used to be together all the time," he says, "and then suddenly, they were both gone, which was weird, and then after a year, we had Ana back. At first it felt like there was a piece of her missing, but after a little while…" He shrugs, a slight frown on his face. "I guess we all stopped noticing. It sounds terrible to say, but Sophia kind of kept to herself when she lived here. I think we all figured she'd moved on, but no one ever really talks about it."

"And Anastasia and Sophia aren't close anymore." The words hurt as they leave my mouth.

"I guess not," he admits, and by the way he studies me I know I've chased this topic too far. Then, before I can say goodbye, his gaze shifts to just over my right shoulder, and when I turn, I find Sara's inquisitive face pressed against the car window. When she sees me looking at her, she pulls the door open.

"Who are you?" She directs this question to Cam, one hand on her hip. Aiden is lingering halfway up the driveway, curious but too nervous to come closer.

"I'm Cam," he says politely, waving at Aiden, who waves back. "Who are you?"

"Sara," I whisper, "not now. Can you go back inside?"

"Are you Skylar's boyfriend?" Sara tilts her head to one side, and I feel a violent blush rise in my face.

"Okay," I say very loudly, unbuckling my seat belt and getting out of the car. "Cam has to go now. Say goodbye."

Thankfully, the twins lose interest and sprint across the lawn, deeply involved in some kind of game, and I turn back to Cam, trying to calm the heat in my face.

"Well," I say after a second, "thanks for the ride."

"No worries." Cam leans back in the seat, picks the car keys up again, and flips them a couple of times in his hand. "When is Kaylie coming back?"

I shrug, still a bit surprised that he seems to know her so well. Better than I do. "I'm not sure. I mean, she left us a note, but it wasn't very specific." A thought occurs to me, and since the conversation is clearly not quite finished, I sit back down, legs dan-

gling outside the half-open passenger door. "Does she do this often? Leaving with no warning?"

Cam nods. "Sometimes she's here every week for months, and
sometimes the knitting club meets without her for ages, but she
always comes back eventually."

"Do you think she'll come back this time, too?" We still haven't
heard from her since the letter she left for us.

Cam shrugs. "Eventually. It might not be soon, but I don't
think she could stay away forever. She belongs here, like Ana does.
She's like the whole town's aunt, in a way."

"I didn't know," I say, but it makes sense. Of course she's been
living her own life here, while we've been living ours. I never
thought about what that must have looked like before.

"Is it hard to share?" Cam grins, teasing me the same way he
and Ana tease each other, and I like it. It makes me feel like I be-
long somewhere again.

I'm about to reply when a rusty old pickup pulls into the driveway behind us. Instinctively, I check to make sure Aiden and Sara
aren't anywhere close by, but they've gone inside and left the screen
door swinging on its hinges.

"Is that your car?" Cam asks, eyes narrowed as he watches it
jerk to a halt, almost touching our bumper.

"No." I squint into the glare of the setting sun. "Ours is pulled
up behind the house."

We watch in silence as the passenger door opens and a dark
figure leaps out, just a silhouette in front of the light.

"Oh," I say with some surprise, as the figure reaches Cam's door
and then stops. "That's Mike."

Cam turns enough for me to read his lips, rolling down his
window. "Who?"

"My brother," I say, and Mike pulls his hood back enough that
we can see his face.

"All right, Skylar?" He ignores Cam, looking questioningly

through the window at me, and I don't know whether to be embarrassed or pleased that he's checking on me, making sure I'm okay in a car with some guy he doesn't know. Maybe Mike doesn't like me very much right now, but he stopped anyway, and the warm glow in my chest can't tell the difference.

Cam says something to him, looking away from me, and the two guys shake hands.

"This is Cam," I say, probably too late. "I work with him at the library. We're friends." *Way to go, Skylar. You sound exactly like a six-year-old.*

"Super good friends," Cam says, deadpan, and this flash of dry humor surprises me—he's so quiet at work—but I like it.

"Shut up," I say again, for lack of a better comeback. "I'll see you tomorrow."

"Yup." Cam puts the car in reverse and nods to Mike. "Later, man."

Mike waits for me to round the hood of the car, and we walk up to the front steps together, trying to think of something to say.

"Where were you?" I lean against the doorframe and wait for Mike to open the door for us. He smells odd, like a mixture between a hospital and a dying flower, cloying and heavy. It's too sweet, and I try to breathe through my mouth, but I can feel a headache bloom above my left eye in seconds.

He shrugs, fiddling with his phone rather than reaching for the knob. I know that smell, but I can't place it right now. "Just around. How was your day?"

Good, now that you're speaking to me again, I want to say, but that feels a little pathetic, so I shrug instead.

"Good. I hung out with Cam and Anastasia at the library, and then at lunch I went to the grocery store and bought ice cream for us." We split the tub of Rocky Road three ways, sitting in a circle on the floor behind the counter. There's a perfectly good table in the staff room, but we've never used it.

"That's nice," Mike says, finally opening the door. "He seems nice."

"Thanks," I say. *Nice*. Is that all he can come up with? The same brother who skipped class to come to my track meets, picked me up in the middle of the day when Janie and I had a fight and then bought me fries while I yelled at him in the car, the same brother who painstakingly pours syrup into all the squares of Sara's waffle. The only word he can find for me now is "nice"?

Mike shakes his head like a dog in the front entryway, and I shiver as the air conditioning meets the sweaty skin on the back of my neck. The clock above the door reads only quarter to six, but the thick layer of clouds has made the evening dim.

My skin feels crisp, like I've come in from a fall afternoon, and as the glow seeps inside my skin and settles in my chest, I try to imagine coming home from the local high school to Aunt Kay's house every afternoon, maybe Cam picking me up before work, or walking to the bus stop with Mike. He and Cam are the same age, only a year older than me, just graduated from high school. Would they go to the same university?

I picture them sitting side by side in a lecture hall, exchanging notes and then discussing essay topics on the way to lunch. It's a nice idea, and I stay there, a smile sitting easily on my lips, until Mike bumps my shoulder on his way into the living room. I'd intended to follow my stomach straight into the kitchen, but a flicker of movement catches my eye, and I pause with one foot on the tile, one still resting on the welcome mat of the front entryway.

"Where have you been?" Mom's lips flatten at the end of her sentence, her arms crossed over her chest. Dad appears at her shoulder, glasses on and eyes focused behind the lenses. Clearly, he hasn't done much writing today. In our family, we measure Dad's productiveness by the level of distraction in his eyes at any given time. The less he sees us, the more we know he's living in the world of his characters. Today, he's 100% present, which doesn't bode especially well for Mike.

I can't see my brother's reply, his words just a whisper in my hearing aids, but when he tries to push past my parents into the living room, Dad puts a hand on his chest, holding him in place.

My stomach leaps into my throat, and I swallow convulsively. Dad's so gentle I forget how big he is sometimes, but he towers over my brother, who is almost exactly six feet tall with his shoes on. I haven't paused to notice the difference in their heights lately, but with the two of them standing almost nose to nose, I see it now.

"Answer your mother properly," Dad says, and while the lines on his face are soft, there is no humor in his eyes.

Mike replies again with something I can't read but jerks out of Dad's grip and takes a step back, the line of his shoulders as hard and immovable as rock.

"Mike," I say, stepping forward, but no one hears me.

My brother turns so his back is to the wall, and I can catch just the slightest glimpse of his face. His expression looks like his shoulders—stiff and frozen.

"I told you," he says, spitting out the words. "I went for a walk."

"All day?" Mom puts a hand on Dad's arm, stepping forward. Her eyebrows are drawn up and one long wrinkle crosses her forehead. I imagine her voice, pitched lower and with just the hint of a fissure at the end of each sentence. The more upset she is, the harder she strives for control, and the more measured her sentences are, the more fragile they sound. By buckling her words down tightly, she creates tiny fractures in each one. "Mike, you're not in trouble. We just want to know where you were. We woke up, and you were gone. You didn't call, and you didn't answer your phone." For once, she's not paying attention to me. I just wish it didn't have to be because something's wrong with Mike.

"I'm an adult," Mike says, the muscles in his neck drawn tight. "I don't have to tell you everything anymore."

"You're not an adult yet." I can almost hear Dad's voice in my head. Like water, it doesn't seem strong until you're caught in a current and swept off your feet.

"You're only eighteen," Mom says, and then she seems to think that the conversation is getting out of hand, putting a hand over her mouth as though to physically hold back her words. She says something else behind her hand that I can't see, a faint thrum through my ears, and then pulls it away. "We just want you to talk to us, Mike. We know you're upset—"

"Stop," he says, folding his arms. "I don't want to talk about this. Not with—" He turns so I can't see his lips anymore, but by the way Mom and Dad both look over at me it doesn't take much to guess that he doesn't want me around.

"What's wrong?" I feel my voice catch in my throat and know that it comes out very small and hoarse.

"Nothing," mutters Mike in my direction, and then turns back to our parents. "I got a job today, okay? So just get off my case about not being around as much. I'm making my own decisions, isn't that what you want?"

He rounds the sentence off with a four-letter word dropped heavy into the room, and even being hard of hearing doesn't dampen the bitterness in his voice. Mom looks like she's been slapped in the face, and Mike takes advantage of their startled pause to spin on his heel and hoof it up the stairs.

My parents exchange glances as he reaches the landing, and when Mom winces half a second later I figure he's slammed the bedroom door. How mature.

The three of us stand in an awkward triangle, Mom's arms folded as she runs her fingers up and down her bicep, Dad's hands dangling loosely at his sides. At last he pulls his glasses off, wiping them on the hem of his shirt, but I can tell by the twitch in his jaw that he is furious.

"Well," he says, so calmly I know it must take an incredible effort, "at least the twins didn't hear him this time."

"This time?" I say, and I know by the way he looks up sharply that he's forgotten I'm still here. "You've had this discussion before?"

Mike has disappeared before? Where?

"Mike finds it hard," Mom says, switching on her hyper-enunciation now that she's speaking directly to me. I know I'm being shuffled to the side. They will deal with Mike later, when I'm not around to watch it happen.

"So?" I try not to sound like a jerk, but I have a cramp in my chest and I'm not feeling very gracious toward Mike right now. "Do any of us find it easy?"

No one has to ask what the "it" is we're referring to.

"Skylar," Mom says, but Dad rests a hand on her arm, and she stops, blinking hard. My stomach drops. When will everyone cut the act and start acting normal around me again? It's been months since the accident.

Dad waits until I look away from Mom, my eyes searching for his face. "We'll finish this conversation another time," he says, but I see Mom bite her lip and I'm not sure that I want to. "The twins are playing in their room upstairs. Why don't you go tell them to wash their hands for supper?"

I know a dismissal when I see one. "Sure," I say, and shrug out of my rain jacket.

The inner layer sticks to my skin as I peel it off, damp with the humidity of summer rain. I'm halfway up the stairs, fingers wrapped tightly around the railing, when I chance a look down. My parents are standing in the entryway to the kitchen, locked in an embrace. Mom's head is against Dad's chest, her face turned away from me, but my father is facing the stairs, eyes closed, and the look on his face is so tired that the ache in my chest twists inside of me.

I pause outside my brother's closed—and probably locked—bedroom door. *What are you doing to us, Mike?*

Then I remember the way he looked lying on the couch the morning I came down and found him crying, and I'm not sure if I should be angry with him or not.

"Aiden," I call instead, "Sara, it's suppertime."

The door is flung open under my hand, and the twins rush out, pounding down the stairs in a blur of knees and elbows, and I follow them without a backwards glance, because it's easier this way.

Whatever, Mike. I try to convince myself that I don't care.

It doesn't work.

• ● •

I get dressed in the middle of a thunderstorm the next morning, the sky black and pregnant with clouds. The hairs on my skin feel tingly and charged, although the electricity in the air is nothing compared to the tension in the car when Mike drives me to work, so heavy I have to remind myself to sit up under the weight of it.

"Have a good day," I say when he pulls up to the doors. Mike stretches out a hand to stop me from leaving the car.

"Sky," he says, the only one in my family who shortens my name. "About last night."

I swallow hard, waiting, but he doesn't say anything.

"Mike?"

He shakes his head, pulling his arm away from me. "Never mind."

"Are you sure?" I hover, my hand on the door, hoping he'll change his mind.

He nods to the door, just a jerk of the chin to push me out of the car. "Bye, Skylar."

I feel sick, but I can't do anything except leave him with whatever he was thinking left unsaid. Was it an apology? A confession?

"Bye." I leap out into the downpour and sprint hard for the library doors, my hands clapped protectively over my ears. It's only a few feet to the door, but my shirt is soaked almost through before I land on the mat, gingerly patting my hearing aids to make sure they're still dry. Why hadn't I grabbed my rain jacket?

"It's nasty out there," I proclaim to the almost-empty library. I'm trying to make myself feel better by acting as though nothing is wrong, and Cam nods his head in agreement from behind the front counter. I'm determined to move on from this situation, from Mike being the biggest jerk ever, but after only a few minutes a faint pinpoint of a headache begins to throb behind my left eye. When the lights flicker, a faint rumble in the background, I glance at Cam. "Thunder?"

"Yup," he says, and I think maybe this is the widest I have ever seen him smile. "It's awesome."

"I miss the sound of thunder," I say, approaching the desk.

"You can't hear it?" He looks at my left ear, where he can probably see the tip of my hearing aid under my braid.

Without thinking, I reach back to touch it, and he looks away.

"Sorry," he says, ducking his head a little bit, as though he's embarrassed. "Maybe it's rude to ask."

"I don't care," I say, letting my hand drop. "And I can still hear thunder, kind of, but it's different. Quieter." Before he has a chance to reply, I glance across to the vacant front counter. "Hey, where's Anastasia?"

Cam grins and looks down at his feet, and when I lean over the counter a head full of blonde curls greets me. Ana is sitting cross-legged on the floor beneath the desk, looking up at me.

"Good morning," she says cheerfully, waving a screwdriver at me in greeting.

"What are you doing under there?" I rest my forearms on the counter, trying to remember if there are any logical reasons for head librarians to be sitting under their desks instead of standing behind them. I can't think of any.

"Well," Anastasia says in reply, "my dog is terribly afraid of thunderstorms, and he seems to find that crawling under things makes him feel better. So, in order to really, you know, identify with my dog, I'm sitting under the desk to see if it makes me feel better."

"Are you afraid of thunderstorms?"

"No," she admits, and when Cam taps the desk in front of me, I look up at him.

"She's fixing a loose screw," he explains, grinning. "Not the one in her head, a real one."

Ana slaps his knee, and too late, he jumps out of her reach.

"Ah," I say, scrutinizing the situation. "And is it working?"

"Yes!" says Anastasia, as Cam shakes his head silently above her.

I stifle a laugh and take my nametag when Cam hands it to me.

"We'll probably get a lot of people today," Ana predicts, popping to her feet and whisking a curl out of her eyes with the back of her hand. "When it's rainy, the tourists pour in, and parents bring their kids, and we get lots of coffee groups and book clubs and goodness only knows what else. So put your people face on."

She says this with what I think is supposed to be an encouraging smile, hands raised in the air like a cheerleader, but the smile is more of a grimace and since she's brandishing a screwdriver instead of a pom-pom, the effect is more than a little bit menacing.

"Or not," Cam says, taking the tools from her.

"Maybe we could just put our normal faces on instead," I say, turning in time to see the first few people duck in out of the rain.

"Good morning," I call to them, and maybe my voice doesn't quite reach the front doors, but Cam and Anastasia don't seem to care.

By 11:30, the library is bustling. Anastasia and Cam check books out in two lines, and I'm frantically shelving away as fast as the paperbacks come pouring in through the return slot. My hair is falling out of its braid, I've got sweat stains under both of my armpits and possibly across my back, and I've just become aware of a blister on my toe when somebody's child spills our entire Lego collection all over the floor and then proceeds to scream so loudly I think I'd be able to hear it even without my hearing aids. I decide to test this theory and discover that, although my hypothesis fails, the silence is far preferable to the tantrum. I leave my hearing aids turned off until I see Anastasia waving at me from the front counter some time later, then I turn them back on and leave my cart in the now-empty aisle, skirting the pile of spilled Legos as I approach the counter.

"Are the raspberries in the fridge yours, Skylar?" Cam pokes his head out of the staff room, waving the clear plastic container over his head as Anastasia skips to the front of the library to hang the "closed" sign.

"Yeah," I say, scraping my hair into a ponytail. "You can have some if you want."

"Sweet." He pops it open and scoops some of the fruit into his hand before passing the container to Anastasia as she comes back behind the counter. "Hey," he says. Then around a mouthful of food so I can barely hear what he's saying, "Isn't that your brother?"

This is a translation of what I actually read on his lips, which looks more like "Ihhh ahhh ohhhh buuuthaaa?" I only realize that he's talking about Mike when I follow his outstretched hand to the figure walking by the front window. A thin sliver of sunlight peeks through the covering of clouds, making the street shimmer where the water droplets have pooled. Mike has pulled his hood down, and he's looking toward the library, talking animatedly to the guy next to him.

"Who's that?" I ask, taking a raspberry for myself.

"I don't know," Cam says, and swallows what's in his mouth with a gulp so pronounced I think I can actually hear it.

I put down the raspberries and stare hard out the window after the two of them. Mike's taller, and dark, but the guy with him is muscular, his shirt stretched tight across his back and upper arms. His hair is light brown, and it sticks up in tufts. He lifts a hand to his mouth and then when it relaxes by his side, I see a faint white shape wedged between his fingers. Is he smoking?

I look back at Cam, who has closed the container of raspberries and is very busy tidying the already-neat pencils on the front counter. Anastasia has the phone pressed to her ear and is breaking her potato chips into pieces before putting them into her mouth, gesturing broadly into thin air and paying us no attention.

"You've never seen him before?" I try to keep the disbelief out of my voice.

Cam straightens and turns to me, rubbing the back of his neck with his hand. "I don't know for sure. He looks like someone I know, but I could be wrong."

He makes eye contact with me, but I can tell the effort costs him.

"What's wrong?"

"Probably nothing."

"Stop dodging my questions." I smile to cushion my words, but it feels forced.

"He looks like a guy I went to school with," Cam says, sighing. "Eric."

"And…?" As I push for details, for the first time I feel the newness of our friendship. There's a line, somewhere, where I'll have to stop digging for answers, and I don't know where it is.

"It's probably not a big deal, Skylar." Cam reopens the raspberries, but he hasn't looked back out the front window. This makes me feel better, although I'm not sure why. "And maybe it's not even him. He just…we didn't really get along in high school."

"What do you mean?" I think about my high school, and suddenly I'm missing Janie and Gavin.

When Cam takes a little longer to answer, I look away from the window. He's still picking through the raspberries, but he's got a weird look on his face, like he put one in his mouth and it was sour.

"Cam?"

"Sorry," he says. "I really hated high school." He forces the words out, and I notice the tension in his shoulders. "Eric and I had beef a couple of times in ninth and tenth grade. It's not really a big deal."

"What kind of beef?" I ask this without thinking, and then by Cam's stung look, I realize too late that I should have left him alone.

"He had friends and I didn't," Cam says abruptly. "They'd spend the weekend partying and getting high, and then he'd come after me to do his homework. Or he'd just take my assignments, change the name, and hand them in as his. I didn't have anyone to back me up, so for a while I just let it happen. Eventually at the end of tenth grade I got tired of it and said no, and we got in a fight, and after that, he didn't bother me anymore. That's it."

He finishes, but I can practically see the words *Are you happy now, Skylar?* hovering around the edges of his lips.

"I'm sorry," I say, and for a minute I feel so bad about asking him that I forget that my brother is now hanging out with this guy and that this is a HUGE problem.

"It's okay." Cam sets down the raspberries, looking me in the eye. "Seriously, I shouldn't still be upset about it. It was a couple of years ago, and high school is over now, and I overreacted about the whole thing."

There's a brief pause, and then I have to ask one more question. "Are you sure it was him?"

Cam glances at me sideways but doesn't answer right away.

"Not that I don't believe you," I rush on, "but Mike's not like that. He wouldn't hang out with a guy like Eric."

"So maybe it's not him." Cam shrugs, as though putting the matter behind him. I wish he had come to my high school. He would have fit right in with all of us. Janie would love him.

He opens a box of Smarties and tosses me a handful, most of which I fail to catch. "Or if it is Eric," he continues, crouching to scoop up a stray candy, "maybe he's changed."

"Maybe," I say, thinking that Cam is far more willing to forgive than I am. "I just don't know what to do about him."

"Who, now?" Cam throws away the discarded candy and pours me a fresh handful.

"You're a guy," I say, and toss the whole handful straight into my mouth. I think about my words while I chew, waiting until I swallow to speak them. "Why is my brother being so weird?" I want him to give me a normal answer, say that all teenage boys act like this, tell me it has nothing to do with the accident at all.

"I don't really know him. If he's anything like you, though," he says, throwing the now-empty box over my head and into the garbage can, before heading out onto the floor, "he can handle Eric."

I study him, searching for a clue that he's aimed a jab at me, but he seems sincere. "Well, thanks," I say to his retreating back. I look out the window in time to see the last lonely ray of sunshine disappear as the rain starts again.

Chapter
FIVE

"AGH!" ANA SLAMS THE LIBRARY PHONE BACK INTO ITS CRADLE WITH SUCH force that the whole desk shakes. Heads turn by the front windows, and I accidentally click "log out" in the middle of my first transaction and have to restart the whole computer before I can finish checking out a customer's books. It feels as though seeing Mike yesterday hasn't just thrown me off, it's put the whole library into some weird kind of funk this morning.

"What's wrong?" I ask, after I've printed the receipt and it's clear that Cam won't be showing up to intervene. He probably has his head buried somewhere in the children's section, where the books are in constant disarray, shoved back into place by parents who don't have the time or the hands to spare for shelving them properly.

"Nothing," Anastasia says, and then before I can say, *Oh, good, just checking, wonderful, great,* and make my escape, she barrels straight on. "Do you have siblings, Skylar?"

I already don't like where this conversation is going. "Yes," I say, "two younger, they're twins."

She waits.

"And," I say, dragging the words out, "an older brother. Mike."

"Well." Ana yanks the book cart over with such force that it tips up onto two wheels. "Good luck, that's all I have to say."

"Was that who was on the phone?" I scoop up a few titles from the top of the cart and scan them in, fingers finding the barcodes so I can keep my eyes on Ana's face.

She looks confused. "What phone?"

"You were talking on the phone, and then you started talking about siblings," I say, "so I just wondered, were you talking to Sophia?"

"Oh," Anastasia pauses, her hands in midair, and she looks as though someone has taken the wind out of her sails. "No, that was a book distributor from the States. I can never get through a conversation with him without yelling about something." She says this absently, without animation.

"So," I say slowly, thinking through my words before I say them. "You started talking about my siblings because…?" I'm thinking that maybe her sister is married to a book distributor, or knows one, or wants to be one, looking for any possible connections between the phone call and the sibling-related interrogation, but Anastasia shakes her head.

"I think about her all the time," she says, her gaze far away. "That's the thing about siblings, Skylar." She says my name, but she doesn't see me, not really. "You can leave them, but you can't really lose them. I've been trying not to think about her for years, but it doesn't work. I just can't help it."

I want to find some reassurance in that "can't really lose them," but looking at her face does nothing to convince me that Mike and I will turn out okay. She's had all this time and still hasn't been able to fix whatever went wrong between them. The pain of it aches within me, mixed with the fear that I'm looking at my own future. This is not how I want to end up. I stand there, fingertips resting on the barcode of my next book, watching Ana stare out the front windows, until at last someone approaches her with a question about Agatha Christie mysteries.

"Oh!" she says then, and goes off to help them, but her words weigh on me for the rest of the afternoon. The sense of limpness hangs over Ana all day, and then at four o'clock, when we lock the front doors and begin to tidy up for the night, she hands Cam the master key ring.

"I have a headache," she says, peering at him through an exaggerated squint. "Can you lock up for me tonight?"

"Sure." Cam takes the keys from her and tosses them to me. I catch them and twirl them around my finger a few times before sliding them into my pocket.

"Are you okay?"

Ana hoists her purse over one shoulder and glances out the window. "Of course!" Her cheeriness feels forced. "Now that the rain's stopped, I'm perfect! Wonderful!"

Cam and I watch in silence as she trips her way down the center aisle toward the front. She waves at us before stepping outside, but as soon as the door closes behind her, her shoulders slump and she puts a hand over her face, like she's forgotten we can still see her. My stomach twists as she leans against the window, a hand over her eyes, before sucking in her breath and striding to her little car on the edge of the parking lot.

"That was weird," Cam says, and we watch as she fumbles for her keys before finally

getting her car unlocked. She chucks her purse unceremoniously into the backseat and then flops down through the driver's side door. "Ana never gets headaches."

"Yeah," I say, my skin bare and prickly like I've just seen somebody naked. Maybe, in a

way, I have.

"You can go if you like," he says, still staring thoughtfully at Ana's car, which is peeling away toward Main Street at what looks like twice the speed limit. "I'm not going to do much tidying, I'll just lock up the windows and then go."

"Thanks," I say, handing him the keys. "I want to make it to the grocery store before the rain starts again."

"Later." He waves as I trace Ana's path to the front door.

The air hangs heavy with thunder, and I look up anxiously, checking for more rain. The food market is only a couple of storefronts away, but stray droplets skitter across my arms, a cold wind blowing in off the lake, and I don't think I have more than a few seconds before the next downpour. I tug my braids forward so they're covering more of my hearing aids to protect them from spare drops, and then something explodes behind me. For one split second, I think I'm about to be struck by lightning, and then I look around and realize that it must have been a horn, since there's a car pulled over beside me.

The window rolls down, and I hover between the door and the sidewalk, hand still outstretched. I should turn and go inside, but whoever's in the car will know that I've seen them, and I don't want to be rude. The driver leans across the guy in the passenger seat, busy on his phone, and grins up at me. A smattering of freckles dusts his nose, and when he grins, two perfect dimples appear on either side of his mouth. His shirt looks familiar, and I can't shake the feeling that I've seen this guy before. There is a faint smell of cigarette smoke wafting out the open window, mixed with something sweet and toxic, the same smell Mike came home with the other night. This time, I recognize the odor of freshly-smoked weed, and my muscles clench at the bottom of my stomach.

As the guy in the front opens his mouth to speak, I put the pieces together from earlier. This must be Eric.

"Hey," he says, and I'm frozen, trying to decide whether to run or scream or just stand and see what he wants. *Leave Mike alone!* I want to yell, but I restrain myself.

"Do you need a ride somewhere? I've got space in the back."

"No," I say, folding my arms, and then unfolding them, in case it makes me look defensive. "I mean, no thanks, I'm here already."

"Too bad," he says, and winks at me—actually winks at me!—before jabbing his finger to the backseat. "Your brother said you'd say that, but when I see a pretty girl, I just can't help myself."

His words leave a faintly bitter taste in my mouth, but nothing compared to the queasiness that squirms into my throat when I see who's in the backseat. My brother lifts a hand to wave, but the tips of his ears are red.

I swallow hard.

"Roll down your window," I say to Mike, pointing, but whether it's because they didn't hear me or Eric said goodbye when I wasn't paying attention, the car pulls away from the curb instead. "Mike!"

Eric sticks his hand out the window in farewell, but my brother's face remains turned forward as the car pulls an illegal U-turn and then careens off down the street to goodness only knows where. The boys are heading toward Aunt Kay's house, but the sick feeling in my stomach says Mike won't be home when I get back.

I refuse to let our story end like Anastasia and Sophia's. No matter what Mike thinks, I'm not going to let him cut me out of his life. I'm willing to fight for him, even if Ana can't find the energy to do anything about the rift between her and Sophia.

I stand outside the store for so long that the manager comes to the door, a questioning look on his face. "Sorry," I blurt out, and then instead of going inside to buy milk like I'm supposed to, I turn on my heel and sprint back to the library. I haven't figured out how to fix what's going on with Mike, but suddenly I have another idea. Maybe Ana hasn't been able to forget her sister because she never figured out what to do about her. Maybe all she needs is a little extra help.

It's not far to the front doors of the library, and I skid to a halt right as Cam is locking the door, my hair blowing in my eyes.

"Cam!" I gasp out, more for show than because I'm very winded.

He says something to me as he turns, but I can't hear through the wind feedback in my speakers, so I talk over him. "Do you have Sophia's phone number?"

"Yeah," he says, and his shoulders relax. He flips a stray curl out of his eyes and then taps two long fingers against the bridge of his nose. "You scared me, running out of nowhere like that."

"Sorry," I say, "I'm fine." This isn't strictly the truth, but I'm so embarrassed about my encounter with Eric that I decide it's probably better not to mention that he spoke to me at all. I'd like to think I came across as strong and intimidating, but I feel cowed instead, and insecure.

I drag myself back to the present and look at Cam, who is waiting for me to keep talking. "I have an idea," I say, shutting down the last thoughts about Eric and Mike and the car outside the grocery store. With one last half-hearted flip, my stomach settles again.

"Shoot," he says, yanking on the door to make sure it's locked before turning his full attention to me.

"I think you should call Sophia," I say, the idea taking shape as the words fly out of my mouth. "Maybe suggest she come for a visit, or call Anastasia, or something. I mean, it's been so long since she was here, everyone misses her. Ana misses her," I say. "She said something to me today, about how she can't stop thinking about her. And I just thought that maybe if Sophia were to come back, then maybe…" I make my best hopeful face at him, but he doesn't look convinced.

"I don't know, Skylar," he says, but I see his hand reaching for his phone. "Sophia and I didn't know each other that well, I think it'd be kinda weird if I called her up out of nowhere."

"You don't even have to mention Ana's name," I say, twisting my fingers into knots behind my back. Maybe if she stops and remembers Anastasia, she'll want to come back. Maybe if all Ana needs is a little push, she'll step forward and fix things. And if Ana can solve this problem, then I know I can figure mine out, too. "And I mean, it's probably not that weird. If she called you today, just to be like, 'Hey, I really miss Golden Sound…'" I stop talking when Cam coughs into his hand, trying to hide his smile. I sigh. "Okay, maybe that would be kind of weird."

"Yeah," he agrees.

"But she used to know Elyse," I say, "so, maybe it wouldn't be that strange? Like, you could say Elyse asked you to call or something?"

"Why is this so important to you?" Cam's hand is now in the same pocket as his phone, but he makes no move to take it out. He's staring at me, eyes slightly narrowed, and I have an unexpected urge to cross my hands over my chest, as though Cam's steady gaze could bore straight through my skin and into the heart beneath as it cries my brother's name.

"It's not that important," I say, unconvincingly.

He studies me for a minute more, and I try to look like this was just a casual idea I came up with while on my way to the grocery store. I'm in the process of realizing that maybe abandoning my shopping and sprinting to the library might have been why Cam assumed this was important to me, when he pulls out his phone.

"Okay," he says, and his thumb taps the screen. "I don't get why it matters so much to you, but I'll give her a call."

"Thank you," I blurt out, and then add, "I thought it might be, um, a good idea." Cam doesn't need to know all the details about Mike, but I can't think of a more reasonable explanation for my irrational behavior, so I'm relieved that he doesn't ask.

"Right," he says, and shoves me with his shoulder as he lifts the phone to his ear, and I know that Cam does not for one second believe the lie that this phone call doesn't matter.

"Are you still going to the grocery store?"

"Yeah," I say, and the dirty feeling returns as I remember Eric winking at me. I'd rather just go home.

"I'm just asking," he says, squinting at the sky, "because it's starting to rain again, and I really don't want to open the whole library for one phone call."

As if in response to his statement, a large droplet of water plops onto the top of my head.

"Let's go," I say, and step slightly ahead of him so I can read his lips as he makes the call.

It's ringing, he mouths to me, the outlines of his words softer than if he'd spoken aloud. I bounce from foot to foot across the sidewalk, dodging the hesitant raindrops as we climb the short hill to the grocery store.

"Hey," Cam says into the phone, standing up a little straighter. "It's Cam calling, from Golden Sound."

There's a short pause, and then, "Yeah." A relaxed grin spreads crookedly across his face, the right side of his lip lifting slightly higher than the left. "Elyse's brother. I'm not that little anymore."

A cool breeze lifts my hair off the back of my neck, and I almost forget to breathe as I watch Cam's lips.

"No, nothing's wrong," he says, and then scratches his forehead, tilting his head to one side to balance the phone against his shoulder as his fingers unhook the strap of his watch and then do it back up again. Unhook, re-buckle. The movement is practiced and fluid. "I'm mostly calling to say hi. No one's heard from you in a while. We miss you."

Say it, I want to scream at him. I take a deep breath in through my nose, and the air smells like summers spent with Janie and Gavin, racing down the street to the local pool, climbing the tree in my backyard, and calling each other's parents to beg to be allowed to stay overnight. I touch the tip of my nose with my fingers. I breathe again, trying to find that elusive scent, but now the air just smells like air, warm and sandy in my lungs. Cam is still beside me, his shirtsleeve brushing against my arm as we walk, and the warm feeling inside me grows, instead of shrinking away.

"Ana misses you." He tucks his chin down when he says it, and I imagine his voice projected lower, since most vocal nuances are lost to me, flattened into a monotone with the occasional crackle to add flavour. He's looking down at the ground, so I miss the next few sentences, staring instead at the swirl of hair right on the back of his head. If I were to trace the path of the hair with my finger, I could make almost a full circle before it begins to wave, falling out of pattern.

"Yeah," he says, looking up again. He startles when he sees me standing there, as though he's forgotten me, and I wish I could see both sides of the conversation. "Okay. You too. Bye."

Cam pockets his phone, and then stops outside the grocery store, playing with his watch strap again, his gaze directed somewhere over my head. Unhook, re-buckle. Pause. Repeat.

"Well?" I ask at last, the word exploding out of me.

"That was weird," he admits, and the faraway look in his eyes disappears.

"What did she say?" I dance from one foot to the next, and twist my ankle, teetering dangerously on the edge of the curb before Cam grabs my arm.

"She asked if I was Elyse's little brother," he says, grinning, and I can feel five places on my wrist where his fingers have touched me. "And if Golden Sound was still Golden Sound."

"And Ana?"

Cam swings the door open and holds it for me. A little brass bell trembles silently at the top of the doorframe as I step across the threshold. He waits to reply until we're standing side by side in the aisle.

"She didn't say too much." He reaches for his watch and then slides his hands back into his pockets. "Did you say you needed milk?"

"Yes," I say reluctantly and follow him down an aisle to the left, my eyes level with the broad part of his back.

I wait as a lady with a shopping basket cuts between us, my gaze darting from the bin overflowing with oranges, to the bright red curtains, to the wind chimes that dangle from the ceiling. So many colors pop, and even though the movements are soundless, like a TV on mute, I can almost imagine what Cam must hear as he walks by. It's magical.

"I love this store," I gasp out to Cam's back when I finally catch up with him again, bent forward to pick up two bags of milk.

"So did Elyse," he says, passing one of the bags to me. "But she wouldn't tell me why."

I shift the freezing cold milk from arm to arm, the bags sagging from one side to another as they leave condensation droplets on my skin, and I think of Elyse. It must have been hard to grow up deaf, to live in a world that no one around you ever understood, to know what it must feel like to be them while wondering if anyone else knows what it feels like to be you.

"I know why," I say, mysteriously, and deposit the bag on the front counter before Cam can ask me to explain.

The cashier is a gangly boy about our age, with his hair spiked up at the front. He's all corners and edges, elbows flying out in all directions as he scans the milk, punches in the code for the debit machine, and flings the cash drawer open for no apparent reason. I tap in the PIN number for my card and watch the cut of his shoulders as he reaches for a bag. His shoulder blades are razor-sharp underneath his T-shirt, and I almost expect to see a rip appear as they scissor back and forth along with the movement of his arms.

"Hey, ham?" he says, turning from the register. One eyebrow cocks like he's asking a question, and I slide my card out of the machine and reach for the bags.

"No, thanks," I say, and then feel Cam turn sharply beside me. "I mean," I continue, a little prickle at the back of my neck warning me that I should probably stop talking, "I'm sure it's delicious, but no."

The cashier stares at me, his mouth hanging open and I count the seconds as they go by. *One, two, three,* before Cam bumps my arm.

"Skylar," he says, enunciating carefully, "this is a friend of mine."

Oh. Not ham. Cam. The difference is in the back of the tongue, a movement I can only catch if I'm looking at someone head-on, and even then, only sometimes. The cocked eyebrow must have been a muscle twitch.

"Um, hi." I waggle my fingers at him and then scoop my milk off the counter, the back of my neck burning. *Excellent job, Skylar.* I'm glad no one from my family is here to witness this.

Cam says something else to him that I don't bother trying to read and then follows me out the door, where the little bell swings cheerfully as we step down onto the pavement.

"Sorry," I say, tucking my chin down to my chest. "I thought he said 'ham,' instead of your name, and then I couldn't figure out why he was trying to sell me meat after I'd already paid, but I should have figured—"

A faint movement from Cam out of the corner of my eye makes me pause, and when I glance to the side I realize that his shoulders are shaking, one hand over his mouth as he glances at me.

He's laughing.

"Sorry, Skylar," he says in between gasps, pulling his hand away from his mouth so I can read his lips. "I'm not laughing at you, I promise."

"Okay," I say, and then I picture the cashier's face, wide eyes and mouth open like a fish, and I get it.

"The look on his face," Cam says, and I see a laugh explode into the space between us. "I have never seen him that thrown off in my entire life."

The disparaging little voice in my head that says, *You suck,*

Skylar, shrivels up and dissolves into dust as I feel a giggle bubble up inside my chest. "I guess it was kind of funny," I say, and Cam shakes his head. Our feet touch the pavement in an identical rhythm as we make our way down the street.

Chapter SIX

I'M IN THE KITCHEN EARLY THE NEXT MORNING, FRYING EGGS FOR MY BREAK-fast before work, when Mike slinks down the stairs. Just as I'd guessed, he wasn't home in time for supper. He didn't reappear when Mom scooped ice cream into five bowls instead of six, a worry wrinkle creased across her forehead. And no light flickered on in his bedroom when I climbed the stairs at 11:00 for bed.

"Where were you?" I demand, not thinking that perhaps it would be better not to antagonize him when my hearing aids are still sitting on my bedside table instead of tucked inside my ears.

"I went to Eric's after work," he says, not meeting my eyes. "Lost track of time, didn't get home till late."

"Who is this Eric guy, anyway?" I put my hands on my hips, trying not to feel hurt about the scene with the car yesterday, try-ing not to remember Mike's face as he sat there, staring past me out the window. "You've never mentioned him before." I don't say anything about the smell of weed. Maybe Mike's not smoking. Maybe he just brings it home on his clothing.

I'm not sure I believe that.

"Maybe it's none of your business," he snaps, and then when I recoil, he rubs his eyes with the pads of his fingers. "I didn't mean

… …." He mumbles something into the back of his hand, so I can't read his lips. "I don't know what's wrong with me. I didn't mean to get mad."

"It's okay," I say, and realize that the two times I can remember Mike yelling at me have occurred right here in Aunt Kay's kitchen. "Where did you meet him?" I'm determined not to lose this topic. I need to know where the brother I know has gone, because maybe then I can figure out how to get him back.

"He works with me at the McDonald's by the highway."

"Is that why you were in the car with him the other day?"

"They're sizzling." Mike points to the eggs behind me, and I whirl around to find the undersides turning a crispy shade of black. By the time I flip them, the damage is done, and Aiden and Sara have entered the kitchen, closing off any more conversation about Eric, at least for now.

Mike drums his fingers on the table, sending a scurry of vibrations through the floor until I look up at him. "Are you taking the car to the library today?"

"I could." I let the words crawl out of my mouth, picturing myself behind the wheel of a car again. I earned my license a few weeks before the accident but haven't driven much since. I mean, I've done it, but it's weird, driving without being able to hear properly. My eyes dart constantly up, down, from mirror to mirror again and again and again, searching for swerving vehicles, flashing lights, or people walking along the side of the road who aren't paying attention.

Every time I see a red car, my hands snap shut, fingers turning white on the wheel even though I take slow, deep breaths. *In the nose*, I coach myself, feeling my back arch, shoulders drawn up to my ears, foot hovering over the brake. *And out the mouth*, as Mom or Dad or Mike or whoever's driving with me pretends they don't notice. Mom clasps her hands together so tightly she cuts off the circulation in her fingers; I guess that's where I get it from. Dad stares out the window, and Mike glares at his feet until I relax again.

A hand grips my arm, and I jump, throwing my spatula arm out to the side before I realize that it's just Mike, trying to get my attention.

"Skylar," he says again, for what must be the fourth or fifth time. His hand tugs the spatula free and uses it to scoop my eggs onto a plate. "Are you driving, or not?"

"I'll drop you off somewhere," I say, and the words feel like ash in my mouth. "At Eric's?"

"No," he replies, too quickly. "The grocery store is fine."

"I was there yesterday," I say, sprinkling pepper on my eggs and trying to keep the challenge out of my voice.

"So?"

I shouldn't keep talking, but I do anyway. "So, why are you going to the grocery store again?"

Mike's lips tighten at the corners, so I can hardly understand him when he speaks again. "Are you giving me a ride or not?"

"Why can't you drop me off on the way?"

Mike squints at me and doesn't say anything.

"Did you get grounded?"

Still nothing. I scrape my fork along the edge of my plate, collecting a few stray pieces of egg. "Did Mom and Dad say you can't take the car?"

"What do you think?"

I allow myself a brief moment of triumph for getting *something* right. "Why?"

"Good grief," he says, yanking the plate out of my hands. "Would you stop making that awful squeaking noise?"

I stare at him for a minute before I realize that he means the sound of my fork against my plate. "Sorry."

"Call me when you're ready." He grabs an apple from the counter before turning his back on me and making for the stairs.

"Five minutes," I yell, and then set my plate down hard, feeling the contact jar through my hand, watching the eggs jiggle unhappily, and then settle again, and I try to convince myself that I hear the thick "clump" of porcelain against wood, the gentle "sloop" of egg against egg, that the air whooshing out of my mouth has substance beyond my tactile knowledge.

It doesn't work. I miss being able to hear.

The thought washes over me like a wave, nibbling at my toes and then suddenly up around my neck, threatening to drag me under. I will never be able to hear again.

If I have children, I won't be able to hear them crying at night, after my hearing aids are lying on the table beside me.

I'll miss their first words. I'll only be able to hear bits and pieces of their little baby voices.

I swallow hard, knuckles white against the table. The sight of my breakfast nauseates me.

"Mike," I call to the empty room, my voice scraping against my throat. "Let's just go, I'm ready."

I tip what remains of my eggs into the garbage can on my way out the door.

•●•

By the time I've dropped Mike off and parked the car, my fingers hurt from clenching the steering wheel, my neck is sweating, and I've realized that the spare batteries for my hearing aids are still at home. The hearing aid behind my left ear is dying and beeps every minute, startling me, until finally I pull it off. I feel lopsided only being able to hear out of one ear, but for now, it will have to do. The automatic doors of the Golden Sound Public Library slide open to greet me, and I match my steps in time to the subdued "lub-dub" inside my chest.

Cam and Anastasia are chatting by the front desk, Cam leaning forward on one elbow, Anastasia sitting with her legs dangling over the counter. Both of them are facing me, so as I draw closer to the desk, I can see enough of their lips to read the whole exchange, aided by the lone hearing aid behind my right ear.

" … … to church with me this weekend?" Cam is asking her, his eyes crinkled up at the corners. "It's only Friday, that gives you a whole two days to think about it."

"I think I have a hair appointment." Ana delivers this line deadpan, and a faint flicker of recognition stirs within me. They've had this conversation before.

"How about next week? We're having a children's choir."

"Oh." Ana's mouth twists to one side. "I really wish I could, but I think maybe I'm getting a cold and I don't want to make the kiddies sick."

"The week after that?" He's laughing now.

"Sometimes it takes me a long time to recover," she says firmly, but her lips are twitching.

"Okay." Cam lifts his hands in surrender and then sees me coming up the aisle. "How about you, Skylar?"

I have never properly heard you speak before, screams the little pain inside of me. *I am so hungry for the sound of your voice.*

"What?" I feel the stillness of my expression as the word bursts out of me, harsh. Oops. "I mean, pardon me?"

"Wanna come to church with me on Sunday?" Cam drums his fingers on the countertop. "I told Ana she couldn't have any coffee, but they serve it after the service, if you're interested."

She smacks his arm, but I'm overcome with a wave of fury. *God.* What a horrible thought. The rawness inside me is stinging and sore, torn like the skin on my hands and knees when I fell off my bike at age six.

"Why do you say that?" Cam's fingers are still, and both he and Ana are looking at me, the easy humour swiped clean off their faces. Both of them look worried. About me?

"Oh, crap," I say eloquently. I said that out loud.

Anastasia looks anxiously between us, and then pops out of sight beneath the counter. Maybe her dog doesn't like arguments, either. I have an itchy feeling that Cam and I are about to have one.

"Skylar?"

"I don't really believe in God," I say, trying to tamp down the anger inside of me. I'm irritated at Mike and Eric, mad at myself for being afraid to drive, hurt that I can't hear. There is some emotion churning inside me about the accident, but I couldn't put a name to it if I wanted to. I'm not sure I should try.

Cam doesn't say anything. I decide to wait for him to make the next move, and then suddenly I realize that more words are pouring out of my mouth.

"I shouldn't say I don't believe in God," I feel my lips say. "Maybe there's a God. I don't know. But if he's up there, I don't think I like him very much."

Okay, that's enough. Let Cam make some sort of argument, and then agree to disagree. You don't need to say anything else. You don't have to explain yourself to him.

"I just don't get it," I continue, and feel vaguely like a freight train charging loose down the tracks. "Like, what is his deal? Why would he create a world, and people, and stuff, and then let such terrible things happen to them?"

Stop it. I don't need Cam knowing the rest of the story.

"My life was so good," I say, and by the tension in my throat I think maybe I'm yelling. My chest buzzes like I have a whole swarm of bees trapped inside my ribcage. "I had so many friends, and Mike and I used to be so close, and I ran track, and I listened to music every morning when I ran. I used to wake up early and hear the birds chirping, and the wind rustling in the leaves, and that gravelly sound when your running shoes hit the pavement.

Mike and I used to talk, sometimes, and I always knew when he was getting tired because his voice would sound lower."

Cam is suspiciously blurry.

"And then," I say, and push my voice through the lump in my throat. "Then the accident happened, and I'm halfway across the province and I can't even pick up the phone and call my friends. I can't run half as long as I used to without getting dizzy, and Mike won't talk to me, ever, and he's probably smoking pot, and I can't hear my running shoes, and I don't even know what your voice sounds like."

The threads of logic holding my monologue together are beginning to come undone, so I take a deep breath. "Sorry."

Cam still doesn't say anything, leaning forward against the counter.

"I didn't mean to…" I rub my eyes with one hand, blink back the moisture. "You'll understand when I say that I'm not that fond of the idea of God right now."

"That makes sense," Cam says, looking me unblinkingly in the face. I feel like I'm standing naked before him, like I've not only said too much, but somehow let him into the hurt place deep inside my chest; like by opening my mouth, I opened that part of me, too. I don't want him in there.

"What?" I'm expecting a fight, a counter-argument, maybe even for him to tell me that "Jesus loves me," which I really couldn't stand. I'm not expecting him to get it.

"It makes sense. That you'd feel that way," he says again.

"Are you saying I'm right?" I cross my arms over my chest.

"I'm not agreeing with you," he says, and still his eyes don't leave my face. "I think you're wrong, but I understand why you feel the way you do."

"You don't have some Bible verse or perfect answer or story about God's love for me?" Maybe I'm being unfair.

"I don't have all the answers, Skylar." He doesn't look mad. A little like a deer caught in the headlights, but he's certainly not angry.

"Then why would I believe in your God?"

"Would you believe me if I said that I did?"

"I don't know," I say, my voice pushed through an opening in my throat which now feels no larger than a pinhole. "I'm sorry, Cam," I say, and I really am. "Can we talk about something else?"

Right on cue, Anastasia pops up again from behind the counter. "I have something for you," she says. "I keep some aside for emergencies, or whenever he talks about God too much."

She jabs Cam with her elbow, and he winces, but the startled look he'd had on his face fades a little bit.

"Thanks," I say, accepting the square of milk chocolate that she breaks into my outstretched hand.

"Do you want to go home for today?" Anastasia sets down the chocolate but doesn't let go of my hand.

No. I look at the stacks of books behind the counter and know how many hours it will take for Cam to shelve them all by himself. I look at Anastasia's kind face, the tiny chip in her normally-perfect pink nail polish, the smear of chocolate on her wrist.

And then I glance at Cam, and I see that look on his face again—determined, and startled, and *friendly*. I swear his eyes go straight through me, and even before my heart lags out the next pitiful beat, I know I'll never make it through a whole shift next to someone so kind.

"If you don't mind," I croak out. "I can work the extra hours shelving books on Sunday when we're closed."

"Never mind that," Ana says, handing me the whole bar of chocolate. "Everyone needs a sick day now and then. Go on home and have yourself a nice, long nap."

That's ridiculous. It's not even lunchtime yet.

But by the time I pull into our driveway, my feet find their own way past the kitchen and up the stairs toward my bed. Dad's sitting at his desk, typing furiously away on his laptop computer, and I tiptoe silently by. The rest of the house is still; Mom and the twins must be out for the morning, and Mike clearly isn't home yet.

When I nudge my bedroom door open with my foot, Tom the cat is lying curled up in a ball on the foot of my bed. His black ears twitch when I close the door behind me, but he doesn't turn around, not even when I stroke one finger from the top of his head all the way down his tail.

"Scoot over," I tell him, and then roll onto my back beside him, my feet resting on my pillow like the Pippi Longstocking stories Mom used to read to us when we were younger. The hearing aid behind my right ear is pressing into my skull, so I slip it out, and then take the left one out of my pocket, dropping them on the bedside table.

I wonder where Mike is right now. Imagining him at McDonald's just doesn't work, so I try to picture him going for a run, or sitting in a restaurant somewhere, or even applying for a job on Main Street, but no matter where I throw my imagination, Eric and his friends appear too. In my mind I see a whole group of them tossing a football back and forth on the beach, yelling to each other over the sound of the crashing waves. I try to imagine myself in the scene, maybe chatting with a few other girls, but every conversation I picture is masked by hair in someone's face, the sun in my eyes, or the glare off the water. I just don't fit.

The hands on my wall clock point to 10 and 12, and I lie on my back and watch a full hour tick by before my eyelids start to droop. I should get up and do something, I think, and then Tom rolls onto my stomach and my eyes slide shut for the last time.

> *Birds chirp in the nearby trees as I jog down the gravel road. The sun is just rising in front of me, and when I glance beside me, I find Mike matching his steps to mine. A great surge of relief rushes through me. We're*

okay. The wind makes a hollow rushing sound in my ears, so angry that I almost can't hear Mike's voice. It's low and scratchy like it always is before breakfast, like the gravel crunching unevenly beneath our feet.

"I talked to Gavin today."

I look down so he won't see me blush, watching the ground slide past as I listen. "So?"

I hear the smile in his voice. "So, we talked about you."

"That's a lie." I shrug it off, but my heart leaps within me, accompanied by a rush of heat to my face. A particularly energetic robin goes sailing past, swooping down close to my head with an ecstatic flutter of wings, chirping merrily, twittering away.

"He wanted to know if you were running at Nationals this year."

"I hope so." The thought makes my stomach squiggle up inside me. "I think this is my year, I really do."

"I think so too, kid." He bumps my shoulder affectionately, and then I'm alone on the road, standing still.

Mike screams my name.

Now I'm falling. Hurtling toward the ground that never gets any closer.

"Skylar, get out of the way! Look out!"

What is he talking about? I try to turn, to crawl over to the side of the road, but my muscles have turned to peanut butter.

"Help me!" I scream the words. They reverberate in my throat and hum inside my ears, but Mike's voice is gone.

I'm all alone.

A car horn honks, loud and blaring. Frantic, louder, louder.

Closer.

For a moment I don't know where I am, blinking up at the ceiling. I'm still lying on my back, but Tom has abandoned me, leaving my stomach cold and bare. The sunlight that streams through the blinds is coming from the west, thick and golden as it filters across my face in sharp lines and shadows cast by my window shades. My hair is stuck to the back of my neck with sweat, and my clothes are twisted around my waist, my back damp. A trickle of water runs down my cheek and tunnels straight into my ear, and when I blink hard, another four tears follow.

Stop this. Get out of bed and go find something to do. Yanking the corner of my sheet away from my mattress, I swipe it under my eyes to catch the leftover tears. Today certainly isn't the first time I've woken up after some convoluted dream about the accident, and I don't expect it to be the last.

The screen on my phone is lit up and blinking, and when I stretch to pull it toward me, I'm startled to find that it's midafternoon, and I've been asleep for hours. I have four unread texts from Mom, Ana, and Mike. I tap into my brother's text first, but it's just blank space—a pocket dial. Of course it is. Why would he text me? Ana's text reminds me to "keep my chin up," and "seriously, take that nap."

Mission accomplished, I text back, neglecting to mention the nightmare that haunted my slumber.

Mom's texts just say to come downstairs whenever I wake up—she must have peeked in the door and found me—so we can talk about our plans for tonight. Mom teaches high school classes during the year, so even when she's home, she's normally buried in essays to grade and tests to mark. During her summers off, she stays home and cooks dinners, chats with the neighbors, and plans outings for us in the evenings when Dad has finished writing.

Her texts about tonight were frustratingly vague, but I haul my butt out of bed and down the stairs anyway. Aiden and Sara are running back and forth through the living room to the front door, carrying towels and sunscreen and all manner of beach-related things. Sara's hair flies around her face, less than half of it still in a limp ponytail that sags down her back.

"Hey," I say from the middle step, leaning over the railing, "what's going on?"

" ... ... beach ... ... Mike now!" says Sara, running past me up the stairs.

"What?" I reach behind my ears and realize that I didn't put my hearing aids back in.

Aiden waves at me from the bottom of the stairs to get my attention. "We're having a picnic!"

"On the beach?" I ask, trying to fit all the pieces of information together.

He nods.

"With Mike?"

Mom appears behind him, a bag of potato chips in her hand. "Well," she says, and she's smiling, but the muscles in her face are tight. It looks like she's trying to get a smile to stay on her face for our sake, but it just won't stick. "He's not home right now, so maybe we'll have to start without him." If she holds the threads that tie us all together, I have to wonder how thin the one attached to Mike is stretching. What happens if it snaps completely?

"He's never home anymore," grumbles Aiden, before sprinting into the kitchen, but he doesn't mean anything by it. He didn't pick up on the tension that I see threaded through Mom's words, tight in the cords of her neck and buried deep in the wrinkle on her forehead.

"Is Dad coming?" I come down one more step, and then another, as my father appears beside Mom, placing one hand on her waist.

"Present and ready for departure, Captain," he says, and since his glasses are actually perched on the bridge of his nose for once, I believe him.

"Go grab your bathing suit, Skylar," Mom says, glancing at the watch that sits on her slim wrist. "And then we'll go."

Sara charges down the stairs behind me, turning to yell something as she goes by. I think I catch the words "Cam" and "boyfriend," but when I look to Mom for a translation, all she says is, "Don't forget the sunscreen." She's so busy being worried about Mike that she forgets to turn on her over-protective Skylar radar. I like it better this way.

Even though most of the packing was finished while I was sleeping, it still takes us almost forty-five minutes to get out the door, as the twins keep helpfully reminding everyone to wear sunscreen, adding extra things to our picnic without permission, and bouncing around in an excess of excitement.

The view is worth it, though, even before we reach the beach. Directly in front of us—sinking toward the horizon with an attitude of royalty—is the sun, as crimson as a pool of blood. I didn't even know the sun could turn that color.

We're not the only family heading down to the beach. Mom calls a hello over her shoulder to our neighbors across the street as they follow us with their own coolers, lawn chairs, and towels. The twins run ahead to catch up with another little girl and her brother walking with their family a few houses away from us.

"… … we lived in a small town," Mom says to Dad, looking fondly at the twins, and I catch the tail end of her sentence, the rest of her words swallowed by the howling of the wind. "It's so friendly here."

I kick off my flip-flops as soon as the pavement turns to sand beneath my feet, still warm from the sunshine earlier in the day. The smooth sand on top slips through my toes with every step, and I lag behind my parents, burrowing the soles of my feet down to the hard-packed earth beneath. A few years ago, when we were on vacation, Mike and I went for a barefoot run on the beach, and my calves ached so badly for the rest of the week that it took me almost five minutes to make it up a flight of stairs.

I wish Mike was here, sighs the ever-helpful part of my brain, and then I have to give up on my sand exploration and catch up with my parents again, before I let myself feel too sad. I wish I could talk to him about all of this—go and sit on his bedroom floor while he's playing guitar, nodding his head in time to my explosion of words. He was such a good listener.

Is such a good listener. After all, it's not like he's dead. I'm trying to reassure myself, but for some reason, this actually makes me feel worse.

Mom and Dad spread the blanket out near the family from across the street, Mom—the social butterfly of our family—chatting with the parents. I used to be right up there with her, talking to anyone who would listen, but now, all I can imagine is her eyes on me, constantly translating, until the people I was trying to talk to fade into the background, and it's just Mom trying to fill all the gaps that my hearing loss creates.

The twins play in the water with the neighbors' kids, splashing each other until Sara's shorts turn from light-wash into the royal blue of soggy denim. The breeze off the lake is warm on my skin, and the waves curl lightly against the shore, glowing pink in the reflection from the sun.

Gradually, a question unfurls in my head, as the twins laugh, and my parents talk, and I watch the scene, the patch of blanket next to me empty and alone.

Where is Mike?

Chapter
SEVEN

EVEN THOUGH WE'RE ONE OF THE LAST FAMILIES TO LEAVE THE BEACH, MIKE never shows up. He isn't waiting for us at home when we get back, sandy feet leaving tracks across the tiled floor in the kitchen, and he isn't back by the early hours of the morning, when I wake up to get a drink of water.

where r u? I text him at three A.M., my phone screen blurry in the darkness of my bedroom. I can see a strip of light under Mom and Dad's door, and I'm willing to bet they aren't staying up this late to talk about the twins.

I'm fine, he replies, almost immediately.

you're a jerk, I type out, and don't even realize what I've written until I see his reply.

I know.

ok, I say, and suddenly I'm not mad anymore. *when r u coming back?*

can you pick me up in the morning? tmrw?

fine. I turn my phone face-down before I can see his reply and roll over. Sure, I can come get you. Sure, I don't have anything better to do than bring you home early on a Saturday morning, because you're too inconsiderate to come back at a time when we're all waiting for you to show up. Sure, everything's fine and maybe you're a jerk, but it's okay, no big deal.

I have a hard time falling asleep after that, picturing Mike high, or drunk, or maybe both. Maybe he's sprawled out on someone's couch. Maybe he's puking in a strange bathroom. Maybe he's telling someone else all the things he doesn't want to say to me.

At six o'clock, I give up and yank my blinds open, throwing on a pair of shorts and a tank top before reaching for my phone. No new messages.

Fine. I comb my hair into a messy bun and adjust my hearing aids behind my ears. You wanted a ride home? I'm coming for you right now.

I pull the keys off the kitchen counter and scrawl a note to my parents before letting myself out the front door. It's already hot, so I roll down all the windows in the car before reversing slowly out of the driveway. *You can do this.* I check all my mirrors and slide the car into drive.

I'm halfway down the street before I realize that I don't even know where Mike is. I pull over and hit "call" without thinking about it, my phone pressed to my ear for a solid five seconds before I remember why the dial tone is nothing more than a faint buzz in the back of my head.

I end the call before it goes to voicemail and sit, watching the blinking display. Someday I'll get used to this. As I'm staring at it, my phone vibrates in my hand.

did you call me?

I don't respond.

Skylar?

After a few seconds, he sends a third text.

I'm at Eric's. go left at the end of Main Street and take the 1st right. you'll know which house.

I take a deep breath, turn the key in the ignition, and pull back onto the road. Traffic is busy for Golden Sound, people getting ready to drive to the city for the day, pulling into breakfast places and coffee shops along the way. It takes me twice as long as normal to reach the end of Main Street, but once I turn onto Eric's street, I can see exactly which house Mike is talking about. There are cars parked all along the side of the road, and two pickup trucks sit crookedly on the lawn. The houses on either side are several car lengths away, which is probably the only reason there aren't cop cars parked here too. Bottles litter the lawn and there are several people sleeping in the bed of the pickup trucks.

What a party this must have been. I try to mask my disgust as I drive around what looks suspiciously like a pile of vomit. I wish I could say it takes me a little while to find my brother, but the truth is, I see him right away. He stands a head taller than Eric and the two girls with them, and all four of them are smoking. He doesn't see me, so I turn the car off and watch, resting my chin on the top of the steering wheel. Eric says something to the girl next to him and kisses her cheek. My brother laughs, takes a drag on his cigarette, and does the same. Girl 1 yawns, Girl 2 stares adoringly up at Mike, and I feel like throwing up myself.

That's enough. I reach for the door handle, intending to step out and give them all a piece of my mind. From across the lawn, Eric sees me. I can tell, because he grins, and my stomach flops sickeningly against the bottom of my lungs.

"Wait a sec," I see him say to my brother, clapping him on the shoulder before sauntering across the driveway toward me. My brother doesn't even turn around to see who he's talking to.

Fantastic. I roll down the window. After a moment, I reach out and flip the lock on the driver's door. It's a silly precaution, since we're in plain sight and my brother is right there, but I don't trust Eric, and it makes me feel safer.

"Hi there, beautiful," he tosses out when he gets closer, stubbing his cigarette out on the hood of the car as he crosses to my door.

"Hello," I say, dropping the word hard and cold into the air between us. "You're up early."

"Late, actually," he corrects me, and when he gets closer I can see the lines underneath his bloodshot eyes. He has that too-sweet odor that Mike's been bringing home lately; it gets stronger every time he exhales.

"What do you want?" I try to ask this as non-confrontationally as I can, but I still feel like I'm accusing him of something. Maybe I am.

"Well," Eric says, leaning on the side of the car with one arm, "we've never been formally introduced."

"That's true." I have to crane my neck to look him in the eyes. "But I think I'm okay with that, actually."

He laughs, head tipped back, and my stomach goes cold. What is wrong with me? Did I actually say that out loud? Mike still hasn't noticed that I'm here. I dart a glance at him and miss the first part of Eric's next sentence, his words mumbled and too soft to make out without the aid of lip-reading.

"... ... from around here, or I'd know." He knocks on the roof of the car. I feel the vibrations travel downward in a series of ripples through the back of my seat. "So, hello. I'm Eric, and you must be..."

He waits. I glance over at Mike again. He's still standing with those two girls, and all three of them are still smoking.

Eric laughs again, but the idea that he finds me amusing is infuriating. I'm trying to shut him down and he's not taking me seriously. "Skylar, right?"

"That's me," I say, squinting. Mike drops his cigarette and grinds it into the dirt with his heel. It's a practiced movement, as though he's done it a thousand times before. Has he?

When I turn to Eric, he's studying me, and uncomfortable goose bumps spike up the back of my neck. I don't like the way he's looking at me.

"Well?" He tilts his head to one side, and I resist the urge to roll the window up a few inches, if not all the way.

I remember what Cam said—about how Eric used to push him around—and I can see it now, his cocky attitude, standing with his arms crossed like someone who is very used to getting exactly what he wants from people.

"Well, what?"

"What do you listen to?" His question, one that I clearly didn't hear while I was watching Mike, makes no sense, and since I'm already irritated and preoccupied with my brother, I spout off the first answer that comes into my head, trying to convince myself that the heat on my skin is the weather and not the fury beginning to spin in the pit of my stomach.

"I don't listen to anything. I'm deaf."

"You what?" He laughs again, but when I don't join him, he stops. "You're serious?"

This is not a conversation I enjoy having with anyone, especially not before 8:00 a.m.

"Sorry," I say, trying to play it offhand. "Forget I mentioned it. It's not a big deal."

It is actually a huge deal, but right now I'm more upset about the fact that Mike currently has his arm around Girl 2, and she's staring up at him like he owns the world. Eric reaches in through the car window and taps my arm, and I jump.

"Cool," he says to himself, and then begins to mouth his next sentence to me, the words too softly shaped to be spoken aloud, no muscle tension in his neck to indicate that he's put air behind his sentence. *Can you hear me, Skylar?* The use of my name bugs me more than it should.

"No, of course I can't," I snap, "because you're not actually talking out loud. Can you go and tell Mike that I'm here?"

"Cool," he says again, and I notice that he's holding a lighter.

He flicks it on, and then off again, the flame sucking hungrily for air. It's an absent movement, the same way Cam unbuckled his watch again and again while he was on the phone with Sophia, but infinitely more dangerous. Everything about Eric seems danger- ous and mysterious, and suddenly I'm sick to death of the drama. I wish I was brave enough to punch him myself, like Cam did. Maybe then he'd leave my brother alone too.

"Never mind," I say, flicking the locks on my door again and stepping out with as much confidence as I can muster. Eric's short- er than Mike, but that still leaves him a good head taller than me. "I'll go get him myself."

Eric follows a few steps behind me as I stride across the lawn, the heady scent of beer hanging over the grass, punctuated by cig- arette smoke.

"Mike," I snap as soon as I'm within what I deem to be a rea- sonable hearing distance. "Let's go."

One of the girls says something to my brother. Her bright red lipstick is smeared, and I'm so distracted by the smudge of color on her front teeth that I don't pay any attention to the slurred sen- tence that meanders its way out of her mouth. Mike turns, bleary- eyed, toward me.

"Yeah, that's my little sister."

"Hello," I say, not bothering to smile. "Mike, I've been waiting for you."

"Sorry," he says, but he's smiling at Girl 2 again, and the apol- ogy doesn't reach his eyes. It's hard to tell if the alcohol smell is coming from him or the other three, but it's making me dizzy.

Eric slings an arm across my shoulders, leaning forward to say something to Mike, and I jump. My brother stands a little straighter, pulled from his slouch the moment Eric touched me, but it's too late. If he wanted to be protective, he should have start- ed earlier.

I shrug out of Eric's embrace and take two steps away from him, refusing to make eye contact.

"Mike, I'll be in the car. Nice to meet you," I add, for the benefit of the two girls, since there's no need to be any ruder than I already have been.

I don't bother saying anything to Eric, and he doesn't follow me. When I slide into the driver's seat, I roll up my window and flip my lock, waiting for Mike to detach himself from the others.

When he finally opens the passenger door and flops inside, he brings the reek of beer and weed in with him, and I cough as I reverse down the driveway and head toward Main Street, our little car humming cheerfully through the bottoms of my feet and up my legs. Spikes of sunlight, bright and sharp like slivers of cheddar cheese, filter through the trees.

Mike covers his eyes. "It's so bright."

"That's because you're hungover," I snap, glancing at the road in time to see the stop sign right in front of us. I punch the brakes, and Mike lurches forward. "Or high," I add, like nothing has happened.

"Leave me alone, Skylar," he groans, rubbing his eyes. "I'm eighteen, so it's not like we were breaking the law. And it was just a party."

"Who were those girls?"

He shrugs. "Just girls. Friends of Eric's."

"I don't like him," I say, making the turn onto Main Street.

"I don't care."

He says it softly enough that he thinks I won't hear, but it's his face that gives him away, not his voice. I indicate and pull over onto the soft shoulder, and then angle myself in my seat so I can see his face.

"Why do you hang out with him?"

"Why not?" Mike squints at me. "Skylar, drop it. It's fine."

"It's not fine!"

"Shhh," he begs, putting a hand over his eyes.

"And you're a pothead now, too?" I'm just getting started, and I don't plan on shushing.

"It's none of your business." Mike glares at me, one hand still shading his eyes. "Just shut up and drive."

"What did you say to me?"

My heart pounds, my blood like ice in my veins. I hate him.

"Nothing."

"Look me in the eyes and say that again, Micah." I pull out his whole first name, and then instantly know it was the wrong move.

"Stop trying to be my mom," he says, lips stiff and angry. "One is way more than enough."

"What does that mean?"

"Just drive, Skylar." He turns away so I can't see his face.

"I'm not going anywhere until you talk to me."

He spins around so fast that I flinch, my seat belt chafing my neck. "Then I'm walking home."

Mike unbuckles his seat belt and shoves the door open, extricating himself clumsily from the car. His door bounces fully open and then swings before he catches it with one foot and slams it shut.

"Mike," I say, scrabbling for the passenger window button, but he's already trudging down the street. I pull out again and press the gas lightly until I've caught up to him, but I can't watch the road and his face at the same time. "Please get back in the car." I scan the road for obstacles and then glance at his face.

"You're going to kill someone if you don't stop driving like you're drunk," he says, and I accidentally slam the brakes.

"What?"

His lips are white; he didn't mean to say that to me. I know he didn't. Mike wouldn't talk like that, wouldn't throw the accident in my face on purpose.

"Just go home," he says, not meeting my eyes, and this time I'm mad enough to obey.

I roll up his window and gear the car up to speed, but I get about halfway down Main Street before I realize that there's no way I want to go home and answer questions about why Mike's not with me. I don't want to watch the lines crinkle around Mom's eyes or see Aiden's face drop when he realizes that Mike won't be home in time for breakfast.

I slow the car down as I approach the stoplight, which is—big surprise—red. As I wait for the light to change, I run my eyes up and down the shopfronts to my left. The red canopy on the end building catches my eye, and when I see the café sign for "Milk and Sugar," I remember the friendly employee who waved at me on my first morning here. I still haven't been inside yet. Why not go today? Flicking my indicator on, I pull over and get out, darting one glance back to where I can just barely see the outline of Mike trudging up the road.

My stomach twinges inside me, but even if I wait for him to catch up, would he speak to me? What would we say? For once in my life, I have no idea, so instead of waiting to find out, I lift my chin and push open the café door.

Chapter
EIGHT

I GO IN EXPECTING TO BUY A COFFEE AND SIT LONG ENOUGH TO DRINK IT, BUT even before the screen door swings shut behind me, I'm in love. There are bookshelves lining the walls at the front of the building, next to the window facing Main Street where I saw the girl cleaning tables on my first day here. Chairs and tables are spread haphazardly across the wood floor, and several French-looking paintings hang on the wall. An old creaky organ sits in the corner opposite the fireplace, which looks as though it's burning real wood.

But what really catches my interest is the table tucked into the side of the building. One long window runs down the front of the shop, facing Main Street, and another one runs almost the whole length of the building at the side. There are too many houses in the way to see the water, but I walk over to the table and try anyway, craning my neck to see if I can spot a ribbon of blue right at the edge of the sky. I can't, quite, but I decide to stay anyway.

"You can hear the geese honking out on the water," the girl behind the counter says, jerking her chin toward the window I'd been looking out, and I offer her a smile.

I sit at that side table for almost two hours, long after my coffee grows cold next to the open window, while people come and go. I watch as an elderly couple takes a table by the wall, orders their breakfast, and then pulls out a cribbage board and plays through a whole deck of cards across coffee and bagels. Two girls close to my own age come in and sit by the front window, playing with their hair and giggling, heads bent together, whenever a guy walks by.

When the breeze off the lake changes direction, fluttering the curtains that flank the side window, a family of three walks in, two parents and a boy a little bit younger than me, with his hands buried in his pockets in the classic "I'm too cool for this" posture. Mike still does it when we force him to come along on family outings.

I'm bored of people watching by now and not paying too much attention to the family until the woman starts to sign; then I can't help but watch. The dad has a cochlear implant, I can see now, the silver disk tucked discreetly behind his ear as he watches his wife. She addresses the boy in ASL, and he shrugs and replies without moving his hands. I wonder if this is a slip on his part, or if he intended to say something his dad might not be able to hear. I wonder why they sign, if he has a hearing aid, and how well it works. I wonder if the boy has siblings.

I wonder if this will be me later in life.

A buzzing feeling in my pocket finally grabs my attention, and I fish out my phone to see that I've missed four incoming texts from Mom, each increasing in urgency.

where are you??? reads her last one.

sry, coming now, I text, and with some reluctance take my cup to the front counter.

"Thanks," I say to the girl, who wipes her hands on her apron and hands me a cookie. It warms my hand even through the napkin.

"For the road," she offers with a smile. "Come back anytime."

I nibble on my cookie, and the melted chocolate chips smooth on my tongue as I drive to the house, parking the car on the street in front of the lawn. I'm lost in thought as I walk slowly up Aunt Kay's driveway, barely noticing the strange car parked behind Aunt Kay's four-door. Maybe someone is visiting, although I can't think of anyone we know that might make the drive all the way here just to say hello.

It's as I turn the doorknob that I notice my school's bumper sticker plastered across the trunk. Weird. Or maybe it wasn't— maybe my brain was jus trying to read something familiar into something unexpected.

Shaking it off, I push the front door open and step inside, kicking off my flip-flops. I turn to make sure the door has actually clicked shut behind me, since I can no longer tell for sure just by listening. That sound, like many others, is lost somewhere in the expanse of air between the doorknob and my ears.

Suddenly I'm attacked from behind, someone's arms around my neck and squeezing tightly, a mouth pressed next to my ear; someone is yelling, speaking too quickly to follow, their words blurring together in a flatline of noise. A shot of panic flashes through my blood, and I twist around and pry their arms free, shoving them away. Has Aunt Kay's house been burgled? Is my family lying dead in a closet somewhere? Will I end up on the front cover of the *Golden Sound Chronicle* as the only survivor of a terrible summer tragedy?

Apparently not. My heart pounds as the room swims back into focus, and I find familiar faces looking at me. My whole family has gathered for some reason, and even Mike is standing a little off to the side, hands in his pockets. Everyone is waiting for my reaction. I'm a little sluggish from my early morning, and my surprise at being tackled, so it takes me a minute to realize that there are a few extra bodies. There's a tall, dark-haired boy standing next to Mike, and a ponytailed girl, the one who tackled me, standing against the fridge where I pushed her.

All at once it comes together in my mind—the new car that I hadn't seen before but whose descriptions I'd read about, and these two figures who are not strangers. This time it's me tackling her, screaming her name as we collide again.

"Janie, what are you doing here?"

I'm laughing, seeing my parents' pleased faces over her shoulder. Aiden and Sara are standing on chairs at the kitchen table, craning their necks to see the reunion. Dad chews on one arm of his glasses, but he's smiling as he watches us from the doorway of the living room. For once, his gaze doesn't dart between Mike and me, every emotion tempered by worry over my brother. This one is all for me.

I have to cut our hug short when I hear her first few words, muffled against my shoulder. I step back so I can see her lips.

"I missed you!" she says, her voice reaching a squeal on the last few words.

Mom and Dad tactfully shepherd the twins out of the room at this point, and the four of us are left standing, Gavin and Mike facing Janie and me.

"It feels like forever," she exclaims, and then, all at once, neither of us knows quite what to say. After a pause that travels slowly from funny to awkward, she stretches out an arm and tugs Gavin into view.

My heart jumps into my throat, and I gulp it back down as Janie proudly announces, "Look! I brought Gavin with me."

My heart, beating too fast from the scare, flutters half-heartedly in my chest. And then, nothing. I don't feel butterflies. I don't feel much of anything at all, except the increasing sense of awkwardness that accompanies my lack of verbal response.

"Hi," I say at last, trying to sound nonchalant. "Long time, no see."

After these gems of wit find their way out of my mouth, I decide that I want nothing more than to crawl into a hole and die.

"Hey, Skylar," Gavin says, reaching forward to give me a hug. His arms are skinny and I can feel his elbow against my back and it's *weird*.

"So!" Janie blows a wisp of hair out of her face. "Tell me all about your life. Girl, let's chat. We've had so many parties, and I have to tell you … … and then … …" I follow her fairly well up until this point, but when she launches into her story I have to stop her.

"Sorry," I say, and I begin to feel like I did right after the accident, like I'm slamming into a brick wall at every turn, slow and sluggish in my communication. "Can you slow down a little bit?"

Mike taps my shoulder like we're still friends, as though we didn't have an enormous fight this morning, as if nothing has changed, and nods toward the living room. "Let's go sit down for a minute."

The four of us head into the living room and sprawl across the couches, Janie reclining against Mike's shoulder with her feet in my lap, and Gavin stretched out on the couch opposite.

"So," Janie says again, "your life! This house is awesome, by the way. Oh my goodness, can you imagine the parties we could throw?"

A tiny flicker of excitement worms its way into my stomach. Without Janie, parties seemed pointless, but she's right. Aunt Kay's house is perfect. The lower floor is open concept, the kitchen big and warm.

"And the windows," we say at almost exactly the same time, and then laugh. "The view is perfect!"

Janie's head turns to the side, and I follow her gaze to see that Gavin has begun to speak. I tell myself that of course he wouldn't remember to raise his voice, probably doesn't even think about the fact that unless he gets my attention first, I won't pick out the sound of his speech amid the chorus of background noise that people never realize they're making, but it still smarts when I find out that I've missed half the conversation.

" … … dancing," he finishes, eyes sparkling, but Mike's head turns sharply back to me.

"What?" I ask, and because it seems like he was teasing, I wrinkle my nose at him like I've smelled something bad. I'm hoping Mike will say something next that will give me some context so I can guess at what was said, but Gavin's already stopped speaking, catching his words mid-sentence and paling slightly, like he's just told the queen that he hates her shoes.

"Sorry," Gavin says, cracking his knuckles. He only does that when he's nervous. "I, uh…"

Janie won't look at me either. She suddenly finds a loose thread in her cream summer blouse to be totally enthralling.

"Guys," I say, trying to pretend that this isn't throwing me way off, and unexpectedly wishing that Cam was here, because at least he treats me like a normal human being. "It's not a big deal. It doesn't matter. Dancing would be fun, this house is perfect. You can all stop looking at me like that."

"Sorry," Gavin says again, and the smile he offers me is totally uncomfortable. "Um, so. What have you guys been doing up here? How have you spent your summer?"

Mike and I glance at each other, and all the words we haven't spoken hang between us. All the times we didn't hang out, all the places we didn't go, all the things we didn't do. *Fake it. They don't have to know. Nothing's changed.*

"Well," I say, "I've mostly been working at the library, and Mike has been practicing his guitar. At home. And stuff."

"It's totally boring," Mike says, deadpan, and Gavin and Janie laugh a little bit too gratefully.

"No parties," I say, letting out a deep breath. Mike and I are on the same page; he doesn't want them to know, either. "But the beach is pretty sweet."

"The beach!" Janie stretches her arms way up above her head. "Oh, when can we go?"

"How long are you staying?"

She and Gavin exchange glances. "Well," she says, "we drove up this morning, and we have to be back by Monday at the latest."

It's Friday. I do a quick calculation in my head. "So, three days? Four?"

She looks over at Mike, comfortable so quickly after not seeing either of us in weeks. *I'm* not even that comfortable with my brother anymore. "Do you think you can put up with me for that long?"

He grins, shoves her head off his shoulder; I'm startled to see a flash of pre-accident Mike. I didn't think I'd ever see him again. "It'll be a struggle, but I'm sure I'll manage."

The three of them laugh, and I'm so busy watching them that I don't realize that I'm not laughing along until Janie kicks me. "Sky! What's wrong?"

"Nothing," I protest, wriggling away from her toes. "I'm just tired."

There is an awkward pause, and everything feels stilted until I notice that Gavin and Mike have settled into conversation, and it's Janie and I who aren't talking. Her head is tipped back, resting on Mike's shoulder, but she's studying me.

"So," she says, picking the nail polish off of her forefinger. "Let's do something. Wanna go for a run?"

"Good idea," I say, pushing her feet off my lap and standing. Maybe running in sync will be the perfect activity to sync our souls back together, too. "Where's your stuff?"

"Already in your room," she says, and links arms with me as we climb the stairs. "Which, by the way, is a total mess."

I twist away from the lazy punch that is directed at my shoulder. Janie has always been a clean freak. I'm the messy one. "You should be used to it by now."

"Abysmal," she says as I turn away, and I self-consciously tug down the blind facing the street before yanking on my workout shorts and tank top.

"I'm turning around," I announce before doing so, but she's already changed, and is sitting cross-legged on the floor with Tom in her lap.

"He's so cute," she says, getting to her feet and brushing excess cat hair off her jogging shorts. "But, ugh, he sheds."

"Cats do that," I say wryly, following her out the door.

"Do you run … … ?" she asks, but coughs into her shoulder, turning her face away from me so I can't see her lips.

"Sorry," I interrupt her, "can you say that again? You looked the wrong way."

Janie looks taken aback. "SORRY," she says, but she's speaking too loudly, projecting her voice into my face as though that will help me to understand. "DO YOU EVER RUN ON THE BEACH?"

"Sometimes," I reply, keeping my own voice pitched low, speaking slightly too quiet to make up for her volume. "And you don't have to yell."

"Oh." She turns completely away from me to go down the front stairs, and I hope that she's not talking as she descends, jogging quickly ahead of me and then jumping off the last few steps.

"Wait a sec," I say, reaching for my shoes. It's hard not to feel guilty for being frustrated with her after only half an hour.

When did it get so hard to be around people I thought knew me better than anyone? Where were they when I was learning to live with this new part of myself—changing without even realizing it?

Janie jogs obligingly in place, rolling her shoulders in preparation for our run as I whip my shoelaces into a double knot. We start by jogging left to the beach, and I push away thoughts of Mike and I running at home. I don't feel like battling memories of the accident today.

"So," Janie says, panting beside me, "I'm super out of shape."

"I guess," I tease her. We were ranked first and second at our school—me first, her second—for long-distance running, but I also competed as part of a club outside school. Janie only ever viewed running as a hobby, but for me it was all I was really good at.

"What's your secret?" she asks, and I notice that she is careful to turn toward me so I can hear her more clearly.

I shrug. "Walking to and from work, running sometimes in the mornings. I dunno."

Truth is, it's always been easier for me to stay in shape, to get up earlier to run, to do what was necessary. Mike may have been the one who motivated me, but I was the one who texted Janie after rolling out of bed to remind her to get up and run too. She paid me back by being better at remembering details like water, food, and where to get our racing numbers. It was always a give and take with us, like two halves of a whole.

Now, I can't seem to find the places where my edges match hers. Everywhere I turn I find another smooth corner instead of a jagged edge where another puzzle piece should click right in, like after surviving without her for so long, ever since before the accident, I don't need her quite as much anymore. It's funny—I would have thought I'd need her more.

"Left or right here?" We pause on the edge of the boardwalk, sand sparkling in front of us.

"Right," I decide, and strike out, ploughing past the soft white beach and down to the water where the sand is firmer and more packed down.

"So," she says again, after catching up with me, "fill me in on the boy situation. What's it like seeing Gav again? Or is there someone new in your life?"

I think of Cam, a gentle spray from the lapping waves speckling my ankles with water droplets, leaving a damp sheen across my skin, and know that for some reason, I don't want to discuss him with Janie. I won't tell her about Eric, either. The way my skin crawls, the terrible feeling that he is changing my brother and I can't do anything about it. Even thinking about him makes me feel sick inside—I push any ideas of him to the back of my mind.

"No," I say, because it's easier. "There's no one." I don't admit to liking Gavin. I don't admit to liking anyone.

Janie cocks her head. "So, it's not Gavin anymore? Even after all those texts?"

Inexplicably, I think of Cam again, and how after just a few minutes with Janie and Gavin, it was him that I wanted most of all. Thankful that she can't read my mind, I shrug. "I don't know. I'll figure it out later, I guess."

"Or," she says, grinning wickedly, "maybe by the end of this week, you'll have fallen madly in love with him again."

I groan, twist my ankle, and stumble.

"Curse those hereditarily weak ankles," intones Janie solemnly once I'm upright again, and I can't help it—I crack up. Even though I don't catch the grave tone that has always gone along with her completely straight face, I can't help laughing.

"You have no idea," I say, and then think of the accident and how those exact words came floating through my mind.

I shake my head, wishing I could shrug off these memories as easily.

"So? No cute boys at all?" Her face is teasing, and part of me thinks I should tell her about Cam. After all, isn't that what friends are for? Half a second later, I know I won't, know she'd never understand the idea of being such good friends with someone without wanting to date them. Maybe that's not being fair to her, but I try to picture her in the same room with Cam and keep thinking one word: disaster.

"Depends on your definition of cute," I reply offhandedly, and then feel disloyal to Cam. "I mean, maybe?"

"You suck at keeping secrets," she says, grinning. "But fine. I won't ask you any more questions." Her smile is a little too wide, too bright, and I know she's waiting for me to ask her the same question in return.

"So?" I say, allowing myself to be drawn into the drama of high school, of crushes and boys and gossip, while realizing how relaxing it's been not to have to keep up with who is dating who this week. "What about you?"

"Okay," she says, and stops walking altogether. "Okay, I didn't want to say so in front of the guys, but oh my gosh, Skylar, I met someone."

I squeal and grab her forearms, and we have a little girly freak out right there on the beach, jumping up and down in excitement. "I missed you," I gasp after a second, "so much."

"Oh, me too," she says breathlessly, and then carries straight on. "He's Daria's brother—you remember Daria, don't you?"

The name is vaguely familiar.

"Dark hair, mole on her cheek, kinda pretty but really quiet." She rattles off a list of attributes. "You thought she looked like Zendaya."

Now I remember. Daria was the girl whose invitation Janie sent to my phone by accident. I've never met the girl, but when I tell Janie so, she frowns.

"I could have sworn…whatever. Anyway, her," she says, breezing right past the fact that she obviously mixed me up with someone else. "And wow, her brother. His name's David, and wow. They have a whole bunch of siblings whose names all start with D, because their mom wanted a certain theme or something, and he's doing a gap year."

"Two years older?"

"And a half!" she says, nodding excitedly. "And the rumour is that we're seeing each other."

"Is it true?"

She grins, touches her hair self-consciously, and nods. "I think maybe he's going to ask me out when I get back. I told him I was going away on vacation with Gavin and his friend's family."

And me? Hello, your best friend? But I don't say anything.

"So I'll let him sweat for a few days," she finishes, "and then I'll waltz in and he'll finally ask me. At least, that's the plan. I can't wait for you to meet him when you get back."

I'm starting to feel like I've missed more than I could possibly catch up with.

"When *are* you coming back?" she asks, tilting her head to one side.

"Not sure." I shrug, trying to keep my tone noncommittal. "Aunt Kay didn't really give us much information on her travel plans." Like, nothing.

We fall into a silence that is slightly less than comfortable, still walking. I'm not sure I want to hear all the details of Janie's life without me, and I haven't done many things that she'd be interested in. Besides hanging out with Cam and Ana and fighting with Mike, I haven't done much of anything at all. And that's okay. I don't mind.

I realize, startled, that I believe it.

After maybe half an hour, when the beach pathway curves up to the road, we've settled into an easy conversation about the coming school year. Superficial, maybe, but it's the only thing we can really find to talk about.

"You'll be back in time, right?" Janie glances down Main Street, and on a whim, I keep walking past the road to Aunt Kay's. Maybe we'll go out for ice cream.

"Yeah," I say, picturing long hours stuck in class, the teacher's voice completely inaudible, buried under chairs squeaking against the floor, whispered conversations, sneezes. The cacophony of background noises would make even the loudest teacher's words almost unintelligible. "I think so." It's our last year in high school, when we'll finally be the oldest of the old, the closest to finishing, flaunting the taste of freedom to everyone.

"Prom is this year," Janie says. "Have you thought about your dress?"

"No," I reply, surprised. "I guess I've been thinking about other things."

"Like what?" Janie says this incredulously. "Sky! It's prom!"

There's another awkward pause while I try to feel some sort of emotion about a muffled dance with people I see every day, dressed up in uncomfortable clothing. If you take away the music, the sound of a thousand voices, the excited pitch in everyone's speech during the weeks leading up to the event, it all rings faintly hollow. Like there's a haunting magic in the noise of it all, and when you take that away, get rid of the Pied Piper, there's not a whole lot of reason to run along with the others.

"I think I'll wear green," I say at last, because it's all I can think of to break the silence. "And, maybe silver heels."

Janie makes an excited comment, clapping her hands to her mouth so I can't understand what she's saying.

"Hey," I say, tugging her hands away from her mouth. "Can't see, remember?"

We reach the little booth selling ice cream at last, and I'm able to distract her with the idea of a Turtles cone. She orders for both of us, and the walk back to Aunt Kay's is pleasantly silent, both of us too preoccupied with our food to talk.

Just as we finally reach the driveway, I sense a vehicle pulling up behind us. *What now?* I am exasperated with the universe today. *Leave me alone*, I want to scream to the heavens. And then I turn and see the van, the driver's side window rolled down and Cam's face inside.

"Hey," he says. "Sorry to bug you, but—"

"What are you doing here?" I ask, and then backtrack. "I mean, hi. This is my best friend Janie. Janie, Cam."

"Hey," he repeats, looking a bit sheepish, and Janie wiggles her fingers at him, mouth full of ice cream. "Can I borrow your library key?"

He puts the van in park and climbs out, car keys dangling from one finger. Janie digs her elbow into my back and whispers something that I hope Cam doesn't hear, her hushed words hissing and whooshing against the speaker in my right ear.

"Yeah, upstairs," I say, a hot flush creeping up the back of my neck. I'm not exactly sure what she said to me, but judging by the way Cam is staring up at the sky, cheeks red, he heard every word.

"Why are you still in town?" I ask, imagining that he would have gone home after his shift ended. Friday shifts are shorter, and this week he drew the short stick. I got the day off.

"I wasn't," he says, both he and Janie following me toward the house. "I mean, I went home, but then Ana called and said she forgot to lock up, but she was on her way into the city, so she couldn't come back and do it."

For the first time since we met, Cam actually looks frustrated. "So I got in the car and drove straight back, but when I got to the library I realized that I don't have my key, either."

I try not to laugh.

"So here I am," he finishes. "Can I borrow yours?"

"Sure." Then I realize that going upstairs to get it will mean leaving Cam alone with Janie. "I'll be right back," I say, jogging toward the deck. As I push through the screen door, I try not to think about the fact that Cam called a blush to my face when seeing Gavin couldn't. On my way up the stairs, I tell myself it's just because Gavin and I haven't had a chance to get to know each other again, and after I grab my key and jog back down, I've almost managed to convince myself that nothing has changed at all. By the time I come outside, Aiden and Sara have joined Cam and Janie, the four of them involved in some sort of earnest discussion.

"Here you go." I toss the key to Cam.

"Thanks," he says, pocketing it, and then the front door opens and Mike and Gavin come down the porch steps behind me. Mike says something to Janie, and she steps back. The twins tag along after her, leaving Cam and Gavin and me standing in a circle of utmost awkwardness. For one wild moment I wonder if they've all done it on purpose.

"Cam," I say, "this is Gavin. Mike's friend. I mean, not that he's Mike's friend only, but that he's primarily here to see Mike. He's my friend, too." Since the first half of my introduction has gone so smoothly, I continue. "And Gavin, this is my friend Cam."

The boys do a man-shake and then all eyes are back on me. Cam's curious, and Gavin doesn't really look like anything at all, except awkward.

"Um," I say with as much eloquence as I can muster. "Cam forgot his key."

They both continue to stare at me, and the longer the silence lasts, the more amused Cam looks.

"Um," I say again, twisting my hair onto the top of my head. It's hot today, and I hope that my blush can be attributed to the temperature and not my embarrassment.

"Well," Cam says, saving me. "I guess I'd better go."

"I'll walk you to the car," I reply, and then wonder why I'm so eager to get out of here. Janie and Mike are still deep in conversation with the twins, who probably keep asking if Cam is my boyfriend, and Gavin drifts over to join them, hands in his pockets as they all disappear around the corner of the house. "They won't even miss me."

I walk shoulder to shoulder with Cam until we reach his van, and then he opens the door and stops, one foot in, one out.

"Are you okay?" I venture after a second, when it looks like he's not about to move.

"I just feel stupid about the whole thing," he confesses. His smile more tired than happy, now that he's no longer amused at my awkwardness with my old friends. "It's been one of those days."

"Do you want me to come with you?" I offer this without thinking, but as soon as the words leave my mouth I realize I'd be leaving Janie behind after only a few hours of our visit. And then, which is even more surprising, I realize that I don't care.

"Yes," Cam says instantly, without any pretense. "But you don't have to. Your friends are here."

"They'll survive." I shrug, not knowing what else to say.

"Deal," he says, rubbing the back of his head absently so all his hair stands up on end.

"One sec," I say, and wonder why I can't decide what to do with my hands. "Just let me tell Janie."

I jog around the house and find my three old friends still deep in conversation. It takes them a minute to notice me.

"What's up?" asks Mike, and I know that I have to be careful how I phrase what's coming next.

"I'm going out with Cam," I blurt, and then as Janie screams in delight, I realize how that sounds. "Not romantically," I add desperately, looking anywhere but at Gavin. "Just, right now. To the library. I'll be back in fifteen minutes."

Mike, who I'd hoped would back me up, folds his arms. "Do you need a chaperone?"

"Mike!" I yell, horrified, and Janie doubles over, laughing. I sneak a glance at Gavin, but he's staring at the ground. A flash of irritation turns my skin hot, because I want to know where the interesting boy is that I had a massive crush on back home. Or was he always like this and I just never noticed before?

"You go for it," Janie says, gasping for breath. "Have fun! And make sure you tell me all the details when you get back."

"Maybe I'd better come," Mike says, frowning, and I feel a twinge of indignation. Now, all of a sudden, he decides to play the concerned older brother?

"Okay, not funny." I start backing away slowly. "I'm going now, bye."

I'm still flushed when I slide into the passenger seat beside Cam a few seconds later, slamming the door a little too hard behind me.

"Okay?" he asks, putting the car into reverse.

I click my seat belt into place and nod. "Let's go."

"So, those were your friends." Cam flips the signal, green light blinking on the dashboard.

"Those were them," I agree. "What did you think?"

"They were different than I expected," he admits, turning the radio dial. I watch his fingers play with the settings, and the layered sound behind his voice dies away significantly.

"Different?"

He shrugs. "I just expected friends of yours to be more like you, I guess."

Having been called Janie's twin for the better part of sixteen years, I find this a little hard to comprehend. When we were kids, we liked all the same things and forced our mothers to buy us similar clothes so we could pretend to be sisters. In high school, we grew up a bit and developed separate identities, but we ran track together and hung out with the same crowd of people as we used to.

After the accident, I didn't see her as often. We didn't have as much time for each other, since she was at school writing exams and running track, and I was stuck in bed with the blinds shut and a migraine pounding in my ears, going no farther than down the hall to the bathroom and back. While she and the rest of our friends wrote their eleventh grade standardized tests in the high school gym, I took mine at a computer in my guidance counselor's office, where I could pause the test and lie down if the headache from my concussion returned.

Because of this, for a moment, I think I've heard Cam wrong. "You don't think we're alike?"

"Nah, not really." We coast to a stop and wait at the red light, even though the intersection is empty. "I don't know her, but she's kind of…" He scratches his chin, doesn't finish his sentence.

"Tell me," I say, desperate to know what he means without quite knowing why it's suddenly so important to me.

"She seems kind of fake," he says, and the light goes green. "Like she's saying stuff but you don't know what's going on inside, or if there even is anything inside her head. With you, I can tell you're always thinking about stuff, and when you say something…" He shrugs. "I know you mean it, I know I can just take it at face value. Whatever." He does a shoulder check and makes the turn into the library parking lot. "I didn't mean to be down on your best friend. You obviously have a lot in common, right? Or you wouldn't have stayed friends for so long."

He seems to be waiting for a response from me, but I'm still stuck on the idea that for the first time in our lives, someone not only refuses to think we're identical, but actually sees us as two different people. I can't decide if it's a good feeling or a bad one.

"I missed her a lot when we first came here," I say slowly. "But after a while, I got so busy, and I didn't think about her, or our other friends as much. And then she showed up all of a sudden, and now I don't know what to think. I feel like she doesn't know me anymore. I feel like I'm a different person, and that person doesn't recognize either of us right now."

To say it out loud makes it so much sadder, and as Cam puts the car in park, I have to tell myself very firmly not to start crying. *Pull yourself together, Skylar. For goodness' sake.*

"Sometimes," Cam says slowly, taking the keys out of the ignition and turning to look at me, "you just outgrow people."

"But not her," I say hoarsely. "Not my best friend."

"Don't start crying." Cam looks panicked. "Please, Skylar."

"Sorry," I say, and sniff hard for good measure. "I'm good."

"Why does it matter so much?" He asks me this after a minute where neither of us move, staring at the darkened windows of the library. "I mean, don't you have other friends?"

"Yeah," I say defensively, and then wonder why I suddenly feel vulnerable. "Lots."

"So..." He leaves it open for me to finish.

"But I'm afraid that if it happened with Janie, it'll happen with them too. Everything is different now. I like different things, I sound different."

"So maybe you need different friends too." It all seems to be very simple to Cam. "It doesn't mean you have to abandon your old ones, Skylar. It doesn't mean everything has to change."

"Are you sure?"

"You met me after the accident," he says. "And, I don't know, it seems to be working out." He's teasing me now, and I choose to smile instead of give in to the tears.

"Thanks."

"Just a sec." Cam pats my knee encouragingly before popping his door open and jogging to the front of the building, where he sticks my key into the lock and flips it three times, to reset the automatic doors. Then he slides the alarm keypad open and punches in the six-digit code, fingers flying. He's back in the driver's seat in less than two minutes and pulling into Aunt Kay's driveway exactly four minutes later.

"Well," he says, brushing the hair away from his forehead. "That's done. I guess I should let you get back to your friends."

I look up in time to catch a glimpse of Janie running by the front window, Aiden and Sara in hot pursuit. "Looks like the gang's all together," I say, and then sigh before I realize that I'm going to.

"Sometimes you outgrow people," Cam says again and gives

me what I think is supposed to be a helpful grin, although on him it looks vaguely goofy. "And sometimes that's okay."

"Thanks." I push the door open and let it thud shut behind me before taking a deep breath and walking toward the front door, wondering why I have to brace myself before being with people I'm supposed to love.

•●•

The next few days are a whirlwind, a tsunami, and Janie and I stay up late watching movies with Gavin and Mike. It's fun, even though they don't put the subtitles on and I can't follow the dialogue. On the first morning I wake up with whipped cream on my face; the second morning it's a marker moustache that takes me a ridiculous amount of time to scrub off.

Sunday night I resolve to stay awake but fail miserably and wake up outside on the deck, my three best friends laughing at me from behind the locked door. And at times like these, it's easy to forget the gap that is widening between us. Even Mike is the same as he always was, and since the first day of their visit, he doesn't mention Eric once. It feels the same, the four of us together like we used to be. Sometimes the illusion lasts for hours, and I wonder if I was making up the space between us, if it was just the natural awkwardness as we slide into place next to each other, waiting for the final "click" that will tell us everything is back to normal.

But it never comes—or if it does, I don't hear it—and it only takes one second, one turned head, hand over a mouth, one missed sentence for me to realize that nothing will ever go back to normal. Mike vanished part of the day on Sunday, probably at another party. He left the three of us limping around, lopsided without him. Janie and Gavin have gotten used to me quickly, remember to tap my shoulder or wave from across the room before speaking, but it's hard for them. More than that, it's hard for me. With Cam, with my family, even with Anastasia as I get to know her better, sometimes I get so caught up in being alive, just living and moving and breathing alongside them, that I actually forget that I can't hear. With Janie and Gavin, it's always in my face, like I'm looking through a dirty window or trying to climb a mountain without moving my fingers. It feels impossible.

By the time Janie and Gavin are packing up to leave on Monday, I feel relieved. And then I feel guilty for feeling relieved.

"I'll miss you so much," Janie says and then throws her arms around my neck, which is lucky because I'm not quite sure how I want to reply to her.

"I'll text you when I figure out when we're coming home," I say into the air beside her ear, and thankfully she doesn't push the subject.

When at last she releases me, she bends down to hug Aiden and Sara. Aiden submits to the hug but won't return it, his masculine pride already beyond the reach of her maternal affection.

Sara, on the other hand, throws herself into Janie's arms. "Don't go!"

"I have to," my best friend says, gently freeing herself from my sister's grasp. "But I'll see you again when school starts."

At last the hugging is over, goodbyes are exchanged, and with one short hug from Gavin, who pulls my braid—just like Mike used to—they climb into the car. It's this final movement that undoes me, because it's the only time all weekend that anything truly feels the same. It's an old action buried in both of our childhoods, and it's the moment I know that Cam is right. Everything *is* different now.

"Drive safe," I call past the lump in my throat. It makes me feel like my mother, always looking out for everyone else, but I just can't think of anything else to say. "I'll miss you!" feels a little too much like a lie.

Mike, hands in his pockets, doesn't say anything, but he does look thoughtful. The four of us stand in the driveway, my parents watching respectfully from inside the house, as the car meanders down the road before turning left.

"And that's it," murmurs Mike in words that I'm sure aren't meant for my ears—or my eyes. "There they go."

I open my mouth to reply, still feeling the warmth of Janie's breath against my ear, the gentle tug of Gavin's hand on my braid, and then decide not to say anything at all. Instead, I nudge the twins gently toward the house. Sara is crying, rubbing the tears away with the back of her hand, and I think with something like surprise that this has been hard on them as well as Mike. As well as me. It's been an adjustment for all of us, I guess, and as soon as I think this, I wonder why it hasn't occurred to me before.

I wander upstairs, feeling aimless and wishing I hadn't asked for today off work, and flop face-first onto my bed, the weight of the words spoken in the past few days heavy against my heart. Tom jumps onto my bed and picks his way gently across the covers, first placing one paw on my back, and then the other three, turning one delicate circle before sitting down, tail curled around his haunches, to lick his front paw.

"Get off," I mumble, nudging him aside as I roll onto my back. "And what do you think about all of it? Huh? Do you think I'll ever get home again?"

He doesn't even bother to look at me, ears flicking briefly toward my face before focusing again on his job, on the urgency of whatever it is that he has stuck between his toes.

"Yeah," I say grumpily. "I didn't think so."

My gaze shifts to the ceiling, to the wooden slats running crosswise across the room, and I glare up at them as though being angry at inanimate objects will solve all my problems.

Unfortunately, it doesn't help. Five minutes later I still feel as tumbled around, upside down and just generally confused and mixed up.

"Fine," I say to Tom, tired of myself and only getting grumpier locked away in my room. "Just fine."

I clomp down the stairs expecting to find the house in some kind of chaos, tears or general upheaval. Instead, my family is watching TV, Mom and Dad on the loveseat, and Mike on the couch, the twins lying sprawled across the floor like casualties of a comic battle.

Normally I would rebel against being inside, when it is warm outside and I could be running, but today my soul is weary and suddenly that empty spot on the couch looks inviting and perfectly Skylar-sized. As though reading my thoughts Mike looks up, pats the cushion beside him, and mouths something to me that I don't catch, because Sara leaned forward to cup an explosive sneeze in her elbow and I got distracted at the wrong moment. But I step forward anyway and sink myself into the embrace of the couch.

The cartoon people onscreen dance back and forth, square mouths opening and closing, their words lost in the soundtrack playing along to the action. I lean my head on Mike's bony, yet comforting shoulder and watch the twins watch TV sprawled across the floor, Sara's mouth hanging open and Aiden's stomach moving up and down rhythmically as he breathes. Mom has her feet curled under her, Dad's head in her lap, and as I watch, she laughs at something on the television, her head tipped back. Her dark hair curls down her back as she laughs, her fingers tracing shapes on Dad's forehead.

When did I not see this? I catch myself for the first time thinking something positive about not being able to hear. If I could hear, I never would have seen this. I couldn't see half as clearly with all the noise in the way.

And then I realize, the side of my head throbbing from where the bone of Mike's shoulder is pressed against my ear…

I am happy here.

Chapter NINE

AFTER JANIE AND GAVIN'S VISIT, THINGS BETWEEN MIKE AND ME SEEM BETTER at first. We're nicer to each other, and for the first week after they leave, Mike is home more often. Some days I walk home from work and find him playing soccer with Aiden, or helping Sara master the art of riding a bike without training wheels. Sometimes he meets me at the library after a shift and we walk home together. I don't see Eric at all, and when I wake up in the mornings, Mike is always at home. Mom's frown lines fade, and Dad spends less time losing his glasses and more time writing, a sure sign that he's making progress on his book.

One day after my shift has finished, we walk home down the exact center of Main Street, following the dotted yellow line along the middle of the road. When I look back, I see Mike carefully placing one foot in front of the other. We used to think that if we could get all the way home walking on the white lines, we were granted three wishes. It was rare when we could manage it, one of us always keeping a wary eye out for cars while the other went as fast as they dared, hoping that today would be the day.

"Well?" I ask him when we reach Aunt Kay's street, turning so I can see his reply. I nearly trip over my feet as I do so.

"Well what?" says Mike, laughing at me.

"What'd you wish for?" It was our rule that while we couldn't reveal our wishes to anyone else, we could always tell each other.

He hesitates.

"Tell me," I say, shoving his arm. I say it like I'm kidding, but suddenly this is way too important to joke about.

"I wished for hotdogs for dinner tonight," he says, but I know he's lying. "And that Aunt Kay would hurry up and get back so we can quit housesitting and go home soon."

"Do you miss it that much?"

He shrugs. "There's not much for me to do here. You've got your job and your friends, and I mostly lie around the house all day with your cat."

I realize that this is true; it's always been this way. Mike has never been the outgoing one. But he had his friends, and he had me, and I'm ashamed to find that other than being frustrated with him for abandoning me, I haven't thought much about him at all. I certainly never thought that maybe I was the one who abandoned him. But the job at McDonald's he'd boasted about apparently came to nothing, and that left him...well, with nothing.

He shrugs. "It's okay, Skylar. I'm just ready to go home."

"You could come to the library more," I say as we reach Aunt Kay's driveway. "Or maybe you could get a job there too, doing something. There are other places besides McDonald's."

Mike looks annoyed. "I don't need you to fix things for me, Skylar."

"Sorry," I mumble, biting back another helpful suggestion.

"Let's go to the beach," he says abruptly, pausing before the front door. "Where are the twins?"

I peek in the front window and see them sprawled across the floor playing some kind of board game. "Maybe we'd better go around back, if we want to get in and out without them noticing."

We make it almost all the way inside before the munchkins

descend. I know the exact place in the kitchen that I'm standing when we're discovered, because right as I step over the threshold, I sneeze. It's one of those sneezes that takes you completely by surprise, knocks you to your hands and knees—not literally, unless you're me, then, who knows?—and leaves you wiping your nose distractedly. As I straighten up again, I see Mike's sloped shoulders relax and know that there's no point in trying to be quiet anymore.

Sure enough, into the kitchen charge Aiden and Sara, and Tom slips around the corner and into the newly vacated living room, tail held high.

"Mike!" Sara throws herself into his arms, and he picks her up and swings her around. "Will you take us to the beach?" she asks when he sets her down. "It's too hot to play outside and it's too hot to sit on the couch inside and Dad's writing his book and Mom said … …"

I miss whatever it is that Mom said, because Mike looks over his shoulder at me, eyebrows raised in a question. Do we really want to do this?

"We'll take you," I say, nodding to him. "It'll be fun."

Aiden pumps his fist in celebration the way football players do after a big run, and I grin down at him, affection for his cute little face rising inside of me.

"But you have to make sure it's okay with Mom," I add, feeling proud of myself for being responsible.

"We did already," Sara says, rolling her eyes. "I told you that."

"Well, okay," I say lamely, trying to pretend that her response didn't sting me just a little bit.

Some days I forget I can't hear—I actually forget. Is that even possible?—and then something like this happens and I feel like I'll never get ahead, never really know what's going on or be able to follow a conversation from start to finish ever again.

"Go get changed, then," I say.

"Let's meet back here in ten minutes," Mike says.

"Okay, break!" Aiden turns to sprint for the stairs.

We meet in the kitchen in fifteen minutes, because it takes me almost ten minutes just to find my bathing suit. It was under Sara's bed—I try not to think too hard about what it might have been doing there.

"Girls take forever to change," Aiden says, looking knowingly up at Mike, and I grin, but something pinches a little bit inside my heart. When did he get so old? When did he start looking up to Mike like our older brother was the one who ran the world?

"No kidding," Mike says. "Let's get moving, slowpokes." He holds the door open for us and we traipse out onto the front porch. I can practically feel the sand on my feet, the icy kiss of lake water on my skin.

We make it down to the beach in record time, and Aiden and Sara sprint straight for the water. Jealous of their already-tanned skin, I spread out my towel and slip my hearing aids off, zipping them safely into a sandwich bag, away from wind and lake water. The world around me newly serene and silent, I slather on sunscreen, handing the bottle to Mike as I smear a stripe down my nose.

"They're lucky they've got Mom's ability to tan," I grumble, massaging the oily cream into my forehead. "Have they ever had a sunburn in either of their lives?"

Mike half-heartedly slaps some onto his shoulders. He's usually the darkest out of all of us, but this year, his skin is pasty white under his T-shirt. "I dunno."

He jogs after them, diving head-first into the spray, and I wait for the allotted fifteen minutes to pass before I'm officially sunsafe, digging my feet deep into the sand, searching for the cold, hard earth beneath. A gentle breeze blows sand across my sunscreened legs, and it sticks there, glittering like tiny shards of glass on my skin. I try to wipe it away but only end up getting sand on my hands, so, giving up, I lay back and close my eyes.

But it's too quiet and I can't see anything, so I have to open them again, sitting up and shuddering slightly, as though to rid myself of that other place, the silent world where all is dark and still.

When at last enough time has passed, I get to my feet and jog down to the water, a single drop of sweat running down my back. My feet hit the water right as a wave comes crashing down to the shoreline, and a fine mist from the contact sprays my legs. I gasp as the cold burns, and then push in a little deeper as relief sets in. At last, when the waves lap around my waist, I throw myself under completely, feeling the water caress my scalp, push across all my skin, and wipe away any traces of sweat or grime that the day has left behind.

Finally, I put my feet down and stand up, puncturing the surface and feeling the broken shards of water explode across my skin. Mike has found a football—or maybe Aiden brought it with him, I don't know—and my three siblings are tossing it back and forth, being careful to stay where it's shallow. Mike and I are good swimmers, but Aiden and Sara haven't quite mastered the skill yet. They know enough to float and doggy paddle, but nothing so fancy as front crawl has entered their physical vocabulary yet.

"Throw it to me," I call, and then when no one hears, I push my voice a little harder. "Mike!"

He turns, arcs the football up in a perfect spiral, and when I reach out it falls neatly into my grasp. I feel the wet leather sticky in my hands, find the lacing with my fingertips, and send it soaring—albeit, a little crookedly—toward Aiden. He leaps for it, disappears underwater in a dramatic splash, and pops up again, shaking his head like a dog. I can see Sara jumping up and down out of the corner of my eye, probably shrieking for him to pass to her, but he reaches back and funnels it straight to Mike.

We play around in the water for almost an hour on the quiet stretch of beach, long after I feel my shoulders start to burn and shrug away the idea of reapplying sunscreen. Aiden and Sara are flushed from the exertion, Mike's shoulders and upper back are already a fiery shade of pink, and I'm almost positive I've grown a racoon shaped sunglasses tan, but it feels good. The sky is still cloudless, but the breeze has grown stronger and the waves are white-capped as they tip and fall before crashing against the beach. If you stand perfectly still, you can feel the baby fingers of the undertow tugging at your legs as the lake rushes in, and then slips silently back out onto itself.

"Skylar," Mike's lips say, and he waves at me until I'm paying attention. "Go long." He motions with his hand that he's going to throw the ball over my head—why do boys always do that?—and I start to run through the water, shoving my weight against the waves until I'm in almost to my armpits. The ball arcs overhead and I leap up for it, missing completely as I crash down in a tremendous belly flop.

I push off the bottom and emerge, the football bobbing in front of me, tauntingly. I was so close to catching it. "Just a few more inches," I mutter under my breath, stroking a confident front crawl and enjoying the feeling of power as I reach out and clasp the ball with my right hand.

When I turn around, Mike is charging through the water toward me, his lips moving in a silent shout, invisible words spewing far too fast to catch. Sara is standing by herself in the shallow end, her face puckered up in a shriek, or a sob, I can't tell which.

"What?" I yell, dropping the football, and then I see. A few feet behind me, barely out of arms' reach, is Aiden, his eyes wide in terror as he struggles to stay afloat, mouth dipping perilously underwater again and again. His hands paddle uselessly, reaching up out of the water, searching for anything to grab. He is so close, almost close enough for me to touch, but I'm frozen, staring at his eyes. They're huge, so big they make the rest of his face look tiny and pale and young and alone.

He sinks, reappears, and I launch into action at the same time that Mike reaches him, yanks him above the surface and into his arms, his own eyes wide and frightened. How long was he struggling there, drowning, and I didn't notice? If Mike crossed the entire beach before I turned around…

I shiver, goose bumps rising on my skin, but I'm too scared to cry. Mike clutches Aiden to his chest, fingers trembling as our little brother coughs and coughs and coughs, his hair plastered to his forehead.

"Are you okay?" Mike asks, his lips forming the words over and over again before Aiden has a chance to answer. He dips his face down so he can look Aiden in the eye, and because I can't see either of their faces, I have no idea what he's saying anymore.

Aiden nods, shakes his head, spews up a mouthful of water, and starts to cry, burying his face in Mike's neck. Both my older and my younger brother are trembling, water droplets running in crooked rivulets down their skin.

"It's okay." Mike's teeth are chattering, and I realize that I'm shaking, too, my whole body wracked with shudders.

"What happened?" I ask, breathlessly, and Mike turns to me, the cords in his neck tensed so I know he's yelling. Whether it's because I'm in shock or he's speaking too quickly, I can't read his lips, but he's still shaking, and Aiden's arms tighten around his neck.

"Stop!" I yell back at him, and still I don't cry. "Mike, I can't hear you! Slow down!"

"What were you thinking?" He enunciates each word clearly and they fall like bricks against my chest. "He was right there! He was right …… and you didn't …… anything!"

I think again of Aiden's eyes, wide and terrified, and swallow a wave of bile that rolls in my throat. "I didn't see him," I offer, but it feels weak, a limp excuse because what could I say that could possibly carry the weight of my little brother's life?

"I don't care," Mike explodes, and I see the faint shadow of a vein outlined in his neck. "You should have...something! For the—" He curses under his breath, but I read every foul word on his lips. I've never seen Mike swear before this summer. "It's not good enough, Skylar!"

I stare at him, eyes defiantly dry, and know that he is right.

"I'm sorry," I whisper, because what else is there to say?

Aiden, hiccupping, says something to Mike that I don't catch; they both turn toward the beach, where Sara is still standing. Her face is red from crying and tears run freely down her cheeks, panic written in every tight muscle and obvious in the way she stands as though frozen to the ground.

"Is he...?" She chokes on the word "dead," but I don't have to see it on her lips to feel the taste of it on my own. I can see her struggling to swallow it back down, the bitterness of it overwhelming.

"No," calls Mike, his throat tense, his lips tight. Even though I want to look away, I force myself to stare at his lips so I can follow at least part of the conversation. "He's okay. We're all okay."

Except me, I think numbly, still standing in the same place as Mike begins to wade back to the beach. Aiden has mostly stopped crying and is just hiccupping now, his white fingers still locked around Mike's neck.

I stay standing in the middle of the lake, feeling the mucky sand drift and settle over my feet, like I've put down roots here, like I'm going to stay. Maybe I will.

When Mike reaches the shore, he tries to set Aiden down, but he won't let go. Sara charges up to him and buries her face in his stomach, clutching at Aiden as though touching any piece of him will make him real, will assure her that he's okay. After a moment of hesitation, Mike picks her up too. Loaded down with a twin on each arm, he looks strong, and capable, and everything else that I don't feel and am convinced I'll never feel again. He stands there for a minute, with his back to the lake, and after a few moments I can see that he's still shaking, water droplets dappled across his back.

At last, he turns. "Come on, Skylar," he says, and with the sun in his face I can read his lips from even this far out. For a moment I contemplate staying here forever. The numbness is starting to fade, and other emotions begin to creep in.

Embarrassment. Guilt. Shame.

"Skylar," Mike says again, and I wish I could see understanding or even empathy in his face, but it is like a mask to me.

Finally, I yank one foot free of the muck and trudge toward the beach, Mike and Aiden and Sara silently watching my approach. My hair, caked with lake water and sand, feels like straw down my back, the skin on my face pulled tight and raw, burned by the sun and wind.

No one says anything when I at last stand on two feet across from them, the four of us all contemplating each other.

Sara, still sniffling, is the first to speak. "I want to go home."

I wonder if that's it, if we will simply never mention this incident again.

Mike looks at me, shoulders drooping, and I know he's thinking the same thing. Do we really need to tell Mom and Dad?

"Me too," Aiden says, and I reach up to wipe a tear off his cheek.

"Let's go, then," I say, my own voice feeling hoarse and raw inside my throat. "I'll get the towels."

Mike stands perfectly still as I drape towels over the twins, like he's some overgrown coat tree, but at last we're ready to go. I pull a towel across my own shoulders, wincing as it rubs against my burned skin, the glory of the day long gone, descending with the setting sun. I carry the case that holds my hearing aids. It feels like a punishment not to put them in, but I think I deserve it.

We are a despondent group as we hike up the dune toward Aunt Kay's house, the unspoken words between us hanging heavy in my stomach. I don't want to have this conversation with my parents.

By the time we walk up the front steps, Sara is walking by herself, clinging tightly to my hand. Aiden has claimed both towels, and Mike still holds him in his arms. The rest of us have stopped shivering as the sun warmed us, but Aiden is still shaking, his body racked with tremors.

"Shock," Mike mouths to me over his shoulder, so Sara won't see. He hesitates for a moment at the front door as though unsure if he really wants to go in—and then he opens the door.

Mom and Dad are sitting together at the kitchen table, and as one they look up toward us, Mom already smiling, and Dad squinting a little bit as though he doesn't quite recognize us.

"How was the beach?" Mom asks, her smile faltering as she takes in our silent forms, the unusually subdued Sara, and Aiden all bundled up in towels. "What happened? What's wrong?"

My eyes start to burn, and I gulp back a sob, breathing in deeply through my nose to still the trembling that starts again. "We were playing football," I say, and then start to cry. "And Mike threw it over my head, and I—"

"Skylar, wait," Mom says, holding out a hand to me. Her skin is browned from mornings spent outdoors with the twins, although I don't know why I notice this now. "I can't hear you, you're speaking too quietly."

The room blurs in front of me and then I can't see anything, can't make out any details. I see the hazy shape of Mike setting Aiden down on the floor, my little brother running for Mom. I see Sara start to cry again, both of them clinging to our mother as she stares in bewilderment at Mike, who is probably offering an explanation.

And that's all I can stand, so as the sobs start in earnest I sprint for the stairs, tripping over the first step and then flying past the rest of them, sand in the cracks of my skin feeling gritty against the wood of the banister.

I collapse onto my bed and bury my face in the pillow, unable to stop the wail buried in my stomach from ripping free, praying that they can't hear me downstairs. *Stupid!* I think to myself furiously, and that's the last thing I know for a while, carried away by the rush of tears.

After a few minutes, when the flow has waned, I roll onto my back. Still choking back sobs, I close my eyes and picture his face, imagining that terrible moment over and over, and hating myself for doing it. Like a sore you can't help poking or picking at until finally it gives up and bleeds, I picture Aiden's wide eyes, the terror in Mike's face as he sprinted through the water, the tears on Sara's cheeks and the way her ponytail came loose in the wind.

He could have died, I tell myself, vicious in my self-loathing. *And it would have been my fault. He could have died.*

Dead.

Death.

My fault.

After a few minutes of this, my door slowly opens. I instinctively roll away from it, hiding my face from view. Then, after half a second, I realize that I still don't have my hearing aids in and I won't be able to hear who it is. Wiping my eyes, I roll over. Dad is standing in the doorway, with his glasses on for once, my hearing aid case in his hands.

"Mike told us what happened," he says, tossing the case gently onto the bed beside me, and I hiccup.

"I'm sorry," I whisper, my guilt-charred heart heaving inside of me.

"Skylar," my father says, and then stops. I fumble for the case without looking away, choking back the remnants of a sob. "Oh, Skylar."

I feel a tiny moan eke out of me, lips pressed together, and Dad wipes his own eyes, leaning against the doorjamb.

"Are you okay, kiddo?"

Finally, I wrangle the hearing aids free and slide them into my ears, making sure the volume is turned up.

"I'm sorry," I say again, once they're turned on and the dull background noise of an empty room hums away in both of my ears. My voice feels ragged and sore. "Mike told you…I didn't mean to, I should have been paying more attention."

"Skylar," he says, holding up a hand, and I choke back the torrent of apologies. "I need you to listen to me."

A tiny hysterical laugh bubbles out of me. If only. How much easier would my life be if that were possible?

Dad sighs and rubs his forehead. "I'm sorry, that was tactless of me."

"Sorry," I say for the third time.

"I need you to know something." He sits beside me on the bed to make sure that I can see his lips very, very clearly.

"'Kay," I mumble, wiping my nose with the back of my hand.

"This," he says, enunciating very clearly, "was not your fault. What happened today was one of those things that happens because it happens, not because you weren't paying enough attention or because you don't love your brother."

"If I could hear—" I start, but he holds up a hand.

"But you can't," he says, and the words are blunt, but his face is kind. "There's no point in thinking about a what-if, Skylar, you know that. This has been…this is new for all of us. And we'll get through it. We all will." He puts a hand on my knee. "But you need to know that no one is holding you responsible for what happened today."

"But Mike," I say, my lips trembling.

"Mike," my father says, and then sighs, and now I think that he looks very tired. "Mike has his own life to sort out, and I can't speak to that, but I don't think he blames you either. I think he'd like to, I think he'd find that easier. But I don't think he believes you're at fault."

"But I do," I whisper. "I think it's my fault. Even after I turned around and saw him, I didn't do anything. He was right there, and I just watched him—"

Dad puts his arm around me, and I lean into his chest. The smell of his cologne makes me need to cry all over again, so I do, chest heaving. My snot makes a wet little puddle on his shoulder.

"Is he going to be okay?" I manage to gulp out finally, after maybe five minutes.

"I think he'll be fine." Dad peels off his glasses and places them on my nightstand. "He's a little shaken up, like we all are. Your mom's got the twins downstairs, I think they're watching cartoons together."

"And he doesn't hate me?"

"No," Dad says and picks up his glasses again. "No one hates you, Skylar." And then he adds, "Except maybe you."

I have the uncomfortable feeling that someone has peeled aside my ribcage and is staring openly at the vulnerable beating of my heart. Suddenly I feel very fragile. I am conscious of my veins, tiny capillaries, all the miniscule pathways through which my blood travels. What are arteries? Because I am not strong enough to send anything else out. I am not strong enough to have anything left to give.

And I know that he has found me out.

Dad gets to his feet and places his hand on my shoulder, giving it a squeeze before walking over to my door. "Come down whenever you're ready. And know that we love you very much."

This doesn't make me feel any better. Tired from crying, I roll over so my face is to the window, the sinking sun warm on my face. And then, in about five minutes flat, I fall asleep.

• ● •

When I wake up, my bedroom is dark, the light from a single streetlamp shining in through my open window. I'm exhausted, but in the relaxing way that makes your muscles feel like peanut butter, slow and totally limp. For a long time, I lie perfectly still, feeling the total elasticity of my body, blinking sleepily. I am too tired to even feel worried or guilty. The events of the previous day seem unreal, and even though I poke at the thought of Aiden for a moment, I can't bring about any emotional reaction.

It is the dull throbbing in my bladder that eventually calls me to action. Reluctantly, I force my body into a sitting position, swing my legs over the side of the bed, and stand up, the floorboards cool against my bare feet. When I rub my eyes with my fingers, I can feel sand caught in my eyelashes, but just as I wonder if I should care, I yawn and decide that I can worry about it tomorrow. One of my hearing aids has fallen out and is lying on the pillow, so I set it on the nightstand and take the other one out, too, pulling open my door with my free hand.

I tiptoe down the hallway and then can't resist a peek into the twins' room. It's between mine and Mike's, and opposite our parents' room and the bathroom, so I reconcile my actions by arguing that it's on the way, anyway. For my midnight brain, the argument is more than adequate.

When I crack open their door, I see the twins curled up together in Sara's bed, the lower of the two bunks. They stopped sleeping together a few years ago, but every so often Aiden will crawl into bed with Sara, especially if one of them is sick or upset about something.

Not wanting to wake them, I withdraw again, but pause in

front of Mike's door rather than the bathroom. It feels silly to check on my older brother, but something in me needs to see him. I need to see that everyone is safe, that there's nothing I'm missing out on by not being able to hear.

Thankfully, his door is unlatched, hanging slightly ajar, and I only have to nudge it open with the tips of my fingers. Mike has his curtains closed, and it takes my eyes a minute to adjust to the darkness. For a minute, I'm not sure what I'm seeing, not sure where my brother is or why his bed is still made up, obviously not slept in since Mom changed his sheets this morning.

He's probably at Eric's, I realize, and then I see a faint light glowing from downstairs. My protesting bladder forgotten, I tiptoe to the top of the stairs and step gently down until the living room is in view, one lamp lit. I slide to a sitting position, resting my face in between the bannisters, and see Mike sitting on the couch, with his head in his hands.

He stays like that for so long that I wonder if he's fallen asleep. Just as I'm consider going down and waking him, his body explodes into action, and he whirls to the side, striking out, fists pummeling the back of the couch, the cushions, anything his hands will reach. I don't realize I'm holding my breath until his fist strikes the wooden armrest and he recoils in pain, cradling his left hand against his body.

I watch as he slumps over, shoulders shaking, and then I stand up and climb the stairs alone. I don't realize until I'm in bed staring at the ceiling that I've forgotten to go to the bathroom, after all.

Chapter
TEN

I THOUGHT IT WOULD TAKE WEEKS FOR US TO RECOVER FROM THE BEACH scare, that it might linger over our heads in the mornings and afternoons following the almost-tragedy, but by the time we all wake up on the morning after, the drama has faded. It takes Aiden and Sara approximately two seconds to forget how scared they'd been and decide that "almost dying" is pretty high on their list of "really cool things." We finally decide that they've suffered no negative trauma when Mom catches them re-enacting the scare on the front lawn a few days later. It was a game they'd christened "Lifeguard Me," and one that Mom quickly put a stop to, in case it happened to occur to them that it might be a wonderful idea to make their game more realistic by adding water.

At the beginning of the second week in August, exactly one month after we arrived in Golden Sound, Ontario, we receive a second letter from Aunt Kay. Aiden and Sara insist on being allowed in the kitchen while Dad reads the note aloud during breakfast, even though they both share a fever from the summer cold that plagues our entire family, and Mom has ordered them to bed for the day. The letter is dated almost three weeks prior and postmarked from a country in Africa that no one in my family has ever heard of, and most frustrating of all, it contains no information of importance.

Well, I suppose that's a matter of opinion. But rather than include any information on her travel plans, or when she's hoping to come home, Aunt Kay has written us a short note telling us that she hopes we're having a wonderful time, to tell everyone in town "hello" from Africa, and to remind us that she always keeps a stash of marshmallows in the back of the bottom kitchen cabinet.

When Dad finishes reading this note aloud to all of us, me peering over his shoulder at my aunt's big bubbly writing, he takes his glasses off again and sighs.

Mike leans against the kitchen counter with his arms folded. "Is she ever coming home?" He's frowning, but I think that has more to do with the dubious contents of the letter than it does any real anger. I open my mouth to speak, think of his potential reaction to my voice, and shut my mouth again.

I wish he would just talk to me. Things seemed so much better between us, at least until the beach incident. When I'm at work I don't think about it so much, but here, at home, when normally we'd be exchanging eye rolls or groans or something, the gap between us is so noticeable. Maybe I'll march over and grab him by the front of his shirt and force him to look at me.

But maybe I'm a little afraid of what I might see in return.

"Who knows?" Mom reaches for the milk at the back of the fridge. "Maybe we should call the embassy and try to get hold of her that way."

"It'll never work," Dad says wearily. "My sister will come home when she's ready—or maybe she won't come back at all."

"Why not?" Aiden asks this very seriously, wiping his nose with the back of his hand. "Doesn't she like it here?"

"Yes," my father says, slowly. "But she doesn't just like it here, she likes it everywhere. And so, she has to divide her time between all of the different places that she loves, and she's already spent quite a bit of time here. She probably thinks it's time that she lived and loved somewhere a bit different."

"Oh." Aiden accepts this answer without a second thought. "Can we stay here, then?"

"Yeah!" Sara jumps into the conversation, the bags under her eyes belying her excited expression. "Let's move here. We can keep the cat."

In a moment of poor timing on his part, Tom stalks into the room, sees Sara coming around the table toward him, and quickly flees in the other direction.

"Sweetie," Mom says, brushing a hand across her forehead as she walks by, "we can't just pack up and move here."

"Why not?"

"What about your friends?"

"They can move here, too."

Sara shrugs, pours milk over her cereal, and then knocks the bowl over with her elbow, sending a cascade of milk and cornflakes across the kitchen table. Aiden's face screws up in a yell as a milky Niagara Falls cascades straight into his lap, and I take the moment of chaos to slip out the door.

"I'll be back before dinner," I call over my shoulder, my flip-flops slapping against the already-hot pavement. I have extra tissues in my pocket, since my nose is the only part of me not yet healed from my own bout with the Brady family virus.

Mom waves me back from the doorway, a milky cloth in hand. "Skylar, wait!"

I pause, wondering if she's going to tell me to be safe, or remind me to look both ways before I cross the street.

"Did Mike tell you about the book launch?"

"No," I say, reaching for a tissue. "What book launch?"

"For Dad's new book," she answers, a wrinkle between her eyebrows. As I watch, four drops of milk fall from the cloth to the floor.

Dad is always working on a new book, so it takes me a minute to figure out which one she's talking about. "The one about the dog and the swing set?"

"That's the one," she says, nodding. "We'll be gone overnight, but we'll be back in the morning."

"Tonight?" I ask. "Like, this is happening today?"

"I'm so sorry." I wonder how many thoughts are running through the back of her mind that she's not saying out loud. "Mike was supposed to tell you."

You should know better than to depend on Mike for anything these days, I want to say, but I hold myself in check. "Okay," I reply instead, sniffing. My nose feels red and swollen. "I'll see you tomorrow, then?"

She comes down the front steps to give me a one-armed hug, and it's casual, like before the accident. "Love you."

"You too," I mumble back, but I squeeze her around the waist extra hard before letting go. How are Mike and I going to survive in the house together for a full twenty-four hours? I try—unsuccessfully—not to think about it, and by the time I reach the library, I'm sweating and more than grateful for the air-conditioned shock when I step through the front doors.

Cam waves at me from the paperback section, the sticker machine in hand as he re-catalogues titles, and I make a beeline for the front counter.

"Hey, Ana," I call, glancing at her computer screen as I walk by.

With one swift click of her mouse, she closes the tab, fiddling with the keyboard as though she's been typing all along, but I catch a glimpse of what she was looking at. A picture of a little girl on a swing, maybe five or six years old, her hair swept into two tufty pigtails. She's laughing, looking toward the camera, and there are strong hands reaching for her from behind, ready to push her—tanned hands, with long tapered fingers, the nails unpainted.

"Morning," Anastasia says, the word rushed and ill-formed.

"Did you have a nice weekend?"

I clip my nametag to the front of my shirt and begin sorting the recently returned books, glancing up at Ana as I do so. She looks preoccupied, picking at the polish on her fingernails where it has begun to chip at the corners.

She murmurs an affirmative, not meeting my eyes, and I let the matter drop. She's strangely quiet for the rest of the morning. Cam can't draw her out of her shell when he presents the stacks of reorganized books, and the "Favorite Childhood Reads" display that I stocked before our lunch break only seems to make her feel worse.

"I can't figure it out," I say to Cam, the two of us perched on the front counter eating strawberries as Ana traipses toward the front doors, heading out to buy lunch somewhere during her hour off. "Have you ever seen her like this before?"

"Not really," he says, crossing his legs. Mine are dangled over the edge, and I kick my flip-flops off and let my feet swing. "It's a little strange, even for her."

I laugh, pull the green head off a ripe berry, and pop it into my mouth. The coolness of the berry feels nice against the roof of my mouth, even if my ability to taste is deadened by my poor stuffed nose. "Maybe it's just—" I'm about to say *her period* when I remember that I'm talking to a boy.

"Just what?" Cam likes to bite the tops off his strawberries, spitting them into the garbage which I find, frankly, disgusting.

"Just…temporary," I finish rather lamely, but he nods.

"I hope so."

We fall into a companionable silence, the pile of green tops growing as the strawberries themselves diminish.

"Let's play a game," I say, kicking my feet.

"Okay." Cam leans back, fingers splayed out across the countertop. "What kind of game?"

"Let's play Truth or Lie," I say, feeling brave. "If you guess wrong, I get to ask you any question I want. If you guess right, you ask me a question."

"Okay," he says again, tilting his head to one side. "I'll go first." He thinks for a minute, and then suddenly leans forward and claps his hands together. I imagine the invisible reverberations rippling through the air. "One: I have four other siblings besides Elyse; and two: I was homeschooled until the beginning of grade nine."

"Oh." I remember suddenly that I don't actually like this game. "Um, I think one is true."

"Nope," he says, grinning. "Homeschooled is true. I get a question."

"Fine, then." I watch his lips closely to make sure that I don't miss anything.

"Have you ever…" He considers. "Have you ever thrown up in public?"

"That's a disgusting question," I say, punching his arm as though he were Mike.

"Well? Have you?"

I sigh. "Yes. At a track meet, but only one time."

"That's disgusting," he says, deadpan, and I lean forward to smack him again. "Your turn."

I suggested the game without thinking about it first, so it takes me a minute to gather my thoughts. "Number one," I say, trying to blow my nose without making any noise. I have no idea if I pull it off or not, but it feels quiet. I hope.

"I came in second place at Nationals three years ago for track." This one is the lie; I actually came in sixth. "Number two. Until last year, everyone thought I was older than Mike because he's so skinny." It used to make him furious.

"Two," he guesses, and when I nod, he grins. "I guessed. I haven't seen Mike enough to know. Did people really think he was younger?"

I laugh. "All the time. He hated it."

Cam twists one of the discarded strawberry tops in his fingers. "Are you guys close?"

"Is that your question?" I'm trying to buy myself some time.

"Sure," he says, nudging the last strawberry toward me. "You don't talk about him very much, but when you do you always have this funny look on your face. I'm curious."

"Funny look?" I try to look offended, but I'm struck by his words.

"I don't know." Cam shrugs, the toe of his shoe jiggling absently against the countertop. "I can't figure out what it is."

I stare out the front window, trying to figure out how to answer. My nose is *still* running. "He used to be my best friend. Like, for real. My best friend. And then after the accident, we just..." I shrug. "We don't talk. He doesn't talk to me anymore."

"The accident?" Cam's looking at me at last. "The one that—" For the first time since I've known him, he hesitates before finishing his sentence.

"Yeah," I say. "The one where I lost my hearing."

"How long ago was that?"

I count backwards, trying to pinpoint the exact date. "Almost a year ago. In the fall." It doesn't seem very long to say out loud, but when you think that it's all those individual days, each one long and silent, it feels like an eternity.

"Can I ask what happened?" His expression is still hesitant, and suddenly I understand that in order to reach out to me in this place where I am, he's pretty far outside his own comfort zone. For some reason, this makes me feel better.

"Well," I say, and then stop. Do I want to get into this with him? Do I want to get into it with myself, relive the whole thing all over again?

Cam waits, not quite looking at me, but not trying to look away, either.

"Mike and I used to run together all the time," I answer, choosing my words carefully. "Every single day."

He'd come and knock on my door, and if I wasn't downstairs in the kitchen, shoes laced up and ready to go in five minutes, he'd come into my bedroom and rip the covers away from me. I used to whisper-yell at him and call him terrible names, but he'd just laugh and snatch my pillow out from under my head.

"Mike loved the mornings," I say, and then wonder why I'm using past tense. Presumably, Mike still loves mornings the best, but the fact that I don't know for sure throws me off. When's the last time he knocked on my door to get me up for a run?

Technically, drawls a nasty little voice inside my head, *he could knock on your door every morning, just for old times' sake, and with your hearing aids out, you'd never know the difference.*

I pretend that I'm not listening.

"Before the accident," I say, drawing myself to the present, "I could always beat Mike in a sprint, but he was faster than me over long distances. If I took two jogging steps every time he took one, we could stay shoulder-to-shoulder. We'd run to the end of our street, still half-asleep, and then turn left."

Left. That direction haunts me still sometimes. "We'd jog away from the city, and after only ten minutes we could run side by side down the country roads. There usually wasn't any traffic."

Cam nods along with me, trying to be encouraging, and I stare firmly down at the counter, pushing the words out, out, out.

"Sometimes we'd race, even though I almost always won. I used to win a lot at school too," I add, remembering. "I did make it all the way to the national competition once—but I came away with sixth place, not second. I remember crossing the finish line that day, everyone cheering, Janie and the rest of our friends and even Gavin jumping up and down and screaming—but the only person I looked for was Mike. I didn't even stop running until

I'd reached him, and then when I skidded to a halt I tripped and almost knocked him over."

I stop for breath, and Cam reaches a hand across the space between us, just resting it there on the counter, palm down. I look up at him, curious, in spite of myself. "You don't have to, Skylar," he says. "It's okay."

I carry straight on, as though he hadn't spoken. "'I could have beat you,' Mike said, squeezing me back, but I could hear the smile in his voice, and I knew that he was proud of me. He'd driven to the meet all by himself, skipped a day of school, and waited, standing just outside my group of friends, for me to sprint across the finish line." I remember that day, because I got a wicked sunburn on my shoulders from not putting on enough sunscreen. Janie never let me forget it, either.

"On the day of the accident, we weren't even racing."

I don't look at Cam, and he doesn't try to tap my arm or get my attention. It had been a good run, the sun was struggling to shine out from behind a light dusting of clouds, and a gentle rain had begun to fall, just the way Mike liked it. We'd run at a good clip out of town and down the road, not a single car passing us for the first half hour. The soft shoulder was still firm and dry, although there were tiny beads of moisture on the grass in the ditch beside. I'd slowed to point one of these out, both of our sneakers squeaking against the damp pavement as Mike matched his pace to mine.

"We were just messing around," I say out loud. "It was raining. I made him slow down so I could look at the way the water pooled in the ditch."

I pause again, chewing on my bottom lip. I've never told anyone this part before. I don't know if I've ever said it out loud. It's funny now to think of that moment and not know what was to follow after. If I'd known that in only five minutes my hearing would be gone forever, would I have paid more attention? Would I have listened for a thousand words to describe the sound of raindrops falling? Would I have paid more attention to the gravel of my brother's morning voice, and the way he clears his throat as though his words are locked somewhere deep inside his chest?

Or would I simply have asked him to say my name? Or the words "I love you"?

It doesn't matter now.

Even my memories of what happened next are fragmented, in bits and pieces—some have sound, and a few are silent, even though I know that technically, scientifically, physically, at that point I was still able to hear.

What I don't remember: whatever it was that caused me to start falling in the first place. Did I trip? Was I running too far away from the curb? Mike remembers, I know he does, but as much as I'd like to, I've never asked him about it. I can't look him in the eyes and bring myself to do it.

What I do remember: the entire process of falling, from the moment I lost my balance until the second my head hit the pavement.

What I don't remember: any thoughts or reactions other than "curse my hereditarily weak ankles," which was a sentence that I had been fond of repeating at times like that.

I shake myself out of this reverie and look at Cam, who is pretending to be very busy with the empty strawberry container. "I don't remember anything before the actual falling part. I just know we left the house that morning, and then I ended up on the ground."

I remember thinking *ouch* and *Am I bleeding?* But I don't tell Cam this part.

I remember that there was a whooshing noise, a roaring, and for a moment all I could hear was my own pulse, *lub-dub*, in my ears.

I remember hearing my brother scream. At the time, I didn't know what it was, where the sound was coming from, but now when I dream about that morning, that's all I hear. Mike asked me in the kitchen if I had sound in my dreams, and I said I didn't remember, but that's only because I didn't want to tell him the truth.

The only noise I ever hear is the scream that was ripped from his still-sleepy throat, cutting through the countryside like the ragged edge of a dull knife. Sometimes I don't even dream of the impact, I just dream of falling and hearing him scream, endlessly. When I wake up from those dreams, I'm curled in a ball with tears on my cheeks and my own mouth wide open. The first few times this happened I thought I'd been screaming, too, but when no one ever came in to check on me, I figured my remembered agony must have been as silent as it was on the morning of.

I glance at Cam to see if he's bothered by the halting way I'm telling this story, more in gaps of silence than actual sentences, but he's still fiddling with the container, giving me space to tell the story without making himself my audience. Thankful, I say, "I don't remember the car actually hitting me. Because I'd fallen facing forward, I never actually saw it. I couldn't tell you what size it was, what type or make or year. In my nightmares, it's a red sports car, but I don't know if it was. All I know is that even though it was early morning, the driver was drunk."

"Wow," Cam says. I only see the word escape him because I am waiting for it, watching for a reaction. I nod, slowly.

I don't tell him that I remember my shoulder slamming into the ground. I felt my ponytail elastic snap, hair flying across my face, Mike's scream ringing in my ears—and then I woke up two days later with a monster headache and a world full of silently moving lips, empty gestures, and confusing facial expressions. For the first few weeks my whole head hurt too much for me to read the signs and papers held out to me, written words intended to help but only hurting.

Later, when I got the whole story and the rest of my injuries had faded, my eyes captured the words about the one that wouldn't go away:

Damage.

Moderate to severe hearing loss.

Permanent.

A harsh reality full of "no," "sorry," and "not possible," I closed my eyes and realized that the world around me had vanished with one flick of my eyelids. Suddenly I had the power to shut people out when the last thing I wanted was to be alone. I hated it, stayed awake long after the nurses had dimmed the lights in the hallway, blinking hard and fast but fighting sleep.

This part I also don't tell Cam: that I waited for Mike to come to the hospital, but he never did. Before too long I was discharged, with a doctor's appointment and a phone number for a hearing aid specialist in my pocket, which I thought was hilarious. What did they think I was going to do, call her?

I thought that getting home would make it better, thought that I'd feel safer in my own house, that maybe I'd at last be able to sleep—but it was worse. Every time I closed my eyes, I'd wonder what I was missing. Who could have walked in, or left without me seeing? What was taking place right in front of me that I could no longer be a part of? How was I supposed to protect myself if the world was out there, and I was trapped in the black and silent space of my own head?

That's when I started dreaming about it. The first time, when I woke up I stood straight out of bed and made it halfway down the hall before getting dizzy and slumping to the ground outside Mike's doorway. No one heard me, and after a few minutes I got up and went back to bed, where I lay awake for the next six hours.

The second time I had the dream, I woke up crying, stumbled down the hall and to Mike's doorway, where I knocked without thinking about what I was doing, that it was three o'clock in the morning and people only wake other people up at that time of night when something's seriously wrong.

Anyway, he came to the door, face tense and wide awake and, to my surprise, scared. He'd said something to me that at the time I didn't understand, and when he saw my tears he yelled for our parents and shut the door in my face.

"And," I say, brought suddenly back into the present by the knowledge that it's been a long time since I said anything out loud, "Mike has been shutting me out ever since." I look down at my fingers, where I've ripped one of the strawberry tops into shreds.

Cam doesn't say anything at all, chin resting in his hands, staring out the front window as people walk by, some glancing in at us, most looking straight ahead.

"Wow," he says again, and then, softly, "I thought when we first met that I had a pretty good idea of what it must be like. Growing up with Elyse…I don't know." He shrugs. "Deafness was just a part of my life. I thought I understood how it worked."

I wait for him to finish his thought, my gaze trained on his lips.

"But this." He shakes his head. "It's different. I thought it was mostly the same thing, but it's not."

"Yeah," I say, and feel the word catch on a lump in my throat that I hadn't even known existed. "It's different."

Cam sighs, still looking out the front window, and as I watch him, I feel a thousand questions roll inside of me. Why me? I am desperate for the answers no one at the hospital could give me. Why Mike? Why something permanent, instead of just a broken leg?

"You believe in God," I say to him, before I can stop myself.

He looks away from the window and straight into my eyes. I expect to see uncertainty or confusion, and when I'm met with strength instead, a firm gaze and a set jaw, the clash rings deep in my chest. "Yeah," Cam says, and his eyes are still searching mine. "I do."

"So," I say, struggling to find the words. "I just don't get it. I don't understand."

Cam tugs at the strap of his watch, eyebrows narrowed in concentration, but before he can speak, my mouth jumps ahead of us both.

"Does God hate me?"

Cam doesn't look startled, but I feel like someone's sucked the insides right out of my body. Almost without thinking about it, I reach for my pulse, dig two fingers into the base of my wrist until I can feel my heartbeat. I don't know what I'm expecting—maybe for God to strike me dead on the spot?—but my heart goes on beating, and my lungs keep breathing, and after a few seconds I feel okay again.

It's a big question, a heavy one, and now that it rests between us, I can feel the light spot between my shoulder blades where it used to sit. I've been carrying the weight of that one lonely question, and until now I haven't even known it.

"No," Cam says, very slowly. "He doesn't hate you, Skylar."

"What did I do?" I say and then choke. My throat closes up in defiance, locking my words deep inside my chest, and my nose feels like it's packed with cement. "Cam," I try again, clearing my throat. "What did I do wrong to deserve this?"

His eyes are very wide, and suspiciously shiny. I feel a tear drip off my chin and realize, suddenly, that I'm crying.

"Hang on," I say, and my words feel muffled and clumsy in my mouth, my lips trembling and quivery. I reach for the tissue in my pocket, but Cam hands me a whole box full of them, his fingers warm when they brush mine. For a few minutes, he doesn't say anything.

"I don't have all of the answers," he continues eventually, leaning forward so his hands are on the counter in between us, fingers tapping restlessly, relentlessly. "It wouldn't be fair to pretend that I do."

"Okay." I wipe my eyes so I can see his face clearly.

The weight begins to leech back onto me. I can feel the moment it presses against my ribcage, because my lungs won't inflate all the way, and I can't draw a full breath.

"But," he continues, and I think that I have never seen a more hopeful word in my life. "You're looking at it the wrong way."

"I am?" I wish I could pretend that these words sounded strong and confident, even though I'm pretty sure they came out in a squeak.

"God is not punishing you." Cam looks me dead in the face, his hands still, and for a moment I feel like I'm falling. "That's not how He does things."

"It's not?"

"If you did something awful," Cam says, and he's still looking at me with that unsettlingly earnest expression, "like, really bad, would your dad throw you into a car accident to punish you?"

I recoil from the thought. "How could you even say that?"

"Because he loves you, right?" Cam taps the counter for emphasis. "Your dad would never look at you and say, 'Oh, well, Skylar screwed up, I guess I'm done with her.' And God doesn't do that, either."

"Are you going to tell me that God loves me?" Suddenly that place where I carried the weight of my question feels bare and vulnerable and naked.

"Yes, I am," Cam says with more ferocity than I've ever seen in him. "God loves you, Skylar. I don't care if it's cliché to say so."

"And yet…" I have to look away from him when I say this. "I still have hearing loss. I can't hear. And you said that God loves me like my dad does, but my dad would never have let this happen to me if he had the choice. And maybe God loves me, but if His love doesn't keep me safe, then what's the point?"

"God's love can keep you safe." Now both of his hands are

moving across the counter, desperate for me to understand. "But only if you adjust your definition of danger."

I stare at him.

"It's not like a seat belt," he says, "God's love isn't a preventative measure. It's like there are more important things than physical safety." He doesn't look at me when he says it, like he knows he's treading dangerous ground. "So the really important stuff—your soul, what happens after you die—that's all safe. But nothing else is really guaranteed.

"This whole God-thing," he goes on, "it's not easy. It's not safe the way you want it to be safe. It's not comfortable. In the blink of an eye, I could give you a thousand logical reasons not to be a Christian."

I snort.

"I could!" He is so serious about this, meeting my gaze again, but now I'm the one who doesn't know where to look. "But your life wouldn't be worth it. It wouldn't be worth anything. Life without God is just…" He raises his hands, and then lets them fall again. "What's the point? God's love is wild and untameable and crazy. Sometimes it hurts. It's like riding a wild horse—dangerous and beautiful and unlike anything else, but you don't expect it to be safe. You expect to get bounced around and thrown off, and you expect to maybe break a leg, but you do it anyway, because how could you stand there, looking at something so amazing, and say no?"

He rubs at a patch of dirt on the toe of his shoe. "I don't know why the accident happened to you, Skylar. I don't know why bad things happen to good people. All I can say is that I know God isn't punishing you, and He isn't safe, not like a helmet or seat belt. His love for you isn't easy or comfortable, but it is strong. His love for you is so strong."

I'm reeling, my heart pounding like a shockwave through my body, mouth open and gaping, searching for words to reply to him.

They don't come. I don't know what to say to this idea of dangerous safety, and I don't know what to do with Cam's version of God's love.

"I just don't know, Cam," I say, and I have a sneaking suspicion that the words might have come out as a whimper. "I don't know what to do with this."

He opens his mouth to reply, elbows resting on his knees as he leans toward me, and then, out of the corner of my eye, I see the front doors swing open. Cam glances up and away from me, and the moment shatters, our connection broken. Someone comes running down the center aisle, hair obscuring their face, a smartphone clutched in their right hand.

"What—" I say to Cam, but he's already vaulted off the counter to meet the figure halfway, brushing the hair out of her eyes in one frantic gesture to reveal the panicked face of Anastasia.

Chapter
ELEVEN

"WHAT'S WRONG?"

My words dissolve into thin air as Ana sobs, Cam holding her by the shoulders in a vain attempt to get her to focus. Her words are choppy and broken, obscured by hiccups and sobs and shaking lips, but I manage to catch a few words.

" … … called me this morning, but I didn't … … so then now … … starts ringing … … at the grocery store and it's her … … come and visit me! Here!"

Cam says something to her, his head bent low so he can speak straight into her ear, but whatever he says only makes it worse. She shakes her head and pushes him away, eyes wide, but her lips have stopped trembling. Now they're white and stiff.

"What happened?" I say, sliding down from the counter to stand beside Cam, and Anastasia turns to me.

"My sister," she says clearly, although with significant effort. "She called me this morning and left a message, and then while I was at the grocery store she called again, and said…"

"She wants to visit?" I say. I'm putting together the pieces of Anastasia's earlier sentence, and thinking of Cam's call to Sophia a few weeks ago.

Ana puts one hand to her mouth, swallowing back another sob.

"I'm confused," I say, glancing at Cam, who looks just as lost as I do. Poor guy, he's had two of us in tears within the span of forty-five minutes. "Isn't that a good thing? Don't you miss her?"

Anastasia reaches for my extra tissues on the counter and pulls out a fistful. "I think I'd better go home," she says.

The words look forced, and I touch my throat almost without thinking about it, as though I can feel her pain. Cam reaches for my arm, and I look up at him in time to catch his next few words.

"… … take you home," he says. "Skylar, can you lock up? We'll just close early for today."

"Sure."

He puts an arm around Anastasia, guiding her back toward the door. Standing by the counter, I watch them go, and when they reach the door he turns back.

I'll text you, he mouths over Ana's head. *When I figure out what's going on.*

Thanks. I offer a half-hearted wave as the doors slide shut behind them.

The building feels lonely without Ana and Cam, and I close up as quickly as I can, pulling the blinds down without thinking about how much noise they make as they clatter shut. In less than ten minutes, I'm setting the alarm code and slipping my key into the lock for the automatic doors, the heat making the back of my neck sticky with sweat.

A piece of gravel slaps against the back of my leg, and I spin, my key flying from my fingertips, to find a car pulled over by the side of the road—Aunt Kay's car, and Mike's driving.

"Hey," I say, shielding my eyes against the afternoon sunlight. "What do you want?"

"Need a ride?" asks my brother, pointing to the spot on the sidewalk where my key now lies. "Are you done early today?"

"Kind of," I say, snagging the key and then walking around the front of the car to slide into the passenger side. "What are you doing here?"

"I'm on my way home," he says, one hand on the wheel. "Remember, Mom and Dad are going to that book promotion thing tonight? I'm supposed to watch the twins while you're at work, but I saw you locking up early."

"Oh." I buckle my seat belt as the car pulls away from the curb. My nose feels swollen, but as I probe it gingerly with my fingers, at least it doesn't start running again. "Right. I forgot about that. Where is it?"

He shrugs, speeding through the yellow light at the intersection, making this the first time I haven't been stuck at a red for almost five minutes. "Somewhere not too far from home, I think. A couple of hours away."

"Huh."

I wonder why the idea of spending almost twenty-four hours without our parents as a barrier between us frightens me so much. This is ridiculous.

The car bounces as it rolls over the curb and up Aunt Kay's driveway, and when Mike yanks the gear into park, I pop open my door. Before I can step out of the car, he grabs my arm.

"Uh, wait," he says, forehead wrinkled. "Look, Skylar, is it okay with you if I take off for a bit?"

"Now?" I say, trying to make light of the situation even as my heart does a belly flop inside my chest. "We just got here."

Mike fiddles with the car keys, not meeting my eyes. "But now you're here, so I can go, right?"

I feel off-balance, caught off guard and not sure how to proceed. The wheels haven't stopped rolling for even two minutes, and already Mike is a thousand miles away.

"Where are you going?" *Not Eric's again, please.*

He doesn't answer right away, staring down at the steering wheel.

"Mike!"

"Just…" he says, after I give him my best bossy-sister look. "You know, out. With some of the guys."

"Oh." I feel a little bit lonely at the thought. "So I guess I'll just stay with Aiden and Sara then?"

"If you don't mind," he says, after a pause just a few seconds too long.

"Whatever." I'm a little irritated but do my best to swallow it back. "Maybe I'll make brownies or something. Since they're probably too sick to hang out with."

Mike glances up at the house. "Mom said they were both asleep when she and Dad left."

"How long did you leave them here alone?" I don't mean to sound accusatory, but judging by the glare I get in return, I might not have judged my tone very well.

"Only like five minutes," he says, not quite looking into my eyes. "Come on, give me some credit. Mom and Dad waited until I said I was on my way before they left."

"Sorry," I say, and I really am. "So will I see you later? Are you coming home in time for dinner?"

He shrugs. "Maybe. Maybe not. I'm just going to Eric's."

I probably shouldn't ask, but I do. "Are you going to drink?"

"Of course not," he growls, lips tight. "I'm driving, Skylar, what kind of idiot do you think I am?"

"Sorry," I say again, but Mike shifts the car into reverse without looking at me.

"See you later." He turns his head away from me, a clear indication that our conversation is over.

I mutter several choice words under my breath and watch the car as it glides down the driveway, but I'm not really angry. Something in my chest feels all rough and torn, but there's no point in staying outside, so after Mike drives to the end of the street, I open the front door.

The house is silent and still, and after I drop my purse onto the kitchen table, tugging off my hearing aids, which are uncomfortably hot behind my ears, I'm not sure what to do next. The quiet gnaws at my skin, and I pick away at a scab on my elbow, considering, before I decide to go ahead and make brownies.

It takes me almost ten minutes just to find a mixing bowl. Apparently, Aunt Kay keeps them under the sink, where normal people toss their recycling. And then another five to find dishwashing soap to clean it—in the fridge, for no apparent reason. Thankfully, I find the ingredients in relatively normal places, and the recipe is one I know by heart.

I finish mixing the batter together and slide the pan into the oven, not bothering to double check the dials to make sure I've got the heat set right. After I've done that, I clean the kitchen, just killing time and trying not to think about what Mike might be doing. It's just Aiden and Sara and me, at least for this afternoon.

Tom winds himself between my ankles in reproach, and I bend down to scratch him between his ears. "And a cat," I say reassuringly. "Just me, two sickies, and a cat."

And for a while, as the afternoon shadows grow longer on the wall, that's really all it is. At least until the fire trucks show up.

I don't even know they've driven by, much less knocked at the front door or even entered the house until Tom, who has refused to sit still but keeps pacing between the kitchen and the sofa, sprints past me and up the stairs, the fur on his tail stuck straight up on end. Startled, I place a finger in my book and look up to see a tall figure enveloped in the baggy uniform of a firefighter, helmet pulled low over his eyes and an actual real live axe clutched in his hands.

"What?" I gasp this out convulsively and leap to my feet, dropping my book on the floor.

We stare at each other for a minute, and I wonder if he's an axe murderer who has escaped from jail and intends to butcher me and then abandon his fireman's regalia to cast the blame onto someone else.

At this point he flips the visor up on his helmet and I realize, with a guilty pang, that (a) those are not the eyes of an axe murderer, and (b) he's been speaking to me the whole time because I haven't bothered to (c) tell him that I can't hear and that my hearing aids are, yet again, not in my ears when I really, REALLY need them to be.

"I'm deaf," I say, just to get it out of the way. "What's going on?"

It occurs to me as the words leave my mouth that maybe I should feel a little bit more concerned than I currently do. But the fact that there's a firefighter standing in the living room is just too crazy, too much like a dream, and try as I might, I can't muster up any feelings of panic.

Another firefighter emerges from the kitchen. This one is shorter, and as the first man turns to give an order—or perhaps to receive one—I can see that the second figure coming out of the kitchen is a woman. She pulls off her helmet, wipes her forehead with the back of her gloved hand, and says something about an oven.

"The oven!" I say, and by the way they both jerk around I know I've probably yelled it. "My brownies!"

Suddenly my comfortable inability to feel fear is gone, and spikes of panic crawl up my belly, tickling the bottom of my heart until it pounds.

"They're not brown anymore," the female firefighter says with a frown, and then rattles off a full sentence that I don't catch except for the word "wiring." "Were you *trying* to burn the house down?"

"No." I realize too late that it was probably a rhetorical question. "I mean, why are you here?"

The man says something to me, pointing at my hair—or possibly the wall behind me—but since he hasn't taken off his helmet, I can't tell what he's saying.

"Sorry," I say and shift my weight from foot to foot. "Um, if I don't have my hearing aids in, then I don't know what you're saying to me."

Of course, it doesn't occur to me to simply go to the kitchen and get them.

He tugs his collar down, away from his reddened face, and enunciates very clearly. "Your fire alarms … … Station … … fifteen minutes."

Although I don't understand every single word, I catch enough to piece together his sentence.

"They've been going off at the station? For *fifteen* minutes?"

I think of the sick twins, deep in their flu-induced sleep sixteen long stairs away from the front door, and my stomach goes cold.

He says something else, but now it's starting to sink in, and as a third and then a fourth firefighter come stomping in the front door, I forget to focus on paying attention and just stare. One of them goes clomping heavily up the stairs, and I leap forward.

"My siblings are up there—he'll scare them!"

The first firefighter reaches out an arm as hard as rock and holds me back, but it's the woman whose words catch my eye. Though spoken heedlessly and without malice, they cut me all the same.

"… … deaf girl to watch the kids? … … could have burned down … … never would have noticed."

I open my mouth to reply, and then for once in my life think better of it and say nothing at all, even though I have a thousand retorts—being hard of hearing is not the same as being deaf, I still have eyes, and if it wasn't for this cold, I could still smell, too, which would have completely eliminated this problem before it started. The issue is not my ears so much as it is that *I wasn't paying attention*—but none of this is reassuring at all. In fact, it's pretty much the opposite. Instead of speaking aloud, I step back so I can see the face of the firefighter who seems to be in charge.

"My name is Chief ... ..." he says, but as always, the name is lost to me, floating away in a sea of silent letters and lazy pronunciations.

Why are people always so careless when they speak their own name? It's the most important word, the one I am so dying to capture, and yet it is the first to fall by the wayside, abandoned by those who don't think twice about the hazards and casualties of lip-reading.

"Is there someone we can call for you?"

"Why?" I say, frantically trying to think of someone.

My parents are too far away, and I don't want Mike to know. Not yet, anyway. I don't want to bother Anastasia, and even though Cam would understand, I don't want to tell him, either. I'd rather hold the shame of it all inside and tell them about it sometime in the distant future, when the pain is but a pang in my memory and I can laugh about that time a fire truck showed up at the front door and all the neighbors came around to look.

I glance out the window and count not one but three fire trucks. I didn't even know Golden Sound had a fire station to begin with. An entire crowd of neighbors stare curiously up at Aunt Kay's big old house, still standing, and I want to give up on everything.

"Well," the chief says as another firefighter pushes past me to check the rest of the living room, "once my team is done giving the house a go-through, we'll be returning to the station, and you look a little too shaken up to be left alone."

"I'm okay," I say, but I know it comes out thick and numb, which is exactly how I feel.

The firefighter who went to check the upper floors comes jogging back downstairs and flashes the chief an "okay" sign.

"Are the twins all right?"

"Still sleeping," the chief says, and I breathe a sigh of relief, feeling unusually thankful for congested throats, blocked ears, and the heavy sleep that accompanies a light fever.

"Miss," the chief says, waving an awkward hand in front of my face. "Are you going to be all right?"

I try my best to look like a mature and responsible adult. "I feel fine, Officer."

Do you call firefighters "officer"? By the way the corners of his lips are twitching, I guess not.

"… … feel better if I knew that … … call someone for you."

I glance outside again at the crowd of neighbors, which seems to be growing rather than shrinking, and imagine calling Mike. Him marching back in here to a crowd of people and four fire-fighters in the living room along with his younger sister, who can't seem to do anything right.

Nope, not looking to my older brother for help with this one.

After flipping through my options—this doesn't take long since most of the people I know are either (a) currently on the other side of the province, (b) having some sort of crisis and crying at home in their living room, or (c) not people I want to bring into this particularly messy part of my life, ever—I decide what to do. Sighing to myself, I cave and scrawl down Cam's number, careful to give them his home phone rather than his cell. If they actually do call him, by the time he gets the message things will be under control here.

I hope.

It only takes ten minutes for the firefighters to pour out of the house, emerging from what seems like a thousand corners. Even after they're all gone, I jump every time I walk into a new room, because suddenly all the shadows are shaped like firemen. How-ever, it takes far longer for the crowd congregated on Aunt Kay's front lawn to decide that the neighborhood is not, in fact, in dan-ger, and moreover, no one from inside the house is going to come out and offer details to satisfy their raging curiosity. I'd say it's because I won't give them the pleasure, but really, I'm just not up for any more embarrassment today.

I pull the front curtains shut and lock both the front and back door, feeling paranoid, before finding my hearing aids and slipping them carefully into place. Then I allow myself to slide to the floor where I lie on my back, staring up at the ceiling.

"Awesome," I say softly to myself, and when Tom slinks over to me and curls up on my stomach, I rub his head absently. Yet another strike against Cam's wonderful idea of God. I feel pretty bitter about it, but also sort of ashamed. I mean, I did burn the brownies all by myself. But God could have stopped it, and He didn't. Another reason we're not friends.

Sunset light pours in from the back doors that lead to the deck, and I watch the shadows dance, straight slat-lines where the sun filters through Aunt Kay's window blinds. With nothing else to distract me—not even the scent of burned brownies, which I can't force my congested nose to smell, no matter how hard I try—I imagine what could have happened if there had been a fire. Me lost in my book until either the smoke or the flames roused me, then running up the stairs and realizing that I can only carry one twin at a time. Which twin? In my daydream, I try to take both of them at once and trip halfway down the stairs, the three of us wedged against the bannister, and both of them too tired to help.

Just as I'm picturing myself gagging on the sharp taste of fire, woozy from smoke inhalation, my eyes sliding shut for the last time, Cam appears in the kitchen doorway.

Chapter
TWELVE

I SIT UP ABRUPTLY, KNOCKING TOM OFF MY STOMACH AND GIVING MYSELF A pressure headache from moving too quickly. "How did you get here so fast? How did you get in?"

"Kay gave my mom a key." Cam raises his hands and then adds, "And you didn't hear me when I knocked, so I let myself in."

"Well," I reply, and discover with some surprise that I'm angry. "You could have come to the window. Or something."

Cam looks startled.

"Did you feel like you needed to come over here and fix everything because you think I can't handle this on my own?" I plant my hands on my hips, trying to keep my voice low. "Because I can! Everything's fine, no one got hurt, and the twins didn't even wake up." I swallow back the angry lump that has sprung up in my throat. "I can do this, Cam."

"I never said you couldn't," he says slowly, palms out, eyes wide, that deer-in-the-headlights look. I seem to cause that look a lot. "And no one called me, Skylar. I came because I wanted to."

"Because you wanted to?"

"Yeah." He glances down at Tom, who is licking one paw as though all is right with the world. Cam's eyes are still too wide.

"Like, 'Hey, friend, I told you I'd tell you what was up with Anastasia, and I was in town anyway, so here I am.' Like that."

After a long pause, he speaks again, shoving his keys into his pocket. "Do you want me to go?"

"No." I sag against the counter. "You might as well stay, since you're here."

Cam frowns.

"I mean," I say, feeling bad, "please stay. That came out wrong. And the firemen didn't call you?"

"What firemen?" he asks, and I notice him casting surreptitious glances around the kitchen. "Is that what smells?"

I bury my face in my hands, mostly to be dramatic, but also because I can feel my face flaming. "I made brownies." Of course, then I have to take my hands away from my face in order to see his response and feel admittedly silly doing it.

"Brownies, huh?" he says, after a long pause, and when at last he sees the blackened remains of the baking dish on the stove, his eyebrows leap up in surprise. "Yum."

I giggle before I can help myself. "Delicious. Want one?" Crossing the kitchen floor, I scratch at the rock-hard surface of the dessert with my thumbnail, but all that comes off is charcoal. "Yuck." I sigh, and then in a moment of impulse, pull the dish towel free from its hook over the oven and throw it on top of the remains. Now no one has to see it anymore.

"Mike," I announce, trying to sound flippant and not totally succeeding, "is going to kill me. Like, actual murder. Homicide. Manslaughter. Possibly all three at once."

"I'll speak at your funeral," Cam says, deadpan, and I laugh again. "Are you alone?"

"Yeah," I say, and my stomach drops as I remember. "Mike went to Eric's."

Cam is studying his hands intently when I look over, fingers reaching again for the buckle of his watch.

"What is it?"

"Nothing," he says too quickly, curling the fingers of his right hand into a fist before they can touch the leather strap.

"Cam?" I take a step closer so he has to look at me. "Did you see him on your way here?"

He shrugs. "There were a bunch of guys hanging out in the park, but it might not have been him."

The slight pause before he says "hanging out" means that's probably not all they were doing.

Mike told me he wouldn't drink today. Something in my face must give away the fury inside, because Cam puts a steadying hand on my arm.

"Skylar," he says, and I notice the shape of my name on his lips twice in five minutes. It looks nice there. "Maybe he just…"

"No, Cam," I say, and am distracted by wondering what his name looks like on my mouth. "I'm done with his excuses and second chances and stuff. We never used to be the kind of family who lied to each other. Mike and I don't do that to each other."

He doesn't say anything, but there's a slight frown on his face, and I wonder if he's thinking about Eric.

"How's Ana?" I say, and then follow Cam into the living room, where he flops down onto the couch.

"She's…" He shrugs, fiddles with his watch and shakes his head, a crooked smile on his face. I lie down on the floor and put my feet on the couch beside him. "I don't know. She's stressed."

"I don't get it," I say, scratching the tip of my nose. "I thought it would be a good thing if Sophia came back. I thought she'd like it."

Cam shrugs, making sure to look down at me so I can read his lips. "So did I. Serves us right for trying to predict Ana, I guess."

"Do you think we shouldn't have done it?" I stare at the ceiling, thinking. I only wanted to help, wanted to know that I'm still capable of fixing something, since my own life has spun so wildly out of control. "I feel like we made everything worse."

"I don't know," Cam says. "I'm not sure what we started."

I focus on a spot just above his left shoulder, where I'll be able to see his lips if he starts to speak again, but just far enough away that I'm not actually staring at his face. Because that would be weird.

"She's like…" I try to come up with a comparison. "She reminds me of my aunt." From what I know of her, anyway.

"Hah," he says, and pinches the bottom of my foot. "Yes, but more so."

"When is Sophia coming?"

I picture Anastasia's face, the wide eyes, tears and oily mascara streaming down her cheeks. The guilt scrapes raw against my ribcage.

"Next week." Cam's words break me out of the memory. "You want to do something?"

"The twins are upstairs."

"I want food," he says, suddenly. "Can I raid the fridge?"

"Yeah, but don't use the oven." I don't mean it as a joke, but he laughs anyway, pushing my feet out of the way so he can stand up.

"I'm serious," I call as he lopes into the kitchen, but I can't tell if he's heard me.

I lie there, looking thoughtfully at my bare feet against the faded flower print on the couch, for approximately five seconds before Cam materializes by my side, pointing up the stairs.

"One of the twins is calling for you."

I mean to groan quietly as I roll onto all fours and clamber ungracefully into a standing position, but by the barely concealed laughter on Cam's face my guess is that it came out a little louder than planned.

"Are you good?" he asks, lips twitching, and I think grumpily that as soon as I turn my back he'll start to laugh, and I'll never know the difference.

"Just great," I snap, not unkindly, and take the stairs two at a time. Being with Cam makes this day a little less terrible, pushes the firemen incident into the back of my mind a little bit, like it's already fading away into yesterday.

The light is on in the twins' room, and when I ease the door open, I see two identically disgruntled faces staring up at me from the bottom bunk.

"I'm bored," cries Sara, at the same time Aiden says, "Can we come downstairs and watch TV?"

"You can't be that bored," I say, imagining myself as a patient and all-knowing mother. "You've been asleep for hours."

"Have not!" Sara pouts, folding her arms across her chest. "And it's too hot up here."

Aiden just wipes his nose on his sleeve and looks pathetically up at me.

"You have too been asleep that long," I retort, before remembering that I'm trying to be motherly. "But," I add, as a compromise, "it is really hot up here. You guys can come downstairs now if you want."

"Where's Mike?" Aiden asks this right as I'm turning around, and I make a snap decision to pretend I didn't hear his question, because I don't feel like answering it.

I pause at the doorway, my back still to the twins, and realize with something almost like pleasure that they could be saying anything to me right now, and I have the power to choose simply not to see their questions.

That is, until someone grabs my arm from behind and yanks me around, forcing me to look at them again.

"I'm hungry!"

I decide to become a mother later, and for now throw my patience out the window. "Just because you're sick doesn't mean you have to act like a…" I almost say "brat," but then figure that wouldn't be helpful. "Like a really sick person!"

The twins stare at me.

"Just go downstairs," I say, defeated. "Cam's here, too."

"Cam!" shrieks Sara, and sprints for the stairs.

Aiden takes my hand like he used to when he was younger and looks up at me with big, brown eyes.

"Skylar," he says, and I imagine the sound of the lisp he'd had as a baby and feel my heart melt. "What's that smell?"

All melting ceases instantly, and I resist the urge to drop his sweaty little hand from my grip.

"I burned the brownies."

He says something in reply, but I honestly don't catch it this time, since he's taken a step down the stairs, his body turned away from me. By the time we reach the bottom step—Aiden has always been a contemplatively slow person but following him down a long flight of stairs is nothing short of agony—Cam is speaking to someone in the entryway, and his shoulders are stiff.

"Hey, man." He licks his lips. Cam never licks his lips, ever.

"What?" I push past Aiden and skip the bottom step, alarmed. "Who is it?"

"Hey, Skylar," my brother says, leaning one shoulder casually against the doorframe, as though everything is fine. "How's it going, Cam?"

I don't bother turning around to see Cam's reply.

"Mike!" Anger flares up in my chest at the sight of him, at the beer can on the floor by his feet, and he flinches, but I don't care. I don't care how loud I'm talking, because my brother *has car keys* in his hand! "You lied to me!"

"What are you talking about?" His words are carefully chosen. My heart does a sickening double bump inside my chest.

Before I can reply, Cam puts a hand on my shoulder.

"What?" I rear back to look him in the face.

"Maybe," he says, and I see worry in his face, "I should go."

"No," I make the word as hard as I can. "I want you here for this."

"… … go, Skylar, if he doesn't want to be here."

I turn in time to get the gist of Mike's sentence, and although he still doesn't look guilty, I see anger in the furrows on his face, tension building in his muscled arms, clenched fists, tight jaw. But this time, I'm angry too.

"Skylar," Cam says, again putting a hand on my arm.

"What?" Now I'm well and truly angry, and it swells to include not only Mike, but everyone in the room. "And stop tapping me all the time. I can see that you're standing right next to me."

"Sorry." He puts his hand in the pocket of his jeans as though it's burned him, and I notice Aiden watching him, his little eyebrows pulled low above his eyes.

"Aiden. Sara." My voice feels thick in my throat, fuzzy in my mouth, and about as gentle as a brick when the words fall from my lips. "Go to the kitchen."

"Why?" asks Sara, never taking her eyes from the TV.

Cam starts to say something to her, but I talk over him as though I haven't noticed. "Because I'm about to yell really loudly at Mike"—actually, I think I've been yelling this whole time—"and I might say a bad word and I don't want you to hear it if I do."

Cam snaps his mouth shut with a motion so pronounced I swear I hear his teeth click together. The twins are staring at me, eyes wide and mouths open.

"What kind of word?" asks Aiden finally, and whatever resolve I have shreds into very tiny particles.

"Just go. Please." My fingernails bite into the palms of my hands, and my heartbeat thumps through my veins.

"… … come with you," Cam says, deftly flicking the TV off on his way over to the couch, where he picks up the blankets and nudges the twins onto their feet, not meeting my gaze as he does so.

"Cam." I start to call him back, but Mike grabs my arm. His hand is cold, and I jerk back from the grasp of his clammy fingers.

Let him go, he mouths, the words softer than if he'd spoken them aloud.

I fold my arms but do as he asks, watching in silence as Cam ushers the twins into the other room, turning to pull the door closed behind them.

"Well, Skylar?" says Mike when I finally do turn around, the muscles in his jaw tense, a faint pulse throbbing at the base of his neck.

"Well what?" I try to pretend that the stench of beer doesn't sting my eyes, and then barrel right on through without waiting for an answer. "You were drinking."

"Does it matter?" He says this almost desperately, the words shooting from his lips as though he's been trying to hold them back for a long time. His eyes are red-rimmed and bloodshot. "Is it really important, Skylar? I needed to get out for a bit. I needed to get away."

"Away from what?" My voice twists upward into a near-scream at the end of the sentence. "This *is* away, Mike. This is as away as we're ever going to get. I don't care if you drink, I really don't." I slide my hands into my pockets then cross my arms, trying not to look as awkward as I feel. *I want Dad.* "But you drove?"

"Not just away from home," he says, brushing past my comment about his driving, and suddenly I'm not sure I want to see the rest of his sentence. His face is set, eyes not meeting my own, and I know that whatever he says next is spoken because I have forced him into it. I have been the annoying younger sister for too long, and Mike is too mad to care if the truth he speaks is not one I want to hear.

If I could hear, of course. Which I can't.

"What, then?" I ask, desperately hoping that the answer he will give is not the one I think is coming.

"Away from the twins," he begins, and I feel a sickening loop in my stomach. "Away from this house, Golden Sound, away from everything that's different. And you." He finally looks at me, and I am shocked.

Shocked, because Mike isn't angry, after all. There is something dark and powerful and hollow inside his eyes, something that I have never seen before and cannot name, but it is not anger, and I am afraid. Anger is something that I understand, something I can deal with, and this…is not. I don't know what this is.

"I can't stop seeing the accident," he says, looking right at me, and his words don't look slurred, but there is something wild in his eyes. The buzz from the alcohol has given him a false courage. Mike would never say this to me otherwise. "I see it in your face, hear it in your voice. I can still see the blood in your hair." He touches my forehead gently with his pointer finger, calloused from years of playing guitar.

"Mike, stop." I push his hand away, breaking our eye contact, trying to end this terrible moment, heavy with things I don't understand and can't hope to explain.

"You're all fine," he says casually, and the moment is shattered.

"What?" I say. I'm trying to hide the fact that in the breaking of this terrible moment, Mike has broken me too. He changes the subject as though he has not torn my soul into a thousand pieces and left me trying to pick myself up. He still thinks about the blood in my hair?

"You. The twins. I was gone for, like, four hours and no one died, the cat didn't run away, you didn't burn the house to the ground…"

I have been focused intently on reading his lips so I don't have to look into his eyes, and as he trails off, I wish I hadn't been paying quite so much attention.

"Skylar," he says, and I can see his nose twitch, know that he is inhaling and no doubt also seeing the hot blush creeping up my neck. "What's that smell?"

"I burned the brownies," I say, and my voice feels very small.

Mike turns without speaking and stalks into the kitchen, ignoring Cam and the twins seated around the table. He marches straight to the stove, pulls aside the dish towel that I had draped over the mess that was supposed to be dessert, and turns to me, eyebrows raised.

"Maybe we should buy some ice cream," I say, attempting levity, especially with Cam here, but Mike ignores it, striding over to the window, which I only now notice is covered with a thick layer of soot.

"Skylar?"

"I guess there was more smoke than I thought."

He turns to face me, the dish towel still clutched in one fist. "What happened?"

I'm flailing inwardly for mature and sensible words to use.

"I tried to make brownies," I say, starting at the beginning. "And there was eggshell in the batter, but other than that, I thought it was going well."

"I don't care if you made brownies," he says, and maybe his anger is familiar but that doesn't mean I have to like it. "What. Happened?"

"Oh," I reply feebly, "right."

There is an ominous pause, heavy and significant like the stillness just before a clap of thunder, and out of the corner of my eye I see Cam usher the twins into the living room, holding the TV remote like a dangling carrot. He's a saint for keeping them out of the way, but he still won't meet my gaze, a muscle twitching in the left side of his jaw.

"Skylar!" Mike yells my name, face flushed, and the sudden burst of noise raises feedback in my hearing aids. The muscles in his neck are tense and short as he snaps out my name in two staccato syllables. "What did you do?"

I flinch at the swear word he sandwiches in the middle of the question, mild though it may be. Mike's angrier than I've ever seen him, and under the heat of his glare, my own fury is waning. Suddenly, I don't want to have this conversation with him. I don't want to fight. I just want to go to bed and sleep.

"Don't yell at me, Mike," I say, each word measured and calm, cooling along with my anger.

"Then tell me what happened." He swipes one finger down the window, leaving a clear line across the smoke-hazy glass.

"I was in the living room," I say, trying to make the events of this afternoon sound logical and normal. "And I forgot to check on the brownies. I just forgot. So, I guess they started burning—"

"Like, how much burning?" Mike pulls open the oven, and both of us reel back in disgust as a thick, charred smell so strong you can almost see it in the air wafts into the kitchen and slaps us both in the face.

"I guess a lot more than I thought," I choke out as Mike slams the door shut again. "The firefighters said—"

Mike interrupts me again, which is actually a good thing because the only words I remember from the hooded figures in my living room was the woman saying, *They left a deaf girl to watch the kids?*

Yes, I think grimly, remembering. *Yes, they did.*

"There were firefighters here?"

"Yeah." Now that the worst is out, I blurt the rest in a few short sentences. "The alarms went off at the station, and the twins were still asleep even though they checked the whole house, and I gave them Cam's number."

Thankfully, Mike doesn't ask any questions, because those words won't stop ringing in my ears. I don't realize I'm staring at the floor until Mike shoves my arm.

"Look at me," he says, and for a moment I see the anger slip to one side. He's scared. Really, really scared. "Don't tell Mom and Dad about this. Any of it. I'll clean the kitchen, wash the windows, whatever. I can make it look like nothing ever happened. Just don't…" He shakes his head. "Do the twins know what happened?"

"No," I say, hoarse. "But Cam does."

"We don't have to tell them." Mike runs a shaking hand through his hair once, twice, and I watch it in fascination. I'm not even shaking—why is my brother? "They don't need to know."

"Why not?"

"Shut up, Skylar." His head snaps back, the anger fully in place, and for one blank moment, I actually think he's going to hit me. "Just shut up! Because I'm supposed to be taking care of all of you and I left for less than four freaking hours and you literally burned the house down. And if this whole thing isn't my fault already, that would be, and I just don't need anything else to be my fault. Okay?"

"I didn't literally burn the house down," I say numbly, because it's the only thing that makes sense right now.

"Shut up," he says again, turning away from me. I wonder if he is swearing where I can't see him, the foul words emptying from his mouth, cupped in the curve of his body as he bends over. "… … can't do anything right," he mumbles, and I don't know if he's talking to himself or to me.

"I didn't," I say again, which doesn't make any sense at all.

"… … leave me alone," he says, his head turned just enough that I can catch the end of his sentence.

"Mike, I—"

"Go away!"

"Fine then!" I yell hollowly at him, my throat aching with the silence of the words that I'm sure come out in a scream. "I will!"

Before he can stop me—or worse, before I realize that he won't—I twist on my heel and sprint out of the kitchen, through the front hall, and out the door without even bothering to put shoes on.

The concrete sidewalk is warm against the bottoms of my feet. Once I'm at the end of our street and sure that it's too late for anyone to come after me, I slow to a walk. I always thought that people who ran away in movies really wanted to be found, kept looking over their shoulder not because they were afraid of someone finding them, but because they really wished anyone would.

Today, though, I don't want anyone to come after me. I don't want to be reassured. I don't want to feel better. I don't even want Mike to apologize. I just want to forget this whole day, the entire summer, and when I'm alone, I almost can.

I don't look over my shoulder once, and I don't go back home for hours.

Chapter
THIRTEEN

"DO I STILL SMELL LIKE SMOKE?" I ASK CAM THIS ON WEDNESDAY MORNING, two days after the firefighter incident—also two days since I last spoke to my brother. "Mom and Dad didn't say anything about it when they got home, but I feel like the whole house just reeks."

Cam leans across the library counter, nose pressed into my shoulder experimentally, and I roll my eyes and shove his head away, glad that he's not still upset.

"Cut it out, dork. If you have to get that close to tell, then it doesn't matter, anyway."

He grins, tugging the key ring free from my fingertips. "When did your parents get home?"

It's early, just before nine, but Cam and I came in early to tidy the library and make sure the computers were up and running. We were closed yesterday because Ana was too "busy" to come in, but she appeared at my front door last night with a printed copy of the week's schedule in hand.

"I gave Cam one too," she'd said, and I was relieved to be able to understand her words. "I thought if you two didn't mind, you could open for me tomorrow morning. I'll try to make it in later, but…" She trailed off, rubbing her hands together, and I noticed that the paint on her nails was chipped, the nails themselves bitten almost to the quick.

"Don't worry about it," I'd told her, and then given her an impulsive hug, wondering at her pinched lips, the wrinkle between her eyebrows. "Are you…is everything okay?"

She hadn't answered.

"Um," I say now, in response to Cam's question. "They came back the morning after the whole thing."

By the time they got home, Mike was up and out of the house, and the twins and I were eating an early lunch in the living room, away from the still-faint smell of charred oven. Mom and Dad either didn't notice the smell or decided not to ask, and I didn't tell them. Mike didn't come home until after dinner, and we've been avoiding each other ever since.

I hang out with the twins downstairs, he barricades himself in his room or goes out for long walks alone, and when we pass each other in the hall, I turn my head the other way, or he does. Family dinner is a little harder to get through, but if I show up a few minutes late and he leaves as soon as he's eaten what's on his plate, the amount of time we spend together is minimal at best.

I watch Cam flick the locks on the front door and saunter up the center aisle to the counter, waiting for him to get close enough to see his response.

"What did they say about it?"

"Um," I repeat, drumming my fingers nervously on the counter and wishing that someone—anyone—would walk through the front doors and demand assistance. Or that a crack would open in the floor and swallow me whole. Or that I would drop down dead on the spot.

Unfortunately, none of those things happen.

"Skylar?"

"Well," I say. "They didn't say much of anything. I don't think they noticed."

Cam waits.

"We didn't, uh…" I scan a paperback from the wrong pile and the computer flashes angrily at me. I reset the scanner and set the book aside. "Mike and I decided not to tell them."

"Oh?"

For once in his life, I wish Cam would have a big reaction to something, instead of just shrugging and asking open-ended questions.

"Yeah," I say a bit grumpily. "And so far, you know, it seems to be working out for us."

"Oh," he says again, which means nothing at all. "How did Mike take it?"

"Oh, fine." I turn to smile at a woman as she approaches the front desk. When I've checked through her books, I turn back to our conversation. "Couldn't you tell by the way he looked when you left?"

I mean for this to be sarcastic, but Cam takes me seriously.

"I left right after you went for a walk, but we didn't really talk on the way out. He was cleaning the windows, I think."

"Right."

Cam studies me, and the way his fingers reach for his watch is the only way I can tell that the tension in this conversation makes him nervous. "So, Mike's fine?"

"I assume so," I say, trying to sound cheerful. "I haven't really talked to him in a while."

"Like, two days?" He asks this dubiously, and I feel a snap of irritation.

Okay, so it's only been two days, but it feels like a lot longer than that. "Whatever." I set down the scanner. To give myself a little breathing room, I stalk around the counter on the premise of straightening the summer reads display, which is currently at 90-degree angles with the front counter and does not need to be straightened in the slightest. "It feels like a while."

"I get that," he says when I finally look up.

"Cool," I mutter, because I feel like I have to say something. "And please don't give me any advice, Cam, because I'm probably not going to listen to it and it'll just make me mad."

He shrugs. "I was just going to say—"

"And I really don't feel like being mad," I say. I have my eyes squeezed tightly shut so I don't have to look at whatever pearls of wisdom he is about to offer me.

This also helps to hide the fact that I feel a hot rush of tears gathering behind my eyes, and the last thing I want to do is let them loose on a day that I've decided to wear mascara. Also, crying in front of Cam is something I've already done, and I'm not feeling eager to relive that particular experience.

"Okay?" I say out loud, and then open my eyes again.

"Yeah," he says. "Sorry." I can tell that he wants to say something else, but he holds it back, and I love him for it.

The rest of our morning is busy, as though everyone who couldn't come earlier on in the week decides to show up at our front doors at exactly 10:03 today. I go from person to person, smiling at each one, and always thinking *Please don't ask me where to find paperback romances that have titles starting with the letter Q. Or where we keep the children's books about potty training. Or anything else at all except how to check out books.* Thankfully, no one does, and by the time our lunch break rolls around, the library is still standing and almost everyone is gone.

"Should we call it?" I ask, the "gone to lunch" sign in my hand as one last patron lingers by the door.

"In a sec." Cam's words are soft, his response in a whisper. The only way I can tell he's spoken at all is the slight tension in his throat, muscles too tight to be mouthing the words.

Both of us watch with bated breath as the last patron takes one step toward the door…and then veers away to look at our window display.

We let out a collective sigh. "So close," I say, and then laugh at us, at how our lives seem to hinge around whether or not somebody's grandmother is going to take her next four steps outside of the library or deeper within.

At last she leaves, and I walk up to the front to place the "Gone to Lunch" sign on the door. When I return to the front desk, Cam is still standing at the computer, frowning into space. I could ask him what he's thinking about, but I have a funny feeling I already know. I've been considering the Anastasia problem a lot lately—when I'm not too busy worrying about my own—and I keep coming back to the idea that this is my fault.

"I think we should go and see her," I say, and he looks up at me, surprised.

"You do?"

"Maybe?" I phrase it as a question. The last time I tried to make a decision for the greater good, someone got hurt. I don't want to see Ana in pain again. "Do you think we should go?"

"Someone should," he says, almost to himself. "But Elyse isn't home and no one else knows the whole story."

"I don't think we know the whole story, either," I say. Without meaning to, I think of the picture on the computer, Ana's panicked sobbing, and the faraway look in her eye when she gave me the schedule.

"Maybe not." Cam taps his pointer fingers on the counter. "I'll go and see her after work."

I rub the toe of my shoe along the tile floor. "Do you want me to come?"

The relief on his face is so palpable that for a moment, I think I can taste it, sweet like the ocean; light at first, and then the sting of salt in an open wound. "Do you want to?"

No. "I think I should," I say instead. "It was my idea."

"Both of us were in on it," he says, fingers moving faster.

"Okay." This one word seals our fate like one of those old wax stamps. I look at him and I can see that we've made some sort of pact. There's no going back now.

I flip the sign in the window to "open" fifteen minutes early, and I can feel myself wishing the afternoon away, trying to rush forward so we can get this day over with. I shelve one cart of children's books in the time it takes Cam to do two from the adult section, and when I try to check out a blonde lady's books, I forget to read her lips as she speaks, and have to ask her to repeat herself. My head is not in Golden Sound Public Library. It's at Ana's house, trying to picture what she's doing and how we should respond.

What will I say? How do I tell her the truth, when the truth is that this is all my fault? Will she get angry? What does Ana look like when she's angry? This thought scares me more than the others, so I decide to stop thinking altogether—not very successfully.

"How are you feeling?" Cam asks me in passing, stepping to the side so I can come behind the counter as he walks out with an armload of books.

"Aghhh," I reply, not even bothering to fit syllables and letters into my frustration, but he only laughs.

"Me too." His thumb juts toward his chest, pinkie finger extended toward me. He doesn't often slip into sign language, but every so often his hands will leap into action, a faint twitch or movement when he speaks, and I know that's where it comes from.

At last, the day is over, and we close up the building. My pulse is rocketing through my veins, and almost without thinking about it, I put two fingers to my wrist. It feels like a hammer pounding against my skin, and after a moment, I pull my fingers away again.

"Ready?" Cam pulls the driver's door of the van open, and I walk around the hood to the passenger side. The heat from within strikes me in the face, and I pause outside, squinting, until my skin no longer burns, before sliding onto the front seat.

We ride in silence down Main Street and through the right

turn to Ana's house. Neither of us says anything until the car is parked in her driveway, and even then, it's several minutes before anyone speaks.

"I owe you one for today," Cam says at last, and both of us look at Anastasia's cheerful little house, unsure about what we'll find within. "Ready to go?"

"Nope," I say, but I unclick my seat belt and open the door of the van. "Let's do it."

We walk up to the front door together and stand shoulder to shoulder in front of it for a minute before I open the screen and rap—hard—on the wood door beneath.

Then we wait.

After a few minutes, Anastasia opens the door. For a moment, I don't recognize her. She's wearing pajama pants and a tank top, her hair hanging limply around a face still coated in this morning's makeup, eyeliner smeared and lipstick on her front teeth.

I exhale sharply, and Cam digs his elbow into my side.

"Hi, Ana!" I say, opting for a greeting instead of "oww." "We, uh…we came to chat."

"Look," she says, and the stillness, the lack of outward emotion, is way scarier than her Halloween-esque makeup. "You guys are so sweet to come, honestly, but I just need to be alone."

"I think that's exactly what you don't need," Cam says, but he doesn't step across the threshold, just looks at her for a moment. She doesn't say anything. "Ana? Can we come in?"

She dips her chin slowly, and then after a moment, steps back to let us in.

Cam follows her, making space for me in the small entryway. "Have you talked to your parents?"

"… … told them yet," Ana says, turning to face us again. "I don't know if I will tell them… Maybe I'll call them when she gets here. Until then, it's just me."

"And me," Cam says, closing the front door.

"And me." I slip my shoes off and fold my arms, trying to look committed and determined, but instantly feeling silly.

"We have a confession to make," Cam begins, after an almost imperceptible pause. "I guess we kind of owe you an apology."

"It was my idea," I say, and see her head turn toward me. "To call Sophia. It wasn't my business."

Ana's face looks stuck in one expression, her tongue caught between her teeth, a faint twitch in her right eyelid. My stomach churns.

"And I'm sorry. I just wanted to help, because you used to be so close and I thought that maybe if you started talking again, it would be okay. I have a brother…"

At this point I break off in confusion, no longer sure what point I'm trying to make.

"Sophia loves you, you know." Cam states this very gently, and I see the tiny shiver that runs through Ana's body as she starts to relent. Cam's one short sentence does what my whole explanation cannot, and her shoulders relax.

"And so do we," I add, and then realize that it's true.

"You don't even know," whispers Ana to herself, and maybe Cam doesn't hear it, but I can see the words on her lips.

"Don't know what?" I ask, and Ana shakes her head.

"A story from a long time ago, that's all."

There's a pause after she says this, and Cam and I glance at each other. *Please do something, please do something, please do something.* I'm praying that he'll develop mind-reading powers, but I'm pretty sure he's trying to communicate the same thing to me.

"Maybe we should sit down," he says finally, and steps forward—elbowed only slightly by me—into the living room where he sits in one corner of the couch. I wait for Anastasia to curl up on the easy chair opposite before settling myself against the armrest across from Cam.

"I don't want to talk about this," Ana says, and starts to cry.

Cam closes his eyes, and I pass her the box of tissues discarded on the floor. Her living room is small but has big windows that face both the street and the small garden out back. It has the look of a room that is normally tidy—the furniture is at right angles to the walls, the photographs are hung straight and there are still lines on the carpet where it has been freshly vacuumed. However, at the moment, the place is a disaster. There are blankets wadded up in the middle of the couch between Cam and me, used tissues scattered across the floor, and one lone high-heeled shoe without a mate sits on the coffee table beside a half-eaten plate of macaroni and cheese.

Ana blows her nose and rubs her forehead with trembling fingers. "I think you should go."

I glance at Cam, and he stands up, but doesn't walk away, like he can't figure out which direction he's supposed to go in.

"No, stay," Ana says, eyes still closed, and after a moment, Cam sits down again.

"This isn't a story you'll like," she says, but she's just warning us now, obviously already resigned to telling us the truth.

"That doesn't matter," Cam says, and I would think that he is very good at this if I couldn't see his left leg twitching anxiously across from me.

"Okay," Anastasia says, and one more tear rolls down her cheek. "Are you hungry? Maybe we should eat first."

"Ana," Cam says, and she shuts her eyes.

No more stalling, I see her say to herself, throat empty of sound, and then, "My sister moved away about five years ago."

"For school," adds Cam.

Anastasia shakes her head. "That's what everyone thought. That's what we wanted them to think."

Cam and I sit, silent.

"I went with her for the first year," Ana says, and then hesitates. "The first year…"

"What happened?" I expect these words to have come from Cam, but when they both turn to look at me, I realize that I am the one who has spoken them aloud.

"I went because…"

She clenches her fists, eyes squeezed shut. Cam and I exchange concerned glances.

With eyes still closed, she takes a deep breath. Calmly, so calmly that I almost don't recognize what she's saying, she finishes her sentence.

"I went because I was pregnant."

She's been building up the moment of truth for so long that when it comes, I'm more shocked by Cam's reaction to it than I am by the declaration itself.

He stands straight up, mouth open.

And then without saying anything, he sits down.

"Ana," he says, and it is not an accusation, and he is very confused. "You?"

I expect her to start to cry again, but she does not.

"Yes," she says simply, and does not clarify or expound as she normally would. "And no one suspected a thing. My parents didn't even know."

Cam says nothing, but when his fingers reach for the buckle of his watch, they're shaking.

"They still don't." And now the words start to pour out of her in earnest, as though the floodgates have opened, and she is helpless to stop them. I am torn away by the passion on her face, and although I miss a word here and there, muffled by a sob or a cough, her face is so expressive that I barely fit words to the feelings that are flowing from her, and yet feel no loss.

"You have to understand," she says, "that my sister and I have always loved each other. And I loved the baby, too, and I loved him. My boyfriend. And it's all a mess now, but you can't think that I didn't love all of them, because I did."

Cam says something to her at this point, but I'm too focused on Anastasia to catch what he says. She takes one final deep breath and at last, the whole story comes pouring forth.

"I was twenty," she says, "so only a little bit older than both of you. Old enough to have made better choices, but young enough to not know or care which was which."

Anastasia hesitates, licks her lips. "We'd been dating for four years, since my sixteenth birthday, and we thought we were in love. We always talked about getting married someday, but it was all like a dream to us then. We weren't ready to live in the reality, and when I got pregnant, we both panicked. I still…" She shakes her head. "I still can barely remember that day. I hadn't had my period in months."

Cam's leg twitches beside me on the couch, and when I look over at him, surprised, I see that the back of his neck is red. Anastasia continues, oblivious to his obvious but endearing discomfort.

"But I was young. I thought, 'These things happen!' You always think it's a missed period, never assume that something like pregnancy will happen to you until it does, and even then, you don't quite know how to believe it. The lines on a stick were just lines, and I remember putting one hand on my stomach and feeling nothing. I don't know what I was expecting, a heartbeat or a kick after just a month and a half, but I sat there in the bathroom for almost half an hour with the test kit in one hand and my other on my stomach. My skin was cold."

She falls silent for a moment.

"My sister," she continues, and then pauses. "You've never met her, Skylar. She's very…" Ana doesn't seems to know how to describe her. "We're opposites," she says finally. "So, if I didn't know what to do, I knew that Sophia would. She was living on her own at the time, way far away from me in the big city, but she was visiting for that weekend. I remember walking down the hall and thinking,

'Thank God, thank God, thank God,' over and over again, even though I don't believe in Him…" She breaks off. "Sorry, Cam."

He motions for her to continue, still fiddling with his watch. He looks stunned. I wonder what's going through his head right now. I wonder if he's praying. I wonder what God thinks of his prayers.

"And then I went into her room and just stood there in the doorway. I watched her read, sitting there on her bed and thinking that this was the last time I would speak to her without her knowing how badly I'd screwed up."

Now she starts to cry, just slightly, and my stomach twists. *She was perfectly happy before you went and tried to fix things.* As much as I try to ignore that thought, it won't leave.

"Sophia was four years older than me, and she looked after me while we were growing up. She always had everything under control, and I didn't want her to know that I'd done something she couldn't fix. Being pregnant in a small town… People wouldn't understand. I didn't want to see their faces as they figured it out, didn't want to have to live the rest of my life as the single mom or any other kind of label." She pauses to blow her nose. "I'm not excusing myself, I promise. You don't know how much I regret…"

I want to go and sit with her, but I know that I won't be able to see her lips if I do. As I'm torn, tense and hovering between listening to her and simply putting an arm around her shoulders, Cam stands up and moves to sit beside her, doing just that. With his long arm draped over her shoulders, she looks even smaller, but it seems to give her strength.

"I told her everything," she says, wiping her nose again. "And I told her first, before I told my boyfriend. I still remember she sat perfectly still and watched me, so calm, that I almost wondered if she was hearing me. And then after a few minutes, when I'd started to cry and threw the test kit onto her bed, she just held up one hand. It was shaking."

Ana is shaking, too, and Cam squeezes her shoulders. "You don't have to tell us this," he says gently, and because he is right next to her, I glance over in time to catch his words. "It's okay."

"I want to," she says, shaking her head but reaching her hand up to grip his for a moment. "Can I keep going?"

And because this is Anastasia, and I realize suddenly that I am crying, too, and because I can't tell if Cam has replied, I slide onto the floor at her feet and say, "Please do."

She licks her lips again. "And she stayed there, holding up her shaking hand, and I stood there looking at her until Mom called from right outside the door. I don't even remember what she said, but I remember that Sophia grabbed the stick with its two little lines, and she shoved it under her mattress before Mom came in. And just like that, we had a secret, and suddenly there was a lie, and all of a sudden I could feel it."

Anastasia doesn't speak for a long time, and at last I reach a hand out and touch her knee. "Could feel...what?"

"I could feel the baby," she says, staring at a point over my left shoulder. "With my mother standing right next to me in the room, suddenly the two lines were real, they meant something, and I had this terrible heaviness right under my belly button and I knew what it meant. I knew that it wasn't a mistake, I knew it was more than a missed period, and even later, when Sophia went to the drug store in the next town over and bought four different test kits, I knew what they'd say. And even though the skin on my stomach was always cold, I felt the baby. The knowledge of the life inside me wasn't something I could touch—didn't even make sense when I had ultrasounds done later, always Sophia holding my hand and never my mom. The pictures and the heartbeats didn't even touch what I *knew* was inside. And it was different, and more beautiful, and more terrible than I'd ever thought possible.

"And I never told her," she says, blinking now, and then looking me full in the face. "Sophia and I told our parents that I wanted to get out of town for a little while, and I went to stay with her for a year. No one understood why, and when they asked too many questions, I just said I was sick of the tininess of this whole place, when really leaving was what made me love it the most. I told my boyfriend the truth when I told him I was leaving. And I told him I thought it would be better if we moved on apart from each other. I didn't know what I was going to do with the child, didn't know what I wanted, but I couldn't…it wasn't going to work, the two of us. I should have given him more of a choice, made him more a part of the decision in the first place, but by the time I told him, all the plans were in place and it was too late. He didn't really care," she says and swallows hard.

"I'm sorry," I say, not knowing what else there is to say.

"He was such a nice guy," she whispers, throat muscles tight, "but when he found out, we both knew it was over. We had so many dreams, and when reality started to happen we realized that it didn't fit, it didn't match what we'd thought we wanted, and what was going to happen to us meant that we wanted completely different things. So I left." Anastasia twists the edge of a discarded blanket between her fingers. "And when I got back a year later, he had moved. After living away from him for a year, I realized that I didn't even care."

Cam seems to be trying to say something, but he can't quite get the words out. "And that's why you left?"

She nods, and when I blink, the blurriness clears, and I realize how tired she looks.

"I left and carried the pregnancy to term in a tiny little apart-ment with Sophia. I got a job to help pay the rent, and at the end of the day we'd sit together, her studying frantically at the table, and me Googling symptoms and recipes and, when she wasn't looking, articles on being a single parent. We never actually talked about what would happen after, just plodded through each day one at a time. I got bigger and bigger, and my clothes stopped fitting…I remember crying one day in a Walmart, because none of the maternity clothes fit properly and I just wanted my mom."

I'm so focused on her face that I don't see her dog enter the room until his cold golden retriever nose is pressed right into my neck. Swallowing a startled yell, I rub his ears, and he flops onto his belly beside me.

"And then," she says, and I can tell by the way she shifts on the couch that her story is drawing to a close. "After my year was up, after giving birth and enduring the hospital stay, all I wanted to do was come home. So about eleven months after I moved out, I moved back in, told everyone that I'd missed them and wanted to stay, completed a few online university courses, and got hired at the library. And I've been here ever since."

Anastasia wipes her eyes, tucks her hair behind her ears, and sighs, and I wonder if now is an appropriate time to ask a question.

"What happened?" Cam beats me to it. "To your…son or daughter?"

"Oh," she says. "Oh. Right."

And then for a minute, no one says anything.

"Do you remember Sophia's wedding?" This is directed to Cam.

"Sure," he says, and shrugs. "It was in the summer, she was wearing a white dress, my mom made me wear a tie—and I wasn't too happy about it, either."

"Okay," replies Ana, "that was about six months after I came back to town. Sophia and Levi got married, and then announced that they had adopted a baby girl."

"I never heard about that," Cam says, and I can see the pieces beginning to snap into place.

"A lot of people didn't," Ana says. "They kept it quiet, because of course it wasn't just any child they had adopted. Sophia told me even before I moved in with her that she would take care of it, just like she always did. She was older, she was in a secure relationship, she was almost done with her schooling, and I had nothing. And because I never knew what to do, and she always did, I said yes. The wedding was the last time I saw any of them," she finishes softly. "We decided it was easier that way, although I don't think either one of us intended to stop talking altogether. That just sort of...happened. We had both created different lies, each built on the same lie, and when we tried to talk, I just could never figure out what to say."

I can see Cam thinking before he speaks. "But she's come to visit before, right?"

Ana shakes her head. "Sometimes my parents go see her. Once she and Levi came by on their way to somewhere else, but for the most part, they keep to themselves." She echoes her earlier sentiment. "It's easier that way."

"What's your daughter's name?" I ask, and Ana sniffs.

"Eva."

The name falls heavily from her lips and sits there in the middle of the room. I feel almost like we're all staring at it there in front of us, no one quite sure what to do now. The sun is a heavy golden color, shadows stretched long outside the back window, and I realize that we've been here for a while. Cam squeezes Ana's arm, and I wonder what he thinks of all of this. What does God think of this?

Maybe He doesn't mind. I can't picture how anyone could hate Anastasia. But then I try to picture her younger, hauling her pregnant belly into a pew at the local church, and I can practically hear the whispers start. Does God whisper with them?

"And I just.... I don't know what to do," Ana says, and opens her hands to us. "I just have no idea what to do. She's coming, and I can't...I don't want to do this. I'll have to tell my parents...I want to tell my parents!" She bursts out with this, and Cam and I exchange glances.

How could you let this happen to her? I wonder if you're even supposed to get this angry at God, because if so, I should probably be dead by now. *What did Anastasia ever do to you?*

He doesn't answer, but I'm not struck down by lightning bolts from heaven, so I decide to call this conversation a draw and tune back in to the real world for a few minutes.

"Then tell them." It seems very simple to Cam, apparently.

"It's not that easy," I say, and I can tell by the way Anastasia rubs her eyes, the tilt of her head as she turns, that she's responded in kind, perhaps in unison with me.

"Sorry," he says, hands up in surrender. "I just thought…you know, talking. Isn't that kind of what families do?"

The words hang in the air for a moment, and my thoughts flash to Mike. Talking. Right. Anastasia appears to have been struck by his insensitive words as well. She winces as though he's physically hurt her, and the back of his neck goes a little redder.

"Sorry," he repeats, looking sheepish, and a little tired. "I'm not very good at this."

"You're doing fine," Ana says gently, and then with an almost imperceptible shift, I feel the balance of power move to its rightful place.

The strange feeling of Cam and I being the adults and Ana the child is gone. As silly and cute and innocent an adult as she may be, she is at last in control again, and I'd be lying if I said I didn't feel totally relieved.

"Thank you," she says and puts her hand on top of mine to be sure that I'm paying attention. "You're the first ones I've told in five years. You're the only ones I've ever told, besides Sophia and—" She hesitates, almost says the name of her boyfriend, and then catches herself in time. "Well, never mind."

Impulsively, I get to my feet and put my arms around her, feeling her shuddery breaths against my shoulder, my hands splayed across her back. She murmurs something into my shoulder and I pull away, studying her face.

"Can you stay for dinner?" There is something open in her face, something pleading, and without even looking at Cam, I know my mouth is saying yes.

"There's not much food … … fridge," she says, wiping her nose through the middle of her sentence with a sniff that is loud in my hearing aid, and I turn toward Cam just in time to see his reply.

"I'll order pizza," he says, putting his phone to his ear, and I lean my head on Ana's shoulder.

"You can do this," I say to the air in front of me, and I don't look at her to see what she says in reply. If she can really start talking to Sophia again…maybe I can patch up me and Mike, too.

Cam nudges my foot and I jump, looking up at him. *Mushrooms?* he mouths, *or pineapple?*

"Not mushrooms," I say, and Ana shakes her head in agreement beside me.

"Pineapple it is, then," he says into the phone, and I feel my lips curve into a smile.

After the tension of the afternoon, it feels good to do something normal again, to talk about pizza toppings instead of life-changing decisions. Back on firm ground, I turn away from Cam's phone call and send a quick text to my parents to let them know I'm hanging with Cam and Ana for a while. Then I reach out to fold the blanket on the couch as Ana picks up the cold plate of mac and cheese and takes it into the kitchen. Nothing is figured out, but everything feels possible again, and the knot in my chest is looser as the streetlights come on across the road.

Chapter FOURTEEN

ANASTASIA COMES BACK FROM THE KITCHEN WITH A NEW KIND OF CALM ON her face, and I decide to chance a question, taking the shoe off the table and placing it discreetly on the floor near my feet. "Do you need any help getting ready? For Sophia coming?"

"No." Ana sits down beside me. "I just don't want to think about it anymore."

Her face reminds me of the twins, with her eyes wide and hands clasped innocently in front of her. I can't picture Ana pregnant, can't see her as a mom with a toddler clinging to her hand, or changing diapers, or blowing noses, which is probably because she hasn't. She hasn't even seen Eva since she was born.

As though she can hear my thoughts—or maybe simply because she's thinking them too—Ana's lips quiver ever-so-slightly.

"Let's play a board game or something," I say quickly, hoping to save the situation, and if I didn't know better, I'd think Cam was going to give me a hug, his own expression panicked. *Thank you*, he mouths to me when Anastasia's back is turned, and I try to smile back.

I expect the evening to drag by, heavy with the weight of the words exchanged, stories told, pain bared…but instead, it's actually kind of fun. It doesn't feel heavy at all, playing cards with Cam and Ana—it feels comfortable and safe and right. I am light inside, like instead of being pinned down by her story, it's a weight that has been taken off my shoulders. Maybe it's one I was carrying without even realizing it.

We play Cheat until the pizza comes, and then War, and Blackjack, all of which I lose, and then after we're all full, Anastasia pulls out Monopoly. Without the twins around to change the rules halfway through, I manage not to go bankrupt, and for the first time ever, I plop three bright red hotels down on my property.

Just as I'm leaning over to pick up the dice, my phone vibrates in my pocket, and by the way Cam and Ana both turn sharply to look at me, I guess that it's ringing, too. Without thinking, I pull it out of my pocket and hold it to my ear.

"Hello?"

It only takes me a second to realize why the voice on the other end is faint and tinny, the words smeared together beyond comprehension.

"Hang on," I say, and only a slight blush accompanies my words. "I'm going to give the phone to Cam."

He's grinning as he takes it from me. "Hey, this is Cam." He listens, and when the smile falls from his face as smoothly as though it had never existed at all, my stomach drops.

"Who is it?"

"Mike," he says, and I can't tell if he's replying to me or my brother, but my heartbeat takes off like a thoroughbred pounding down the track.

"What does he want?"

"Hang on," he says, and again I don't know who he's talking to. I barely feel Anastasia grab my hand. I swear I can actually hear my heartbeat, the first sound to reach my ears in almost a year. "Is anyone hurt?"

Some sort of noise escapes me. I feel it rattle in my chest.

"We can be there in ten minutes."

My hands are shaking.

"Did you call the police?" Cam pauses. His lips are white. "But everyone's okay?"

"Cam," I say, and my voice scrapes against my throat on the way by.

"Stay where you are," he says and takes my phone away from his ear. I accept it with hands that shake so badly I can barely hold the phone.

"What is it? What happened?" I scramble to my feet and nearly fall, the Monopoly board skittering away across the floor.

"I'll tell you in the car." Cam is already reaching for his keys, saying something to Ana, too quick to catch.

"Is he okay?"

"I don't know." His lips are stiff, and the lines in his body are screaming *no, no, no* out at me. No, he's not okay, something's wrong, I'm afraid.

Anastasia walks us to the door, her hand squeezing mine, and I barely feel the ground beneath my feet as I run out to the car. We've been inside for hours, and the street is dusky, dim and full of shadows. The clock in Cam's car flickers to life as he turns the key in the ignition, the blinking numbers reading 10:31 in bright red.

"Tell me where he is." I flick the inside light on so I can read Cam's lips.

"He's out in the country somewhere past Eric's house," he replies, and I read his words like a bullet-pointed list—quick, and to the point. Stark. "He's been in some sort of accident, but he said no one was hurt. They didn't call the police."

A thousand interruptions hover at my lips, but I can't voice any of them, don't want to miss anything.

"There are other guys with him. He said the car's totaled."

I feel sick. Sweat beads on Cam's upper lip, even though the AC is on high, blasts of icy air feathering the hair on my arms.

Cam rubs his nose with the back of his hand, and I can see a vein standing out in his neck.

"Is that it?"

He doesn't look at me, two hands on the wheel, both eyes on the road.

"Cam?" I take a slow breath in, but it gets caught in my throat halfway to my lungs. "What aren't you telling me?"

"He sounded…"

I twist in my seat so I can look straight at Cam. His hands grip the wheel, then loosen, then grip again, and I'd bet anything he wants to let go and unbuckle the strap on his watch, instead. A muscle twitches in his jaw, and his lips are stiff, words hesitant and unsure.

"What?"

"I don't know him very well, so I could be wrong. And I don't want you to think that I'm making a call against him for no reason—"

"Cam!"

I hear his words in my head before I see them escape his mouth. "He sounded pretty drunk to me, Skylar."

"Great," I whisper, and then a curse word slips out unbidden as the last streetlight winks by my window. I flick the inside light off so I can't see Cam anymore, and the night swallows our van. "Was he driving?" I ask after a minute, but I'm looking out the window so I don't see his response. I asked, but I don't actually want to know.

The dark silhouettes of trees towering over the road whizz by in the periodic glare of the streetlights, and I rest my forehead on the cool glass, trying not to worry. Trying not to think at all. I purposefully don't watch the clock, but I can feel the minutes sliding away, scrabbling frantically against my skin as they pass, too fast—until, too soon, Cam pulls off by the side of a road just out of town.

I force myself to look at him as he slides the car into park.

"Are you okay?"

I feel very cold. My eyelashes have turned into glaciers. My fingernails are icicles, and there is a snowbank sitting in my chest where I know my heart ought to be. "I'm fine."

I don't wait to see if he asks anything else before popping the door open and sliding out. The faint outline of a car turned upside down in the ditch swims into view before my eyes, and I'm running before I quite know what I'm doing.

"Mike!"

My hair is in my eyes, and I slip partway down the incline, heart thumping sickeningly into my throat, and then all at once I slam into something hard and tall and reeking of beer. It doesn't look like my brother, but when his hands grab my elbow and haul me upright, something about the way he moves feels familiar.

He says something to me, and I reel back. I don't need to be able to see his lips to know that he's drunk out of his mind.

"What did you do, Mike?" I push his hands away and then step into him, shoving him back with my hands planted firmly on his chest.

He stumbles.

Behind me, Cam's headlights flick on, illuminating my brother's haggard, bloodshot face.

"Hey," he says, holding a trembling hand up in front of his eyes. "Hey, something… something happened." He slurs his way through the next clumsy sentences, but he won't meet my gaze, and I can only make out a word here and there.

"Where's Eric?"

He shrugs. "Not here?" He shrugs again, and then staggers a few steps to the side. "Skylar, I didn't…"

"Didn't think?" I ask, and the ice in my heart cracks. "Didn't care? Didn't what?"

"I was driving," he says, and then starts to cry, as unashamedly as a child. "I'm drunk, I'm so drunk, and I drove."

I stare at him. I am a statue. I am frozen, frozen solid, nothing will ever make me warm again. This is what drove us apart in the first place, this is what carved out the space between us and filled my ears with blank space, this is one bad choice that I never expected Mike to make.

"You what?" I'm hoping that I read his words wrong, but somehow, I know that there has been no mistake. Cam appears at my brother's side and wordlessly hands him a fistful of napkins, which Mike uses to wipe his nose.

"I was taking the guys home," he says, and squints at me through the light. "I think they walked the rest of the way."

My stomach clenches, and I force myself to glance at the overturned car. As though reading my mind, Cam sidles unassumingly over and peers inside, and I feel my heartbeat race. *Please don't let there be anyone inside, please let Mike be right, please don't let him have killed someone.*

Cam looks up at me and shakes his head, hands still in his pockets. *It's okay*, he mouths, and I let myself take a deep breath.

"You suck at choosing friends, Mike," I say, and look from him to Cam, not knowing what to do next.

A chilly nighttime breeze ruffles Cam's hair, and his eyes are closed, lips moving too fast to follow. I wonder if he's praying…I wonder if it would help. What is God supposed to do about my parents' car, upside-down in a ditch? Will He magically adjust Mike's blood alcohol level before the police show up? Is He going to send angels to rescue us from this situation?

"No," I say, under my breath. "He's going to sit back and watch, just like He always does."

"That's not fair," Cam says, the look on his face earnest and scared and young. I must have been speaking more loudly than I thought.

"God's not the one who put your car in the ditch in the first place. Mike handled that just fine all on his own."

As if to demonstrate just how screwed up he is, my brother falls to his knees and pukes on the dry grass at our feet. His hands rest in the dirt, fingers pale against the shadowed ground as he dry-heaves over and over.

"But if He loves me as much as you say He does," I yell back, trying not to breathe through my nose, "why doesn't He…shouldn't I be able to…Mike…"

Mike coughs and spits something into the bushes to his left, one hand pressed trembling to his forehead. I step forward, wanting to touch him, to put my hand on his shoulder and offer comfort, but it feels like more than a few feet of shadows separates us.

I can't find the words to ask the question that is eating me alive, and then as I'm looking at Mike, I start to wonder something else. My brother slides to a sitting position, his knees smearing through the puddle of his own vomit.

"Why does God even want us?" I stare at Mike. I barely even love him right now, and I'm his sister. "Why would God love *that*?"

I stare at Mike for a moment longer, conscious of Cam's gaze on me from three steps away. Finally, I look up at him.

"Will your parents still love him when you bring him home?" He doesn't hesitate, but his expression is the same, as though he's trying to judge where his words will fall before he says them and can't quite figure it out.

My stomach twists at the thought of Mom's face when she sees him. She'll go pale, maybe grab Dad's arm, and then after a moment she'll walk him upstairs, and take off his shoes. She'll probably hug him, too, even though his clothes are covered in vomit, and then she'll turn his light off and come back downstairs to fill up a glass of water and put a couple of aspirin beside his bed.

"Yeah," I say.

"Why?"

"Because he's her son," I say, and it's like the final piece of a puzzle slides together in my head.

Cam says something else, reaching down to lift Mike to his feet. I don't catch his words, thinking instead of the breakfast conversation tomorrow morning. My parents' love won't negate the results of Mike's bad decisions; he probably won't be allowed to leave the house for the rest of the summer, and he definitely won't be taking the car out anytime soon.

"But they still love him," Cam says, like he knows what I'm thinking. He only winces a little bit when Mike rests his head unashamedly on Cam's shoulder. "And so does God." His eyebrows narrow, either with the effort of holding Mike upright or because he's trying so hard to find the right words. "God doesn't make the consequences go away, but that doesn't mean He stops loving Mike, either."

"I get it," I say, my throat worn ragged. "I get it, Cam, and I'm not mad, but can we not talk about this anymore?"

"Let's go home," he says. His shoulders slump either in relief that the conversation is done, or under the pressure of supporting my brother's weight. "Can you open the back door for me?"

It takes a few minutes to hoist all of my brother's six-foot skinny frame into the backseat, and eventually we just shove his legs inside and slam the door shut, glancing back to make sure that his seat belt isn't wrapped around his neck or something.

"I'm done with today." I rub my forehead as Cam turns the car around. "I just want to be in bed."

"I'll call a tow truck for you," he says, and I feel like my chest is going to explode with pain, and with the kindness of the boy sitting in the driver's seat. "After I drop you off."

"Thanks," I say, and a hot tear slips down my cheek. The path it traces burns my skin long after I reach up to wipe it away.

• ● •

Somehow, we manage to get Mike inside the front door without waking anyone up, but when I flick on the lamp over the stove, my brother jerks away from Cam and falls headlong to the floor, where he begins to speak—loudly, judging by the look on Cam's face—with his forehead pressed to the tile.

"Mike," I hiss, dropping to my knees beside him. "Stop! Shh, please be quiet."

He says something to me, but I can't see his face at all, let alone read his lips.

"What?" I look at Cam, who looks as though he's going to laugh, or possibly cry. "What's he saying?"

He shakes his head. "He's just…you know, talking."

I hold back the urge to smack the back of Mike's head and poke him in the shoulder instead.

"Ow," my brother says, turning to look at me, his throat tense with the volume of that one word.

I shove my hand over his mouth, but it's too late—Cam's looking up at the ceiling, his eyes tracing the path of someone's footsteps as they cross the hall and begin to step down the stairs.

"You can go," I say quickly, because there's no need for him to get stuck in the middle of this.

"Do you want me to stay?" He's still watching the stairs.

I glance down at Mike, who appears to have fallen asleep on the floor. "It's okay." Or…it's not. "We'll figure it out." I hope.

A pair of bare feet—Mom's—come down the top step, and when Cam glances at me, I call up, "It's me and Mike."

I leave my mouth open, waiting for the words to explain this situation to pop into the air in front of me. None come to mind, so after a second, I close it again. There's really nothing to say.

"Hi, Mrs. Brady," Cam says, hands in his pockets.

Mom's looking at him, standing in the entryway. She hasn't seen Mike yet. Cam nods in response to something that she says, offers her a panicked smile, and then looks back at me.

"I'll see you at work tomorrow?" His fingers twitch on the doorknob.

"Probably," I say, and then I'm not looking at him anymore, I'm watching Mom's head turn slowly toward us, where Mike is lying on the floor and I'm crouched beside him. I'm surprised she hasn't smelled the alcohol already.

I force myself to meet her gaze. I'm prepared for surprise, shock, anger, or even sadness. What I find—and what I'm not expecting—is resignation.

"Is he drunk?" Her words are measured.

I nod, the grooved tile digging into my knees.

"Where's the car?"

I close my eyes. "Mom, I…" I can't think of anything to say. *He wrecked it? It's in a ditch? No one was hurt?* I can't decide which sentence to start with, what will make her feel better, and then what might make everything worse. The only sentence that rings through my head is *He drove drunk, drove drunk, drove drunk he could have killed someone it could have been me he drove drunk, drunk, drunk.*

After what feels like a long time, I open my eyes again to find Mom crouched down on Mike's other side, speaking into his ear. Her lips are tight, stiff, and brittle like the skin of a porcelain doll, but her hand on his shoulder is gentle, and when he pushes himself to a sitting position and starts to cry again, she pulls him into her lap with no hesitation.

"He drove drunk," I say into a silence that only I can feel, and Mom nods, one hand on Mike's back, smoothing down the creases of his shirt.

"We should have seen this coming," she says, and I look up to find Dad standing behind her, his glasses on, and his hands by his sides. He is staring down at Mike like he doesn't recognize him.

"The car," I continue hoarsely, pushing the words out as they turn to acid in my mouth, "is in a ditch. Upside down."

Mom flinches as though my words have physically struck her. Dad rests one hand on the top of her head.

"Was anyone…?" He swallows, and I see the effort that it costs him.

"No." I shake my head, throwing the thought out, out, out. I want it gone, the idea that he could have done to someone what was done to me, that my own brother could have hurt or even killed someone. I swallow hard, trying not to gag. "No one was hurt, it's okay."

Neither one of my parents are listening. Dad grabs the garbage can from by the stove and holds it out to Mike, who is throwing up again. I close my eyes, grateful that I don't have to listen to him heaving. I imagine his body trying to get rid of the poison that caused all of this. *It's too late, Mike. Not good enough.*

When I open my eyes again, Mike's on his feet, his arm around Dad's neck, and Dad is half-leading, half-carrying him toward the stairs.

"I'll drive out to get the car," Dad says, looking at Mom. "And I'll call a tow truck to meet me there if you can stay with Mike."

"Cam called one," I say, but I'm not sure if they hear me.

"He can sleep it off," Mom says through stiff lips, hard-edged at the corners. I've never seen the wrinkles around her mouth until today. "And then we'll talk in the morning."

I glance up at her. "Are you mad?"

It takes her a long time to answer.

"I'm angry with him," she says, slowly, "because he knows better. But I'm angry with myself, too." She falls silent again, and then when she speaks I wonder if she's forgotten that I'm there. "I should have tried to talk to him more. I should have seen that he was hurting, I should have found some way to put a stop to it before this happened. Thank God he didn't kill anyone."

From my non-religious mother, this sentence comes as somewhat of a surprise. "Thank God," she says again, and I notice the tremble in her hands. "Tomorrow," she says, and her eyes are shining with tears. "Tomorrow he'll wake up, and now he has this to live with this too." *I should have been able to stop this.* Her lips echo these words, but there's no force behind them. She might not even know she's doing it, and I wish I hadn't seen.

I open my mouth to finish the story, to tell her about the brownie incident, the firefighters, and then I close it again. She doesn't need to hear that too. Guilt chews delicately away at my stomach, and when Mom starts up the stairs, still talking—maybe to me, maybe to herself—I follow silently.

At the top of the stairs, she pulls me into a hug. I bury my nose in her shoulder and inhale the smell of safety, warmth, and love. After a moment, I pull away. I want to sleep forever and not have to think anymore.

I pause in the doorway of my bedroom and look back, where the light from beside Mike's bed casts shadows in the hall. Dad comes out of his room carrying his dirty laundry, the pukey shirt wrapped up in a ball. My mother kneels on the floor beside Mike's bed, taking off his shoes.

Chapter
FIFTEEN

WHEN I WAKE UP THE NEXT MORNING, MIKE IS THROWING UP AGAIN. I CAN'T hear it, but when both the twins catapult through my door and under the covers with me, their faces screwed up in disgust, I have a pretty good guess.

"Is Mike sick?" asks Sara, her fingers shoved firmly in her ears and her lips pursed at the end of every word.

"Yeah," I say, and wonder if the clog in my throat is from the early morning or some deep-seated emotion I can't name. "He's sick."

We stay under the covers together for as long as I can bear, and then at last I know I have to get up and face the day. I pull on a blue tank top and twist my hair into a bun, ready for work. I can't imagine shelving books today, but it's better than the alternative.

Mike is sitting at the kitchen table when I go downstairs, a glass of water and a bottle of Advil on the table in front of him. He's pale and won't look at me when I slide into a chair in front of him. We eat breakfast in silence, and then I stand in the middle of the kitchen for a long time, trying to decide what to do. I don't know what to say to him. I don't know if I want to speak to him at all.

Finally, as Dad shoos the twins outside to play and Mom sits at the table, watching Mike stare down at his plate, I figure something out.

"Mike," I say, and he flinches, although he doesn't look up.

"Skylar, maybe not right now," Dad says, one hand on the door, his glasses perched crookedly on his nose, and I wonder how I never realized that loving people could hurt so much. I wonder for a split second, as the sunlight catches a haze of dust in the air and makes it shimmer, if it hurts God to love us, too.

"I love you," I tell my brother, and then I duck out the front door under Dad's outstretched arm, the sun warm on the back of my neck as I stride down the street without looking back.

I'm hoping for a quiet day at work, and I'm hoping that Cam won't ask me for any details about this morning, but as I approach the front doors and see people already inside, I can tell that I'm going to be at least fifty percent disappointed.

Anastasia is behind the counter, a little paler than normal, but with her hair—and personality—back to their springy, bubbly selves.

"How are you feeling?" I ask, clipping my nametag to the front of my shirt and feeling grateful for an excuse not to think about Mike anymore.

"Good," she says, and brushes the hair behind her ears before turning to check through someone's books, her fingers hesitating over the titles as she turns to me. "Cam told me what happened."

"I don't want to talk about it," I say, and resist the urge to close my eyes. "But he's okay. Everyone's okay."

She nods, silent, her hand—nails neatly painted again—reaching out to grab mine for just a moment, the pressure reassuring.

"I cleaned the house for a long time after you two left last night," she continues, and I lean forward to catch a glimpse of her words, grateful for the subject change. "And I called Sophia back and told her that I was ready for her to come."

"Only a week left." I pass her the next stack of books and watch as she rings them through.

"Only a week," she echoes. "Six more days after today."

Six more days. I get so caught up in thinking about the reunion that I shelve an entire cart of books in the wrong section and have to start over, tracing my fingers down the stacks to locate the odd books out, piling them on the cart and feeling silly every time Cam walks by.

Six more days. I wonder why it feels so significant to me and won't let myself think that maybe I'm pinning too much on Ana's sister. I try to remind myself that it doesn't mean Mike and I will automatically be okay again, but that's what I keep coming back to in the end.

• ● •

Cam spends his six days outwardly calm, shelving away as normal, but his fingers are never still and his watch is off his wrist more often than on. When he comes over after one of our shifts, he plays with it so unceasingly that eventually I take it away from him and put it on the table, just so I don't have to look at it anymore. Ana spends her time in constant motion, never standing still, and I spend mine trying to talk to Mike and then falling silent as he turns away from me. I almost preferred it when he was angry, because then I could be angry too. But Mike after the accident is silent and guilty. He won't meet my eyes, tucks his head down when I pass him in the hall, and flat-out ignores me anytime I try to speak to him.

I need something to change. Mom told me to give him time, and Dad sat me down and explained that Mike needs space to deal with the situation, but I can't help feeling restless. If he was younger, I think my parents would have grounded him. As it is, most of his money is going toward repairs for the car. He hasn't mentioned

Eric's name since the night of the accident, and I haven't seen so much as a glimpse of any of his so-called friends.

In the middle of it all, the twins invent a new game called "Play Dead," which lasts for about four hours. At that point, Mom finds jam smeared dramatically across the bathroom walls and puts a stop to their fun. They're so sulky for the rest of the day that they end up sent to bed early, leaving the house quiet but with an air of martyrdom that floats down the stairs, the twins' door firmly shut until breakfast the next morning. Everyone seems to be in a funk, like the whole world is counting down the days until Sophia comes.

At last, the week is over, and the morning of Sophia's arrival dawns rainy and overcast. I wake up too early with a stomach ache that the weather does nothing to cure and spend the time before my shift starts staring out the kitchen window, watching raindrops trace indifferent paths down the glass. They are hesitant to leave each other at first, and then shoot apart like long spindly fingers, joined at the hand but growing ever longer, farther apart.

Sara and Aiden jar the table as they sit, shoveling down mouthfuls of cereal and wiggling in their seats. Sara says something with her mouth full, chewed-up Cheerios visible between her teeth, and I shudder as Mom replies, "Only if you wear your coat."

"But it's hot," she whines and swallows, her face screwed up in true six-year-old agony. "I'll get sweaty which is basically 'zacktly the same as being wet from rain, only rain is also like taking a shower, so actually I'll be cleaner, you know."

Aiden nods hopefully along with her logic, and I'm saved from the ensuing battle by my father, who snags the car keys off their hook. "I'll drive you to work today, if you like."

"Thanks," I say, watching as the last raindrop slides into the sill and disappears, united again with the others.

My stomach is prickly and tense, and every time I start to think about something else, the drama of Sophia's arrival slipping to the back of my mind, the muscles in my abdomen clench and every-thing comes thundering back. I feel responsible. I feel helpless. How did I ever think I could fix this?

The library air is charged with electricity, and the hair on my arms stands up before I'm five steps inside the front doors. I can't tell if it's the thunder in the air or the nervousness pulsing from Ana and Cam, but I have to rub my hands up my arms before my skin quiets down again.

"Good morning," I say, aiming for casual, but Cam's fingers drum the desk, the rhythm so quick I can almost feel the pain in my own fingers, and Anastasia is frozen solid at the front count-er. "Everything okay?" I ask this tentatively, and she nods once, sharply.

"Just a little nervous," Cam says, bringing his fingers to a halt with considerable effort. "And it's quiet today."

I thought an empty library would be relaxing. Instead, it just means that there's more room for our collective anxiety to balloon outwards, swelling until I'm surprised spidery cracks don't appear in the windows. I can feel it pressing on my chest, stuffing my mouth full every time I open it to take a breath.

"What time is she coming?" I burst out, even though I'd told myself not to mention it.

"Tonight," Ana says, tapping furiously away at her computer, which I can see is actually still on standby.

Neither Cam nor I mention this to her, and she keeps pressing the keys, her eyes on the screen, but unfocused and far away.

I glance up at the clock, thinking that maybe fifteen minutes have passed since I walked through the front doors, but the min-ute hand isn't even at the five yet, the second hand ticking away at what I'm sure must be half speed.

"Is the clock broken?" I attach my badge to my shirt with shak-ing fingers. *Pull yourself together, Skylar. This is ridiculous.*

When I look up at Cam, there's a tiny smile playing about his lips, but he just shakes his head. "Not broken."

"Oh," I say, rather lamely. "Well, I guess I'll go check the recently returned shelf."

"Good idea," he says. Over by the counter, Anastasia straightens the pencil jar, wipes away an invisible dust speck, and opens the drawer in front of her before closing it again, having taken nothing out.

The morning drags by. I make my steps as slow as possible, but the clock seems to be moving slower still, as though to taunt me. I even go so far as to count the seconds in my head as I'm shelving, certain that at least ten minutes has passed, and then turning around to find that the minute hand has ticked forward only six times.

Cam and Ana and I don't speak for hours, and the rain never stops, hundreds after hundreds of drops racing down the glass beside me, parting and then meeting at the sill, flowing ever downwards…. I drag out a stool so I can reach the top shelf, climbing up and then down to slide it two steps to the right, and then up and down again, two steps to the right, until I've straightened every single title.

At last, it's five o'clock, and Cam marches to the front to lock up, leaving Ana and me standing awkwardly behind the desk. Ana's hands are twisted in front of her, mine clasped behind in what I think is probably a failed attempt to look casual.

"Are you ready?" I ask, and then I want to hit myself, because *I'm* not even ready, and I'm barely part of this. Not a big part, anyway.

"No," Anastasia says simply, twisting her fingers harder. Her knuckles are white, but her fingertips are bright red. I watch them flush darker until at last she pulls her hands apart and the blood rushes back into her hands, her color smoothing to normal in a matter of seconds.

"Let's go," Cam says, grabbing his keys. "Skylar and I will wait with you, if you want."

"I do," Ana says, almost before he's finished speaking.

Neither one of them asks me how I feel about it, and even in the midst of this crazy day it puts a warm spot in my chest, to be so automatically included. I am a part of them, whatever they are, and this situation involves all three of us, no questions asked.

Even the short drive to Ana's house feels like it lasts forever. Cam's hands are tight on the wheel, Ana's leg jiggling against the back of my seat unevenly until I can feel it inside my head, can almost hear the sound of her nervousness like a swarm of bees whizzing by.

At last, we pull into the driveway, and Ana catapults up the front steps and into the house. By the time Cam and I follow, stopping to pet her dog as he leans against our legs, she's already in the kitchen, yanking bread and cheese out of the fridge to make us sandwiches.

Cam and I exchange a look. "Let's leave her," he says, and sits on the couch.

I slouch down beside him, grateful for the opportunity to put a little space between us and her.

"Wow," I say, mostly to myself, and then neither one of us saying anything at all.

I'm just starting to relax, tucking my feet underneath me on the couch, when Cam's head turns sharply toward the front door. Ana's dog runs down the hall from the kitchen and takes up a wide-legged stance beside me, his whole body shuddering as he barks.

"What is it?" I ask, as Cam gets to his feet, but before he's taken two steps the door opens, and a young woman steps inside.

Her hair is dark and cut sharply at her chin. Her skin is pale, and her eyes are so brown they look almost black. She closes the door behind her, long fingers wrapped tightly around the handle for just a moment too long before she lets go and rests her hand at her side. For a moment we all stand still, looking at each other, and then the dog lunges at her in ecstasy, tail wagging almost faster than I can see.

The stranger crouches and pets the dog before looking up at us again. "Cam," she says, and the smile she gives him looks stiff, as though she hasn't practiced it in a long time.

"Who are you?" I ask, stupidly, even though I know exactly who she is and why she's standing awkwardly in the front entrance. Sophia. She's finally here.

"Sorry," she says, and then pauses, her breath hitched halfway through her throat. "Who are…" She turns to Cam, asks him something with stiff lips that barely move and are impossible to read, her voice a low hum at the base of my skull.

"Skylar," Cam says to her, and then carries on in what I assume is an explanation of who I am and what I'm doing here.

"I thought you weren't coming until tonight." I realize after the sentence has already left my mouth that I've spoken too loudly, the words sharp and strong in my throat, but even as I wince, expecting a similar reaction from the other two, I see they aren't looking at me anymore.

I am lightheaded as I follow both of their shocked expressions to where Anastasia now stands, sandwich in hand, by the couch.

"Ana," the stiff-lipped woman says.

I don't look back to Anastasia in time to catch her words, but I know what name she's spoken without needing to be told. My heartbeat thumps away in my chest; I can see the faint twitch across the top of my blouse every time it pounds. I almost wonder if it's audible.

Still, no one moves.

"Where are the others?" says Anastasia, and then drops the plate as easily as though she'd forgotten she was holding it in the first place.

It shatters as it hits the floor, and the other three jump. I'm captivated, watching the exact moment the plate contacts the hardwood, cracking open and apart instantaneously. One piece shoots straight under the couch, and shards dust the ground around Anastasia's feet. I feel a twinge of recognition pull inside my gut, because I know that crack. I know what it feels like to break, suddenly, pieces of you all over the place, in only a matter of seconds.

As I'm contemplating the feelings that I share with a broken plate, Sophia speaks again.

"I came alone," she says, apparently in response to Ana's question, and I put together a full sentence, tug the words free from her stiff lips, hard and unyielding as concrete. "I wanted to wait…until we'd said hello again."

"Well," Anastasia says, stepping around the ruins of the plate on the floor. "Hello."

This is wrong. My heartbeat rises within me. This isn't how it should be. Then I see Ana's hands shaking. She clutches them together, but too late. Sophia sees them too, and although her hands are steady as she tucks a strand of hair behind her ear, she bites her lip—and I can see tears gathering in her eyes.

"I was so nervous for today," Anastasia says, and then she steps forward, almost falls into Sophia's arms, her back to me, trembling in the embrace of the taller woman.

Sophia hesitates for just a split second and then wraps her skinny arms around her sister, her face toward me, eyes closed, and twin tear tracks line her cheeks.

"Me, too," she says, and then says nothing at all.

I'm frozen, watching them, wondering what Anastasia is saying, if anything. Is it okay? I actually want to ask this out loud, but I hold myself back. Does it feel right? Tell me that you are not too broken to be put back together.

Cam puts a hand on my elbow, and I jump.

We should go, he mouths, and I jump, glancing back to Anastasia and Sophia, who are still hugging. Anastasia's shoulders move, and I wonder if she is crying or speaking.

Cam tugs me gently toward the glass doors that lead onto the back deck, and I turn away, leaving them to their moment. We pause by the door, and then something pulls me back.

Just a second, I mouth. I tug my arm free from his grasp, slipping to my knees beside the couch. I close my eyes and slide one hand beneath, feeling around until the jagged edges of the broken plate meet my fingers. Slowly, trying to stay as quiet as possible, I tug out the small, lost slice of plate, and set it with the other shards, all the broken pieces together in the same place before I rejoin Cam.

We manage to slide the door open without anyone noticing, and Cam closes it again just as the two women pull apart. Even the air feels quiet as we come around the corner of the house, and we don't break it until we're in the driveway.

"Let's walk the rest of the way," Cam says, his head down, and I don't argue.

I keep seeing Anastasia's face in my mind the moment she saw Sophia in the doorway: her hands, as they simply let go of the plate and then started to tremble before it hit the floor. And I wonder what it would be like to be apart from Mike for that long.

Skylar, I say firmly to myself, *you are not Anastasia*. Mike is not Sophia. It's totally different. But…is it? Before this summer, I wouldn't have thought twice about our relationship, would have fought anyone who said we couldn't possibly stay friends forever, and now…Mike and I are totally different people. Who knows what might happen to us over the next few years? Plus, it's not like we would ever keep something like that from our parents.

As though he's heard me—maybe he has, if I was speaking aloud without noticing—Cam's head turns sharply toward me.

Oh.

"You think I should tell them, don't you?"

They still don't know about the firefighter incident. Right now,

I'm still the good child, and maybe it's selfish in the midst of this whole situation, but I'd really like to keep it that way.

Cam just looks at me, and I can tell that we're both thinking about Anastasia and Sophia.

"I should probably tell them."

I say this with such a forceful sigh that it feels like my words are almost lost altogether. I don't want to see the look in Mom's eyes—again. I don't want her to have to worry about me, too, even though I'm sure she already does.

"Will Mike be mad?" Cam slows his pace as we approach the house, and I match mine to his, wanting to finish this conversation before I go inside and my world falls apart.

"No," I say offhandedly, and then remember the haunted look in his eyes.

We don't have to tell them, he'd said. *They don't have to know.*

"Maybe. Probably. At this point, I don't know if he'll care." What else does he have to lose?

Cam digs his hands into his pockets, traces the tip of his shoe in the dirt at the foot of Aunt Kay's driveway. "Well, good luck."

"Thanks," I say, and watch the flicker of curtains as one of the twins pulls it back and sees him standing there. "You'd better go before they get out here."

He looks up, grins. "I'll see you later."

"If I survive the next hour," I say grimly, and turn away before I can see his reply. I just want to get this over with.

My feet are heavy against the driveway, soles of my shoes skidding along the concrete driveway as I approach the house. I go to the kitchen entrance to buy myself a few more seconds. The screen door resists my touch, and I imagine it groaning in protest. Me too.

"Skylar," Mom says, as I come in. "How was your—"

"I have something to tell you," I blurt out, and then spill my story right there in the middle of her sentence. I tell her everything, from the moment Mike left, through the firefighter incident, and finish up by skimming over the details of our fight.

When I finish and look up, she's still standing in front of me, her mouth slightly open, a dish towel dangling from one hand. As awful as it feels to see her struck dumb twice in one week, my stomach is a little less tight, like maybe my piece of the broken plate isn't hidden under the couch any more.

"Are you mad?" I say, but I'm too relieved at having it off my chest to be apprehensive about any kind of punishment.

"There were firefighters in the house?" A wrinkle has appeared between her eyes as she tries to make sense of it all.

"Yes," I say, and force myself to meet her gaze. "A lot of firefighters, actually."

As my eyes meet hers, I notice the outline of another person standing in the entryway. Mom must hear him, because she snaps her mouth closed and turns half away from me to see who it is.

"Mike," she says, and my brother steps into the kitchen for a moment, his shoulders hunched.

He never used to stand like that—I can't remember when it started, only that it hasn't looked strange to me until today. How long has he been slouching like he has a ten-pound weight on each shoulder? I'm afraid that he'll be angry, but the look he gives me is blank, like he's past the point of caring.

"I didn't mean to," he says to Mom, and then glances at me as though to include me in it.

I mean to say, "It's okay," or maybe "I forgive you," but what comes out is, "I know." *I know, Mike.*

I wait for him to say something else, hovering on the edge of what I hope is a reunion similar to that of Anastasia and Sophia, but after a moment, he turns his back on me and leaves the room. His feet climb slowly up the stairs, and Mom and I stay in the kitchen, watching him go, until he reaches the second floor and we can't see him anymore.

Chapter
SIXTEEN

ON THE MONDAY NIGHT THAT MARKS THE BEGINNING OF OUR LAST WEEK IN
Golden Sound, I can't sleep. I'm lying in bed picturing Aunt Kay
walking through the jungle in Africa somewhere, hacking down
weeds with a sizeable machete. The thought of putting a deadly
weapon in her hands scares me so badly that I have to roll over so
my back is against the wall, and I can keep an eye on the shadows
dancing across the doorway of my bedroom.

Not that I think she's going to rush in and murder me on purpose…but if she decided to sleepwalk home, machete in hand, and
do some weed whacking in my bedroom by mistake, I wouldn't
necessarily be surprised. That's just the kind of impossible thing
she'd be likely to do. We haven't heard a thing from her in weeks.
She could show up on the front step tomorrow, or on Christmas
Day, or never come back, for all we know.

I roll onto my back, my skin tingling with late-night insomnia
itches. This isn't helping me to sleep. I picture our house, my bedroom at home, and I feel a sudden rush of homesickness. There's
already a faint chill in the breeze rolling off the lake, and it makes
me want sweaters and jeans and the musty old smell of the school
hallways at lunchtime. I love it here, but I miss being home.

After tossing and turning for several more minutes, I give up on sleep and sit up. The thought of Aunt Kay with a machete freaks me out more than I'd like to admit, so I grab my hearing aids off the side table and slide them in. Just as a precaution.

Moonlight slips through my half-closed blinds and leaves soft strips of light across my floor, and when I swing my feet over the side of the bed, floorboards like ice on my skin, I imagine that I'm leaving footprints behind.

I need a drink, my body heavy with too many hours spent lying awake in bed. As I tiptoe into the kitchen, a curtain flutters. A window has been left open a few inches, and a cool wind whispers gently against my skin, making me shiver. The curtains are all drawn, the kitchen silent and still in the darkness. My hand hovers over the light switch for a second, but I can barely keep my eyes open as it is, and the thought of the florescent lighting is so shrill in my mind that I decide to navigate my way to the sink in the dark.

I take three steps, sliding my feet along the tile floor like I'm cross-country skiing, and then get too cocky on the fourth and slam my hip into the corner of the table with an explosion of pain that goes all the way down to my toes. I yelp in surprise, and then clap a hand over my mouth to hold in the following whimper, but when nothing seems to move upstairs, I decide that I'm safe and keep going, this time with my hands out in front of me.

I manage to pour myself a glass of water without further injuring myself, and as I tip the last few drops into my mouth, a wave of exhaustion washes over me, and my bed seems pretty appealing after all. I'm already imagining how crisp and cool the sheets will feel as I slide between them.

And then something moves in the living room.

Halfway to the stairs, I freeze, my hand already stretched out to grab the railing. Maybe it was just a shadow, maybe something moved outside, or the curtains are being blown by the wind, or…

As my eyes adjust to the darkness, I make out the figure of a person standing in the corner of the room, and then he walks in front of the window, his body silhouetted perfectly in the bright moonlight from the street, and I know him.

"Mike, what are you doing up?"

He goes still, halfway across the room with his shoulders hunched up and his arms crossed, body turned away from me. I let go of the bannister and walk into the living room, putting the window behind me so that the light shines onto my brother's face. A sick kind of determination curls up in the pit of my stomach. If I had been given the choice, I would not have picked the middle of the night to have this conversation. But here we are, and since my opportunity is staring me in the face, I'd be stupid not to take it.

He still hasn't moved, staring down at the floor, and I force myself to look up at his face, expecting anger, or maybe tears, like the last time I caught him out of bed in the middle of the night. What I don't expect, when I finally meet his eyes, is the haunted look that greets me.

We stand there for a minute, facing each other, and he doesn't say anything. He looks so tired…so, so tired, and the longer I watch him the more I realize that he isn't even angry. Mike looks like someone has been chasing him for miles and he will fall straight down if he has to take another step.

He waits for me to say something.

"Did you have another nightmare?" Even as the words leave my mouth I realize what a terrible idea this is. *Way to go, Skylar.* If he wasn't angry before, he will be now.

"I don't sleep long enough to have nightmares anymore," he says, not meeting my gaze.

"What do you mean?"

He hesitates. "I just…I don't really sleep a lot anymore. That's all."

"Why not?" Every time I open my mouth, I cringe. Apparently, late-night discussions aren't one of my natural talents. Go figure.

"Why do you think?" He snaps the words out sharply, but his face is still clear. "I got tired of dreaming all the time, so I stopped sleeping, and now I just can't."

"So, you just…wander? Down here?" In the dark?

"Not always." Mike looks around, and even though my eyes are fully adjusted, I still can't see much. The glass TV screen reflects the faint light from the window, throwing the edges of Aunt Kay's white couch into view, but other than that the room is filled with shadows. "Sometimes I stay in my room. Sometimes I go out for a walk."

I open my mouth and then close it again. Mike still isn't looking at me, but his lips are parted slightly. I can tell he wants to say something else.

He stays silent for so long that I have to pinch my arm behind my back to keep myself from falling asleep on my feet. I have the urgent feeling that this is important, that if I mess this up I might not get another chance to make things right between us—and I so desperately need for things to be right with us again.

"I did have a dream last night, though," he says at last, and then swipes a hand across his eyes so fast I almost miss it. "First one in a few weeks."

"About the accident?"

My leg cramps, and I shift my weight from foot to foot for a few seconds before giving up and sitting down, cross-legged in the middle of the living room. After a second, Mike joins me, his knees pulled up to his chest. I picture him when we were younger, and even though I never thought about it much back then, I realize how small he looks. How young and scared.

"It's the only thing I ever dream about," he answers, staring at my feet. "But yeah."

"Tell me," I say, trying not to make it sound like a command.

I expect another long pause, but he begins to speak almost instantly, as though this has been building inside him for weeks, and he was just waiting to be asked to spill it forth. He starts slowly, but after a few sentences he's talking so quickly I can hardly follow what he's saying.

"It always starts the same," he says, "with us running. Sometimes we're at home, but in this dream, we were here, running down Main Street. I was on the sidewalk, but you were on the road, running in the gutter."

So far it doesn't sound too bad, but judging by the look on his face it's about to get worse.

"And the cars," he says, "there were so many cars, and they were all racing by at highway speeds, and honking at each other, and you were trying to get my attention, because you wanted to get off the road and run on the sidewalk, too, but I kept ignoring you. And you kept screaming at me, calling my name, and I kept getting angrier at you, and angrier…"

His hands are balling into fists, and I feel sick to my stomach just looking at his face.

"And then finally, I couldn't stand it anymore, and I turned around and pushed you, and you fell right into the middle of the road."

Mike won't look at me. I can't breathe. Is that what happened? Did he push me?

"It was like one of those times when you think it's actually happening, you know?" He licks his lips. "I always think it's real. So as soon as you fell I knew I'd screwed up, and I wanted to run into traffic and save you, but my feet wouldn't move and I was stuck on the sidewalk, listening to you scream my name and just watching as the cars came closer and closer—"

"And then you woke up?" I want him to stop talking about the dream so I can ask him about the missing piece, the one I couldn't remember when I was telling Cam what happened. I want to ask him *why*. I want to believe that this has not affected him just as much as it changed me. I don't know if I *can* believe that anymore.

"No," he says, still looking at my feet. "I saw it happen, I see you get hit. Every. Single. Time. And then when the cars stopped and you were lying there by the side of the road, my feet could move again and I ran over, and I saw the blood on your face."

"And then you woke up," I say again, begging it to be true.

"And I called your name," he continues, as though I hadn't spoken, "and you asked, 'why?'" He swallows hard, the Adam's apple jumping in his throat. "The driver of the car got out and started yelling at me, and people came out of the stores and stood on the sidewalk and gasped and held their hands over their mouths and looked at me like I was a murderer and asked me why I did it, and I tried to answer them but my voice wouldn't work."

"Mike," I say, but whether it's because my voice is too low or because he doesn't want to hear me, he keeps talking.

"I usually wake up crying," he says. "Like a little kid, I'm crying in my dream, thinking that I killed you, and then bam, I'm in my bedroom and the pillow is soaking wet and I've got snot all over my face just like a little kid, and I hate it. I just hate it."

He punctuates this last sentence with an expletive before he looks me in the eyes, and I can see that he is on the verge of tears. *Please*, I think desperately, *don't cry*.

I want to fix this, make him feel better, punch him in the arm or put my hand on his knee, or something, but I just can't. If it was Cam, I'd do it in a heartbeat, but this is my brother. This is too important.

"It was just a dream," I say.

"Was it?" The haunted look is back, hidden behind a veil of unshed tears.

"It was just a dream." I look him full in the face, and when I'm confronted with guilt so thick I can barely see my brother beneath it, my questions seem less important. "Right? Mike?"

He doesn't nod, but he doesn't shake his head either.

"We were running," I say, piecing together the bits I remember. "That morning, and I was on the outside, the side closest to the road."

This time, he nods, his head ducked down.

"And then," I grasp for the simplest version, hoping I'm right. "You bumped into me? Or you nudged my arm? And I fell."

"You made a terrible joke," he whispers. "I punched your arm. I didn't see the car."

"And then I tripped," I say, whispering too, and he nods.

"I've dreamed about it so many times, in so many different ways, when I try to remember it more clearly than that…" Mike shrugs and wipes his nose on the back of his hand. "I just can't. I just remember the different dreams, not the actual thing."

The breeze from the kitchen sends a chill down my spine, and I shiver. How long have we been sitting here in the dark? Mike moves, too, and a shadow falls across his face. I can still see his lips, but just barely.

"And then…"

He keeps going, and as much as I know he needs to talk, I don't want to see it. I don't want to know what's going on inside his head, because I thought I was starting to be okay with everything, and his words are driving a knife through my chest all over again. I remember bits and pieces of that day, too, and the nightmares that followed, and reliving the event with him makes the fear burble up inside me again. It chokes me, and I struggle for air.

"Then I wake up, right," he says and swipes a hand across his face again, "and it's morning, so I come downstairs and the nightmare isn't over. Because every single day, I have to see your face, I hear your voice and I know that I did this to you."

He coughs, and I imagine his voice breaking. *Please stop*, I want to tell him, but he keeps plowing on.

"It's my fault, and I ruined your life, and it's like every time I see you, you're lying on the ground again and I think that you're dead. You could have been dead," he says, and I can tell by the way he bites his lip that he is very close to losing control.

You didn't ruin my life. The words don't make it past my throat.

"I feel like ever since that day I can't do anything right." Mike stretches his pajama-clad legs out in front of him, and then lies down on his back and closes his eyes. "We all go to the beach together and I take my eyes off Aiden for one second and suddenly…"

He doesn't finish his sentence. He doesn't need to.

"But that was my fault," I say, and the words hurt my chest.

"Yeah, but Skylar"—Mike raises himself up on one elbow—"you would have grabbed him right away if you could hear. And why can't you hear?"

He doesn't mean to be hurtful, but the point stings. I could have saved him if I could hear. He might have died because I couldn't.

"It's not *your* fault," I say, but it doesn't feel like enough.

Mike lies back down, staring at the ceiling. "And then with the firefighters."

"Which was my fault, too!" I say this with some force, and to my horror, hot tears brim up in my eyes and roll down my cheeks. *It's all my fault!* I could scream at him. *So what's your point? We've established that I suck at being a person, basically! Thanks for that!*

But I don't say it. I don't say anything, because I get it. I understand how he feels because I'm living it, too, and the fact that both of us are carrying guilt for something that was no one's fault isn't going to help anyone, no matter how you phrase it.

"And then," he says, and the lump in his throat bobs up as he licks his lips. "The other night."

"Mike, you don't have to—"

"Yes, I do," he says, fists clenched so tightly the cords in his forearms are stretched taut all the way into his neck. "Please let me get through this, Skylar. I have to tell you."

"Okay," I whisper, but I don't know if he hears me. I don't know how much more I can take.

"We were at Eric's, like always." He coughs as though trying to dislodge the rest of his words. "Just messing around, you know. I had a couple of drinks, smoked a few cigarettes. They were passing a bong around, but I didn't touch it, not that time…"

I didn't know that seeing someone's words could cause physical pain until this moment, when I can feel each one of Mike's words branded into my heart with a white-hot iron.

"But I wasn't really feeling it. I was still thinking about the firefighters, and that day with Aiden at the beach, and no matter how many beers I had it was just like it all came clearer and clearer until it was all I could see."

I watch him, frozen stiff with my legs crossed and my hands clasped in front of me. I feel like I'll never be able to move again.

"Eric was pretty drunk too," he continues, staring at my feet. I can see his pulse throbbing at the base of his neck. "And he wanted to go driving, so I thought, I'm too upset to be drunk. I thought I was still sober, because I couldn't shake the memories, couldn't lose the sadness. Normally drinking is like being in a fog, it just…" He shrugs. "It doesn't matter anymore, and that night it still did, so I thought I was fine."

I should say something, but I don't know what.

"We got out into the country, and I still couldn't shake it. Eric was riding shotgun, dropping everyone's finished beer bottles out the window, and he kept yelling for me to go faster, faster. I guess I was so drunk that it seemed like a good idea. Maybe if I drove fast enough I could stop thinking about it or something." He swipes a hand across his face, cutting out his next few words. "I don't really remember, but all of a sudden it was like it hit me, how fast we were going, and I could see the turn coming up. Like someone had smacked me across the face, or something, and it was just so clear, I knew I had to stop. I knew we were all going to die if I tried to take the turn, so I slammed on the brakes. None of the guys were wearing seat belts, and a couple of them went flying forward, and they all started yelling at me."

I am trying so hard not to picture it, but my stomach is curling tighter and tighter, and I feel like I'm going to be sick.

"Eric was yelling at me, trying to twist the wheel, but I just kept my foot on the brake and tried to make the turn. I had our speed down, we were okay, we might have even made it around the corner…but he got a couple fingers on the wheel and cranked it too far, and we just rolled."

"How did no one get hurt?" I don't mean to say it, but I do.

"I don't know," he says, his eyes wide with the memory. "Honest to God, I don't, Skylar."

God. This single word shocks me like a jolt of electricity. No, I think then, and anger rises in me. *This isn't about you.* And I shove the thought away.

"So we rolled it," he says, and his fingers pull the top of his shirt down, and I see the bruise, the green rash and the red burn from where the seat belt cut him, and I feel it on my own skin. "And after a long time, I guess I kind of clued in that we were upside down, and some of the guys had already crawled out. I unbuckled my seat belt, I'm still not sure how, and then we were all standing there looking at it. Eric handed me the last of his beer and started walking, and it was in my hand so I drank it, and then…" He breaks off and thinks, his forehead furrowed. "I don't remember anything after that. Except throwing up a couple of times, and then I woke up at home, in bed."

"The tow truck brought Dad's car back," I say, unnecessarily, "and they didn't call the police. The mechanic wanted to, but Dad convinced him that we could pay for the damages."

A tear plops off my chin and into my lap, and I realize that I'm still crying. Tears like raindrops run indiscriminately down my face, not so much in paths as in streams, traveling to my chin and then joining up again in the puddle that is my lap.

Mike puts a finger to his lips, glancing toward the stairs, and then when he sees that I'm crying, his face goes slack.

"Skylar," he says—or at least, that's what I think he says—but his face is all blurry and as I gulp back a sob, I know that this conversation is over, at least for the next few minutes.

"I'm sorry," I say, my voice wobbling, and then it explodes out of me, one muffled sob torn raggedly from my chest. My lips are trembling, and as I hold one hand over my mouth to muffle the sound, I can feel my hands shaking, too. *Stop it, Skylar,* I say to myself, but it doesn't help.

Through the blur of tears, I see Mike heave a sigh, and then sit up, scooting over so he's sitting next to me. Gently, he places an arm over my shoulders—not quite a hug, but almost—and rests it there, the weight of it solid and comforting.

I cry like a baby for several minutes, and then when I finally get some breath back, I wipe my eyes and look up. My brother is crying, too.

"It sucks, Sky." He wipes his nose with the back of his free hand.

"Yeah."

We are silent for a minute, and then his hand tightens on my shoulder—I look up.

"I'm sorry," he says, fiercely, teeth gritted. "I really am. For all of it. For being a jerk. For being such a…" He tries to find a word. His lips begin to form a swear word to fill the gap, but he swallows it back, half-formed. "For being such a freaking idiot." Then he is silent.

He has never said this to me. Not at first in the hospital, not when I got home. I try to remember a time when Mike and I have seriously talked about the accident, what happened that day, and I can't. We just don't talk about it.

"I'm sorry, too," I say. *Sorry that this happened to us, sorry that you have to remember what it looked like, sorry that you can hear and I can't. Sorry our lives got screwed up, sorry we didn't talk about it before, sorry I was mad.*

"Can we, like…" I lick my lips. "Talk, and stuff, like we used to? I miss you."

He laughs, and the sick feeling that has been spinning circles in my stomach slows, does a couple of experimental laps, and then eases away, taking the tension from my abdomen with it.

"Maybe," he says, and squeezes my shoulder. "I'll think about it."

It's a sparse bit of humor, but it smooths over the delicacy of our newly mended friendship, and I am grateful.

We sit in silence for a few more minutes, his arm around my shoulders, my head resting against his chest, and I am almost afraid to breathe in case I screw this up too.

Mike stretches his hands over his head, and I look up in time to see his lips moving. "… … time is it?"

When I glance out the window behind him, I'm shocked to see the first faint yellow sunbeams trickling over the tops of the houses. "It's a lot later than I thought," I say and discover that I don't even feel tired. "Maybe five-thirty?"

"How long have we been down here?" he asks, forehead wrinkled as he holds back a yawn.

He still looks exhausted, but the haunted look is gone, and when I look at him, I'm startled to realize that I actually recognize the person looking back at me.

"It didn't feel that long," I murmur, and then wonder if I fell asleep somehow and missed an hour or two—but no. I would have remembered. Maybe. "Look, the sun's coming up."

Both of us turn to peer out the front window. It's not exactly bright outside yet, but you can easily see the houses across from us, and the streetlights are winking out one by one as the light hits them. It's awfully pretty here, and I realize with a pang that I'm going to miss waking up to this every day.

"Mike," I say, looking at the road in front of us. How would it feel under my feet this morning? If I asked him to come...would he say yes? "I'm going for a run. Do you..." I can't breathe. "Do you want to come with me?"

I do my best not to look at him, too afraid of what I might see in his face. I can see the vague shape of him beside me in my peripheral, his shoulders rising and falling as he breathes. Considers.

"Skylar," he says, and I look up at him, my heart pounding. "I can't...yet. Not today."

I force myself to smile, to nod. *Sure, Mike,* I imagine myself saying, to mask the sound of my heart breaking into a thousand pieces. He doesn't want to run with me yet. Will he ever want to again?

"Maybe tomorrow?" He's watching my face, and he knows me too well. Mike is not fooled by my stiff little smile in the dark. "Or sometime when this dream"—he shudders involuntarily—"isn't quite so strong."

"Oh," I say and almost laugh out loud. "You'll come running with me? Like we used to?"

"Eventually, yeah." He shrugs, tracing a line down the carpet between us. And then, after a moment, "I missed it."

"Me, too," I whisper, and if our relationship was less tenuous, I would throw my arms around him...but now, I content myself with just squeezing his shoulder for a moment before getting to my feet as the sun streams in the window behind me.

Chapter
SEVENTEEN

OUR LAST WEEK IN GOLDEN SOUND IS MY FAVORITE OF THE WHOLE SUMmer, because at last Mike and I can pass each other in the hall without feeling like strangers. He smiles at me on Tuesday morning across the breakfast table, and I grab hold of it like a drowning swimmer clutching the hands of her rescuer. It's just a smile, but it's been such a long time since he's directed it at me that I hold the memory of it close to my heart all day.

I'm afraid to ask him to run with me, and he doesn't bring it up again, but on Thursday morning, he asks me to go for a walk. I cling tight to that as I say yes, feet slipped into flip-flops even before I'm done with my cereal.

For a while we walk in silence, but I swear every step feels like balm on the wound that is our relationship, our steps falling into rhythm, turning the corners without stopping to check which way we'll go. We're chatting about going home again, normal things, easy conversations, and then, right as everything starts to feel good again, Mike's face falls. I'm watching him instead of looking where I'm going, so he has to grab my arm to stop me from walking right into whatever has arrested his attention so fully.

"What?" I say, turning, and then I get it.

Eric is standing right in front of me.

"Hey," he says, looking at my face, and then I watch as his eyes travel all the way down my body to the worn flip-flops on my feet. Instinctively, I cross my arms over my chest, but I force myself not to take a step back.

"What do you want?" I say this a half-second too late—my brother has already spoken, stretched up to his full height so he can look down at Eric.

"Relax, man." Eric spreads his hands defensively in front of him. "I was just saying hello."

"Well next time, don't." Mike is not exactly glaring, but if I were Eric, I would choose this moment to walk away.

"So, what hap … … night?" Eric isn't even fazed, hands loosely in his back pockets, but his face is cast into shadow as he watches Mike. I miss snatches of words, torn away by the static of wind in my hearing aids, and have to rely on lip-reading to follow the conversation. "I was so wasted … … remember what … … decided to do. Did … … driving?"

"Yeah," Mike says, and I see him finger the top of his shirt, probably thinking about the bruise again.

"Mike," I say, never taking my eyes off Eric, "I'm going to keep going, is that okay?" I don't want to be here for this, don't want to watch my brother relive that night, or see how much Eric doesn't care. Does that make me a coward?

I don't move, prepared to stay if he wants me to, but so desperately wanting to leave. I never want to see Eric's face again.

Mike nods in my direction, and a muscle twitches in his jaw. "I'll meet you at home."

Without looking back, I stride past Eric, chin up, eyes forward. I take the first turn I can to get a barrier between us and the gross way he looked at me, pumping my legs as hard as they'll go until the thin strap of my flip-flops snaps, and I'm left barefoot on the sidewalk, toes throbbing.

I think of Mike talking to Eric, fielding questions he doesn't even have answers to, and something deep resonates within me, a sweet sort of pain that swells in my stomach until I can't breathe, it's pressing so hard against my lungs.

It takes me a minute to realize that what I'm feeling is love. I love my stupid brother and his stupid decisions. I love him even though picturing his conversation with Eric hurts me so much I can't get enough air into my lungs to feel comfortable. I love him even though he drove drunk, even though the thought of that night still makes me sick to my stomach. I love him because I can't help it; because I always have and because I'm pretty sure I always will.

Is that how God loves us?

The thought comes upon me unbidden, unwelcome, and I stop walking out of pure irritation.

"What do you want from me?" I direct my questions to the bright blue sky above. "I can't get you out of my head and I'm tired of it. Just tell me what you want and then please, leave me alone."

Unsurprisingly, there is no answer from the heavens, so I keep walking. I don't say anything out loud again, but the thoughts keep circling my head like a flock of seagulls around a child with food. I'm not even sure when I decided to believe in God, but I think I do. I just don't know if I like it, yet.

Everything feels the same for so long that I almost forget my question, and then the longer I walk, the more I can feel everything loosening in my chest. I can't figure out what it is at first, but all of the knots, the tension, the stomach ache…everything just melts away, and gradually, I can breathe again.

That was weird, I think, and then it hits me. Like a wave that smacks the breath out of you from behind, this warmth envelops me, surrounds me, this sudden certainty that I am understood, that I am good, that I am *loved*. Something really big loves me, I think in amazement, and I feel completely opened up. It is pulsing through my veins, radiating through every artery and capillary, and when I place two fingers against the heartbeat in my wrist, I can feel it singing to me:

Loved, loved, loved.

My feet pound the pavement, following the rhythm until I'm running, sprinting barefoot up Main Street toward the library. I can't tell if I'm chasing or being chased, but the rush of love is all around me still, and it is so beautiful, and so terrifying, to be so loved, so known, so accepted in all the mess that is my life. I sprint through the library doors, straight up the worn carpet to the front counter, even though Ana told me not to come in today, even though people are staring, even though Cam is halfway through checking someone out and is staring at me with wide eyes as though I've gone crazy. Maybe I have.

"Cam," I gasp out, winded. "I think God loves me, and I don't know what to do."

He starts to say something, the scanner hanging limp in his hand, but I bulldoze straight over him, not even looking at the person beside me in line.

"Something huge loves me, and I don't know why, and I don't get it, and I don't like it because it doesn't make sense to me, but I can't get away from it. I ran all the way here and it followed me— He followed me—and I am such a mess and I just don't know. I don't know anything anymore."

Cam is laughing—his head is tipped back, and his eyes are wide, wide open, and he drops the scanner like he's forgotten it exists, like he doesn't have a nametag on his shirt, like he's not on the clock. He reaches right across the counter in front of the whole library and pulls me into his arms. I throw mine around him and I'm clutching him so hard I'm sure he can feel my heartbeat against his chest, can hear the roar of love that is not mine, but knows me.

"Is this what it feels like?"

I know he can't answer me. I know my question doesn't even make sense, but I have to ask. I can feel him laughing, and his arms tighten around me again before letting go.

"Sometimes," he says, and the lady next to me looks seriously peeved, but I don't care.

It's like someone cracked the universe open and handed it to me on a platter, with everything opened up and laid bare. And the strangest thing is that where I thought there would be hundreds of pieces and pathways, there is only one. The whole universe condenses down to one concept, one idea, one glorious dose of the love of God, the end.

"I should go," I say, breathless, everyone's eyes still on me. I wonder if my skin is glowing with the wonder of it all.

"Okay."

Cam is grinning, and suddenly I recognize the love that surrounds me, because Cam has it, too, and it has been *pouring out of him* this whole summer. I stare at him, at the face that I've been looking at for months without really seeing, until he reaches across the counter and snaps his fingers in front of my face.

"That's enough, Skylar," he says, but he's still laughing. "Get out of here. Go pack up. You only have a few more days, right?"

I have to go home. The thought is like someone has doused me with freezing cold water. God loves me, I think, putting one truth in front of the other much the same way a child takes her first few steps, her feet wobbly and unsure. God loves me, and I have to leave.

"I'll come over tomorrow, if you like," Cam says, clicking away at the computer.

"Okay," I say, trying to reconcile the enormity of everything that is swirling inside of me. "Okay, yeah. That would be…good. You should definitely do that."

The lady standing beside me coughs loudly enough that even

I can hear it, and, still feeling a little shell shocked, I drift toward the front doors of the library.

Cam waves as I near the doors, and I wave back, still rolling this new idea of God over and over inside my head. Eventually, I meet up with Mike again, and we walk back to Aunt Kay's house in silence, he with his thoughts, and me with mine. I think of Cam, and the God he's always known, and how he introduced us without me even realizing it. I think of Anastasia, and her sister's return, and the calm look on her face—so unlike anything I've ever seen in Ana before. And I think, and I wonder about it all…about how we try to do our best, and make mistakes, and how we love each other, but we still get hurt, and how God's love fits into the picture—if it does, at all.

The rest of the day slips away from us, sneaky and silent as the tide running down the beach, away from your toes and miles of sand away before you've realized it's going, and sooner than I can blink it's Friday morning. Our last day.

• ● •

It takes us almost the entire day to pack the car for our trip home. To be honest, if we'd all left Dad alone to do the packing, it probably could have been finished in less than an hour, but between all of us running up and down the stairs, adding and subtracting from the pile of luggage by the door, it becomes an all-day affair. Cam comes over in the morning to help lug all of our suitcases down the long flight of stairs, and Ana pops by around supper with food for everyone. The neighbors are all out on their front lawns, chatting to each other and to Mom, who is being a social butterfly and making friends with everyone. *Mom*, I want to say, *stop. We have to leave soon, anyway.* But I don't; for a while I just sit on the front step, knees tucked under my chest, and watch.

Aiden and Sara have been running in and out of the house all morning in their bare feet, tugging on Dad's arm and begging him to let us stay, or trying to jump on Mike as he's coming down the stairs, or shyly spying on Cam from behind the front hedge. This is mostly Sara, but she ropes Aiden into being her lookout after he gets tired of bugging the guys.

Anastasia is helpfully unpacking the luggage from the car as fast as Dad can jam it in, smoothing imaginary wrinkles from the tops of our suitcases—can suitcases even have wrinkles?—and checking to make sure that everything is zippered shut properly. Finally, in exasperation, Dad asks her to "help" by checking the inside of the house to make sure we haven't missed anything, which she does with so much exuberance that when I finally go inside, none of the furniture is in the same place as it was when I left.

Between the two of them, Cam and Mike manage to bring everything out front, and then Mike disappears down to the beach. Part of me wants to follow him, but I just can't bear to leave now, in the last few minutes of being here. Cam and I swap numbers after realizing that we haven't needed to text each other this whole summer, and then he gets roped into lifting something for Dad, and I'm alone on the front porch.

We're leaving early tomorrow morning—like, so early it almost doesn't count as morning at all—and as the sun begins to set, casting long shadows down the street, I can feel the minutes slipping away. *Wait*, I want to call, *I'm not finished here yet!*

"You can always come back," Cam says, startling me as he walks up the driveway. It's as though he's read my mind. Who knows, maybe he has?

"Yeah, but I have to leave first." I watch as Dad slams the trunk shut and dusts his hands together, his task—finally—completed, no thanks to Ana's helpful contributions. "I can't believe summer's done already."

"Yeah," he says, shoving his hands into his pockets. "Back to school for both of us, I guess."

"But university for you," I say. Summer is such a timeless season, I forget we're not the same age. "Wow."

"Wow," he says.

We enjoy a moment of silence for approximately four seconds, and then Anastasia bursts out of the house like she's being chased by wild dogs. She's yelling something, hair smeared across her face, and for one heart-stopping moment, as all the neighbors turn to look, conversations cut off mid-word, I think someone is dying.

"Ana, what?" I can't read her lips, she's running too fast, head whipping side to side to call to Mom, Dad, anyone who will listen.

"It's your aunt," Cam says, a look of amazement on his face. "She's on the phone."

I notice now that Anastasia is clutching the house phone in her hand. She vaults off the front step and nearly throws it in Dad's face.

"She's here," shrieks Ana, jumping up and down on the driveway. "From Africa!"

"Hello?" says Dad into the phone, clutching it with a white-knuckled hand. "Kay? Is everything all right?"

Mom comes jogging over from across the street, and even Aiden and Sara emerge from the bushes. Just as I notice that Mike's the only one not here, I see his sharp-angled silhouette striding up the hill from the beach toward us.

"What's he saying?" I hiss frantically to Cam, but he shakes his head.

"She's doing all the talking, I don't know. I can't hear her side of it."

We wait, all the people I love best gathered around in a circle—it's funny, to think that at the beginning of the summer, I didn't even know all of them, and now I can't imagine life without them—and all of us are curious.

She's okay, Dad mouths, and then he just listens. "I don't think—" he tries to say at one point. And then, "Okay. Love you too. Bye."

He turns the phone off and stares at it in his hand for a moment, while the rest of us wait.

"Well?" Mike's chin juts forward, and I turn to see what he's saying. "What did she want?"

"She's coming home," Dad says, still staring at the phone, and Mom puts her arm around his waist. "I really didn't think she would."

"She's coming home?" Mom leans her head on his arm. "But she hasn't been gone for that long."

"I know," Dad says and pockets the phone, squinting around the circle at us. "She was hoping she'd catch us, but her flights aren't until next week, and school will have started by then."

Mom opens her mouth to say something else, but the twins decide that now is a good time to see who can climb the highest in Aunt Kay's front tree and then jump out without injury, and she goes running to their rescue. While she's putting a stop to their fun, I turn to Anastasia. She is preoccupied, probably checking her phone for texts from Sophia, who left this morning, and I have to ask her three times if she'll be hiring anyone new at the library in the fall before I can finally get a straight answer out of her.

"I might," she says at last, focusing on my face long enough to spit out the sentence. "It's not so busy in the fall as it is in the summer, so usually Cam and I can manage. The hours go down, too, so that helps."

I like the idea of it being just the two of them. I can remember it as it was, imagine that they're working together like we have all summer, just us. I'm glad no one will have to take my place.

"Maybe I'll come back next summer and help out again," I say, and when they both grin at me, a warm glow spreads through my chest.

"I'd like that," Cam says, but Anastasia bursts forward and gives me a hug, chattering away into my empty ears as she does so.

"… … miss you so much," she's saying as she pulls away. "I

loved meeting you and working … … this summer." She sniffs and covers her mouth halfway through her sentence to mask the tears that I can see are rising again, but I manage to see enough to understand the gist of what she means.

"I did, too," I say. I hope she and Sophia had a nice long talk. I hope she got to meet Eva. I hope, more than anything, that her story has a happier ending than she thought it would. If her cheerfulness over the past few days is anything to go on, I'd venture a guess that my hopes aren't too far away from being reality.

The twins pick this moment to rejoin the conversation. "We can come back, can't we?" asks Sara, tugging on Dad's arm.

"Please?" Aiden puts on his best puppy-dog face, and I feel my own heart begin to melt.

"I don't know," Dad says, and I know he is thinking logically— if Aunt Kay comes back, will we stay with her? Will she sell the house? She might move across the country, for all we know—but then he sees the twins' crestfallen faces and relents. "But we'll see if we can work something out," he finishes, and I smile.

"Well," Anastasia says after a minute, and I know this is it. She will be the first to leave; hers is the first goodbye. "It's getting dark."

Somehow, without me noticing, the sun has sunk below the horizon. There's a chill in the air, and the faint dusk of twilight is settling over the street.

"Goodbye," I say, quickly, giving her a squeeze, and then I stand and watch as she hugs everyone else, even Mike, who she's never met, and Cam, who she'll see at work in the morning.

"I could drive you," Cam says, a little belatedly, but she shakes her head.

"I like the walk," she replies. "And you two haven't said goodbye yet."

I hug her again, breathing in the sweet smell of her shampoo before releasing her. She trots briskly down to the end of the road and then turns left, and I can picture her jogging lightly up her own driveway and letting herself through the front door, where her dog will leap up to welcome her, tail wagging.

The night comes on fast once it has begun, and Mom and Dad start the process of wrestling the twins inside and into bed at the untimely hour of eight o'clock. Mike goes with them, leaving Cam and me alone out front to say goodbye.

"I'm glad you came this summer," he says, kicking the driveway with the toe of his shoe.

"Me, too," I say, and watch the streetlights flick on one by one. "I'm going to miss you."

"I'm not going to miss you," he says flippantly, and I shove him. "Maybe just a little," he concedes, grinning.

We're silent for a little while, and then just as it's almost too dark to see his lips, he asks, "Did you and Mike ever talk? About the accident?"

"Yeah," I say, looking up to see if the stars are out yet. "We did. It's better now." I search for the words to express how much better it is, how clean I feel, how relieved. I have my brother back again. "It's…we're okay."

"I'm glad," he says. "And, Skylar?"

"What?" I think I know what he's about to say.

"He's not safe," he says, and it feels like a quote. "But He is good."

"Thanks," I say softly, and then we just stand together, looking up as the first few stars twinkle at us from a thousand miles away. And then, inevitably, he says, "I'd better go."

Don't cry. For once, my body listens. "I'm going to hug you," I say, and I do, squeezing my arms around him as though somehow a hug could say what my words can't.

He squeezes me back, and then we let go and I know that we've delayed as long as we could. One of us is going to have to say goodbye.

Instead, Cam leans forward. Just as I'm about to ask why his face is so close to mine, he tilts forward a little farther and his lips brush my cheek, very close to my right ear.

"What?" I say, because I am nothing if not coherent at times like these, and he laughs, his teeth a white flash in the twilight.

"Will you come back next summer?"

I realize that my hand is pressed to my face, but I think I'm blushing, so I decide not to pull it away.

"Will you text me?" I say instead, and his grin widens.

"If I say yes, are you coming back?"

I nod and manage to pull my hand away from my face and jam it safely into my pocket instead. My fingers are tingling.

"Then okay."

"I'll give you my number," I say, and then remember that I already did. Cam laughs again, and then takes a step backwards, down the driveway.

"I'll see you next summer, Skylar."

Bye, my lips say, but there's no voice behind it. I wave, and then watch him walk to the end of the driveway before I turn and go inside.

It's warm, and the lights are turned on, and Mom and Dad and Mike are sprawled across the couches in the living room, watching TV. I slide to the floor beside Mike, and even though my chest hurts, it's a sweet bitterness, because this isn't really goodbye. A part of my heart lives in Golden Sound, and even though we're driving away tomorrow, it isn't forever.

I'll be back.

ACKNOWLEDGMENTS

THEY SAY IT TAKES A VILLAGE TO RAISE A CHILD, AND I THINK THE SENTIMENT holds true when you're trying to write a book. The only reason Skylar's story is sitting in your hands today is because of the support of so many incredible people. I couldn't have done any of this without them!

First, I'd like to acknowledge (see what I did there?) something that I mentioned also in the dedication at the front of this book: this is God's book, not mine. Drafting *Seeing Voices* was hard work at the best of times. More than once, I hit a wall and just prayed, asking God for ideas, inspiration, anything that would help this story fit into a book-shaped package. I prayed through the querying process, trusting that this really was God's book and it would end up exactly where He wanted it to be. This has been a team effort all the way, and I've only done a small part of the work. The credit belongs to the Author of the greatest story ever told.

Next, I'd like to thank my immediate family for their endless support, encouragement, and love. Thanks for letting me monopolize the dinner table conversation on more than one occasion… and for letting me spread my outline and storyboard all over the living room when I was figuring out where each scene needed to go!

Mom, thanks for reading me stacks and stacks of books, driving me to the library almost every day, and introducing me to the One Year Adventure Novel curriculum. *Seeing Voices* wouldn't exist without you—and I don't have words to say THANK YOU. You're the best!

Hannah!! My first beta reader and best critique-giver ever! Thanks for saving me from my terrible first draft—Skylar's story would still be boring and drab if it wasn't for you. Thanks for squee-ing with me over every (edited!) page.

Zayya: Thanks for talking me through so many plot holes and querying discouragements, and for believing in me no matter what. I love you forever.

I have so many wonderful friends who supported and encouraged me throughout my publishing journey, and there's no way I'll have enough space to mention them all! Even if I did have space, there certainly wouldn't be words enough to say how grateful I am…but I'll do my best!

Paul and Carolyn, if you hadn't introduced me to Don Pape, I'm not sure this book would have made it this far. Thanks for asking if I had any summer plans…and when I said I was writing a book, for helping me make such an awesome connection in the writing world.

Don, I will never forget how it felt to pick up the phone and hear an industry professional tell me that Skylar's story was something special. I don't have words enough to thank you for believing in me, introducing me to Nancy, and helping me read through my first-ever book contract! Your support and guidance has been invaluable.

Nancy, working with you was an absolute pleasure. I hung onto your words of encouragement (and editorial guidance) every time the doubts crept in. I've learned so much from you! Connecting with you as a fellow author was a dream come true for a girl who grew up reading your books.

Clarissa, thanks for inviting me out for coffee back when I was in second year. If it wasn't for you, Skylar's parents would still be super annoying (and I probably never would have met Rachel McMillan)! Thanks for your wise advice in all the stages of my journey. Having fellow writing friends who GET IT is just the best.

Rachel, you are my favourite "book gusher" and general encourager. Your passion for books is contagious! Thank you for sharing your enthusiasm—and many words of wisdom—with me over the past year and a half.

Brooke, you have answered a million and one questions for me...thanks for being so patient! And for explaining the difference between "hearing" and "feeling" when I just couldn't seem to draw the line between the two.

Miranda G-B: Thank you for offering such calm advice the day I walked into your office and said, "I was just offered a publishing contract and I don't know what to do next." I'm so thankful someone was there to proofread my emails and reassure me that I was on the right track!

Finally, there are several groups of people who are too large to name individually, but who have contributed in such special ways to my publishing journey!

To everyone who read an early copy of *Seeing Voices* and shared their feedback with me, THANK YOU. I could not have prepared for querying without your insight!

To my amazing launch team: what can I say that hasn't already been said? Your support, enthusiasm, and encouragement means the WORLD to me. Thank you for reading *Seeing Voices* and leaving kind reviews even when the world was in crisis mode! You are such special people, and it's been a joy to walk this journey with you.

To the team at WhiteSpark (Roseanna, David, Wendy, and many more!): you made my dream come true. I will never be able to thank you enough.

And at last, to all the numerous friends and extended family members who supported and believed in me from afar. Thanks for signing up for my newsletter and sending me warm wishes!

With all the love in the world,

Olivia

YOU MAY ALSO ENJOY

Victoria Grace, the Jerkface
by S.E. Clancy

A sassy teenager and a woman born before sliced bread. Just add boys. And homework.

Heart of a Royal
by Hannah Currie

Everyone wants her to be their princess... except the ones who matter most.

Gone Too Soon
by Melody Carlson

An icy road. A car crash.
A family changed forever.

CPSIA information can be obtained
at www.ICGtesting.com
Printed in the USA
LVHW020731140420
653368LV00004B/852